THE VAMPIRE'S Masquerade

KIERSTEN FAY

THE VAMPIRE'S MASQUERADE
Published by Kiersten Fay
Copyright 2018 by Kiersten Fay.

www.kierstenfay.com

This book is a work of fiction. All of the characters, names, and events portrayed in this novel are creations of the author's imagination.

ISBN-10: 0-9975491-5-7
ISBN-13: 978-0-9975491-5-7

CHAPTER 1

Kasima Wilder gripped the black-velvet clutch in her lap as if it were a release-triggered bomb set to explode. Downing the last swallow of her wine, she signaled to the bartender. "Another, please."

All around the nightclub, gossamer drapes hung like the spidery webs of a temptress's lair, giving glimpses into dark alcoves, ripe with secret liaisons, while the carnal pulse of sensual music flowed from hidden speakers.

Though Kasima knew all about the infamous nightclub, Ever Nights, and its owner, Cortez, a vampire who had practically founded Riverstone, raising it up from a desolate war-torn patch of land to a rare, thriving destination spot, she never thought her first visit would be attending the annual masquerade ball. This was not a normal night for the club. Tonight was special, catering to guest's baser desires.

The entire town went nuts for tonight's event. Mostly because it drew in rich tourists from all over the continent, both human and vampire, which greatly benefited Riverstone's economy as a whole, but also because in the days leading up to the event, Ever Nights offered a chunk of tickets to locals at a discount. That was how Kasima first assumed Brian had gotten hold of their tickets. Turned out he'd bought them months before.

She was still stewing over that. *And yet here I am.*

There were three types of people here tonight: club members who could afford the astronomical yearly membership fee, friends of those wealthy club members invited to share a single wild night, and a handful of lucky locals. Of all of them, Kasima was probably the only one who regretted coming.

Ass planted firmly on a barstool, she waited for her refill. Coming over, the bartender flashed a movie-star smile, showing off his sharp fangs—of course he was a vampire, as were many of the staff—which he seemed to enjoy showing off, if only for the shock-and-awe reactions he received from some of the out-of-towners.

Though Kasima lived in Riverstone, she didn't make a habit of hanging around the prevalent vampire community, and knowing she was in a den full of them was unnerving. When the bartender once more flashed those pearly whites at her as he refilled her glass, she played it cool, even as the hairs on the back of her neck sizzled. She held her clutch tighter, till her knuckles screamed. She didn't belong here. Surely everyone could tell.

Once more alone, she fiddled with her mask. The pressure around her nose and cheeks wasn't bad, per se. Just a nuisance. When the air around her stirred, the tiny white feathers that lined the edge tickled her skin. She would remove the thing altogether if she didn't think that would draw attention. Maskless at a masquerade? She'd be a goddamned spectacle.

She peeked around the room—one out of many currently in use. Though there were probably hundreds of people in attendance tonight, they were all scattered throughout the many lobbies and lounges within the twenty story club that also doubled as a hotel for its wealthier members. Her dark little room boasted maybe thirty or more guests, many dancing and smiling and otherwise deep in reverie while several others either lounged on a set of sofas that curled around each of the four corners or sat at the booths that lined three of the walls. The three-sixty bar was the centerpiece, though she felt practically invisible sidled up next to it. Perfect.

The atmosphere here was surprisingly subdued compared to some of the other rooms. Before she'd claimed her little out-of-the-way corner, she'd taken a quick tour of the club. She shouldn't have been surprised—she'd heard the rumors about Ever Nights' masquerade ball—but still, she was surprised by the openness with which some individuals groped one another, exploiting the anonymity of their elaborate, bedazzled masks. After stumbling into a room where an orgy was in full swing, she'd ducked in here and hadn't moved since—leaving her far too much time to fret about what her wayward boyfriend was getting up to. She didn't have to wonder for long.

As Brian entered the room, a small gaggle of women in tow, all masked as animals: a cat, an owl, and a peacock. She hated that theirs all looked nicer than her simple dove. Electronic pop music hip-bumped her eardrums, though she could still hear their faint giggles. The four of them found an empty booth near the door. Kasima faced the bar, trying to pretend she hadn't noticed him or his beautiful entourage.

I agreed to this, she reminded herself. *It's just one night.* It had been Brian's idea to come here tonight. For weeks, he'd been talking her into it. Begging, really. *Come on. It will be fun*, he'd told her, acting all nonchalant about testing their relationship in such a fashion. *Like a one-night-only free pass for each of us.* That was how he'd sold it. *A last night of freedom before we take our relationship to the next level.* He'd made a face at the last part, a micro-wince, but she had noticed. Pretended not to. Like always.

Her argument? If two people want to be together, they shouldn't be contemplating sleeping with strangers.

Yet here she was, watching him—trying not to watch him—flirt across the room, potentially gearing up for a ménage.

She'd always been fiercely loyal to whoever she was with, and it hurt that Brian wasn't entirely all in like she was. But she'd promised to give him time, and she could put up with a lot. It was practically her talent. Not a great talent, but you take what you get. Yet, all night she'd been wondering if she could accept this philandering, even for a single night. *If she should.*

This inner debate had been warring all night. She really liked Brian. He was a journalist for the Tribune where Kasima worked as an assistant to the editor. They'd been coworkers for a few of years before dating. Brian had always given her his ridiculously charming smile as he passed her desk on his way to meet with her boss, Mr. Dixon, which, to her great embarrassment, had always made her blush. She suspected he enjoyed her reaction, but he hadn't really pursued her till last year. And she had let him, delighted to have caught the eye of someone like him; charismatic, ambitious, handsome. All the women in the office swooned over him.

To be fair, she and Brian hadn't been dating exclusively until roughly three months ago when she had breached the subject. They were still adjusting to the new dynamics of their relationship. And though Brian had agreed "to try" being exclusive with her, tonight had been one of his exceptions.

She took a sip of her wine, letting the delectable flavor wash over her nerves. *It's just one night.*

She lightly tugged at the silky fabric of her low-cut blouse, chosen in hopes of keeping Brian's attention. The rest of her outfit followed that aim. Her skirt was short, tight, and hugged her ass like plastic wrap. Her fuck-me boots were miles high black leather that wrapped her calves in a cozy embrace. She'd taken extra care with her hair, piling it up in a messy bun with strategic curling tendrils, exposing her delicate neck. One of her best features, in her opinion. It was only after they'd pulled up to the club that it dawned on her that they were about to enter a vampire-rich club. Did someone order the extra juicy neck? Luckily the only one she'd come across was her brawny, my-biceps-are-too-big-for-this-shirt, bartender. Thankfully he remained professional. Not that she'd expected him to leap across the bar and randomly fang-fuck guests, but when you're the meat in a room full of carnivores, you tend to be on guard.

Her ploy to hold Brian's affections had flopped at the start.

As soon as they'd entered Ever Nights, Brian's eyes had flashed with excitement as they'd wandered a sea of skin and tightly bound dresses. He'd hastily kissed the top of her head and then beelined it straight towards a group of scantily dressed women whose outfits made Kasima look downright wholesome. In fact, most everyone here outshined her in some way or another. Even some of the men.

She took another sip of wine and glanced over to

where Brian and the three women cozied up to one another. Which one would he sleep with tonight? Or was he going for a trifecta?

She gritted her teeth and turned away, pain lashing her insides. *I can't do this. I can't watch this. It's too much. How can he not know how much this will hurt me?* She hadn't made it clear to him. That was why. Stupidly, she thought this would be easy. Since they hadn't been exclusive very long, she thought this would be like nothing. And maybe she'd have a little fun too. But she didn't want to have any fun. At least not with a stranger. And watching Brian seduce other women was gutting her.

It's only one night!

I can get through this. One night. Then things go back to normal. The last few months with Brian had been wonderful. He'd been attentive and loving and seemed to be delighted with her. They'd even discussed moving in together.

Just as she was contemplating sneaking away to another room to ride out the rest of the evening, a stout man in a golden-brown fur-lined mask slinked into the seat next to hers, scanning her with open interest. *So not ready for this.* She fidgeted with the stem of her wine glass and avoided eye contact, but she could feel his eyes on her. When she checked to see if he was indeed watching her, he licked his lips suggestively.

Ew!

He asked, "What's your mask supposed to be? Is it a pussycat?"

She kept her body facing away from him. "It's a dove." Cheapest mask she could find. It did the job just fine. Some of the other masks in here were a hundred times more gorgeous and had to be worth three times her annual salary.

"Ah." He leaned in to get a better look. "Well, can you guess mine?" He smiled as if this were a great game they were now playing.

She gave an uninterested shrug. "Um. A dog or something?"

He laughed with exaggerated fervor. "It's a lion." He reached under the bar and patted her on the knee, letting his hand linger. Her muscles stiffened and clenched. She hadn't invited him into her space, and his touch repelled her.

He either didn't notice her distress, or was inclined to ignore it. "You know. Like the king of the jungle." His smile widened.

"O-Oh," she stammered, and tried to swivel her chair away from him.

His grip on her knee tightened, halting her retreat. "Do you want to make me roar, Little Dove?"

Her mouth dropped open at the blatant proposal. "Not in the slightest," she shoved his hand away.

He frowned, surprised by her swift and ardent rejection, but then his lips curled back up into a sly grin. He thought she was playing hard to get. Crap.

"Perhaps you'd rather make me purr like a kitten?"

"I'm here with someone," she blurted.

He cocked his head. "I've been watching you. You've been alone all night."

She shivered, suddenly feeling unsafe. She glanced around the room. How many others watched her even now? Waiting to see how she'd handle this first suitor? Suddenly it was as if a sea of masks faced her way, dead black eyes trained on her.

It was a pretty safe bet that if you attended the masquerade, you were looking for a hookup. A woman sitting alone on a night like this was basically an open invitation. This shouldn't freak her out so much. She just needed to let this guy down.

Even though Brian had encouraged her to find a partner tonight, she realized now she wasn't interested in a one-night stand. Her oats didn't need any sowing. Especially not with this self-proclaimed king of the jungle...whose hand returned to her leg!

A hint of revulsion slithered up her spine. She hadn't invited the touch, and resented that he'd taken the liberty. Just as she was about to slap his hand away, a deep, baritone greeted her from behind. "Darling!" A warm palm landed on her shoulder. For a second, the sense of being surrounded filled her with panic, but then Mr. King of the Jungle yanked his hand away, and she was grateful for the reprieve.

"Sorry I'm late," the stranger behind her continued as if they'd made plans to meet up here. Had someone misidentified her? She was about to tell him he'd confused her with someone else when he bent to kiss her cheek. She was too stunned to react. Then he whispered, "Just go with it."

He sidled around to face her, inserting himself between her and Mr. King of the Jungle.

She gazed up at him, speechless for a whole other reason now. Even with that black strip of loose fabric masking his upper face, she could tell he was gorgeous. His jaw was well-defined with a touch of stubble that rode up his cheeks. His dark hair was tousled around his face and mask, framing an unusual set of green eyes that almost seemed to shine from within. His mouth spread in a small, rakish grin that drew her gaze to his full lips.

He winked at her.

She blinked several times, searching for her voice. Did he still think he knew her now that they were face to face? Or was he...could he be coming to her rescue? *Just go with it*, he'd said.

She cleared her throat. "I was starting to get worried... um...honey." Note to self: learn to act.

The handsome stranger's smile shifted to something that was almost soothing. "My apologies, darling. I got caught up at work." He turned to Mr. King of the Jungle. "Would you mind scooting down so I can sit next to my girlfriend?"

Kasima grasped her mask, fidgeting with it though it didn't need adjusting.

Clearly unhappy by the cock-block, Mr. King of the Jungle grumbled, "Yeah, sure." Then he moved to the other end of the bar.

"Thank you," she whispered to the dark stranger. "You're a lifesaver."

He nodded politely...and then claimed the newly vacated seat next to her.

Her stomach clenched. Had she just traded one problem for another?

The man signaled for a drink. Without even asking, the bartender poured him a full glass of top-shelf whiskey.

Obviously her stranger was a regular here.

She watched the thick muscles of his neck as he took a swig.

He glanced at her from the corner of his eye. Realizing she'd been caught staring, she looked away.

"So." That masculine drawl drew her attention back to him. "Were you lying before?"

She blinked. "Huh?"

"I overheard you tell that man you were here with

someone. Is that true, or did you just say that hoping he'd go away?"

Unconsciously she looked across the room where Brian was now seated between the peacock and the owl. The man followed her gaze, his derisive snort evidence he'd caught on.

That mocking sound kicked her already bruised ego.

The stranger scanned her body from the fuck-me boots to her perfectly curled do. Not quite the same way Mr. King of the Jungle had. This was more of a curious assessment rather than an open ogle. When he shook his head again and quietly sipped his drink, she felt the sharp bite of...rejection?

Which was ridiculous. Surely she didn't care what this man thought of her. She was, however, grateful toward him. It seemed he was polite enough to sit with her until Mr. King of the Jungle found another gazelle to stalk. And because of that, this was now the best place in the club to avoid attention.

She glanced around the room, trying and failing to keep her eyes away from Brian, who was just full of conspiratorial smiles for his neighbors. None of which were meant for her. Had he even looked her way once tonight? Dejected, she took a long pull from her glass.

"So what's the story?" the stranger asked. "You like to watch your man get off with other women?"

She nearly choked on her drink. "I'm sorry, what?"

"Do you like to watch him pick up other chicks and have sex with them? Is that your kink?"

The idea horrified her. "My God, no! And, well, that's really none of your business. And no, that's not my...kink."

He put up both his hands, a tiny smile playing along his lips. "Okay. I was just curious why your guy, I'm assuming he's your guy, is all the way over there and you're all the way over here."

"Again, none of your business."

"Fair enough. I was just wondering if this was some kind of game between you two. Like when couples dress up and pretend to be strangers. If you're waiting for him to mosey on over here and pretend to pick you up, I can leave."

"No!"

He blinked.

Her outburst drew The King's attention from the other side of the bar. She lowered her voice. "I mean...that's not it. I just...If you could stay, just for a while longer, I'd appreciate it."

He contemplated her for a long moment, then nodded, once again checking his watch. She almost asked if he was waiting for someone, but refrained. Obviously that was the case. A man that looked like that did not go stag to a party. He probably had a hot-something-or-other on the way.

For several minutes they sat in silence, and she found her eyes slipping toward him more than a few times. He polished off his drink, ordered a second, and then checked his watch again, displaying no more interest in her.

Which should have been a good thing. So why was she itching to engage him in conversation? In unison, the girls at Brian's table cackled as though he'd said something terribly cleaver. It even drew the stranger's attention. He glanced her way as if to gauge her reaction.

She smiled, though it felt forced. Then an idea tripped into her mind. The dark-masked man wasn't going out of his way to hit on her. He wasn't invading her space. So it was likely he either didn't find her attractive or he did have a girlfriend on the way, which meant it should be safe to engage him in light conversation. Perhaps if Brian saw her chatting up someone as handsome as this stranger, he'd be compelled to leave his groupies to claim his woman.

"Are you waiting for someone?" she asked, smiling as if she were enjoying herself.

"I am," he replied, casually glancing around the room.

Okay. Not a lot of response there.

The peacock's hyena-like laugh grated from across the room. Kasima downed the last of her wine and wiped her mouth. A small amount of lipstick smeared onto her arm. That red hue, originally meant to entice Brian, was now like a stain on this entire night.

She suddenly realized how much she resented this one-night-only free-pass.

Snatching a napkin from the bar, she scrubbed clean her arm, and then wiped the rest of her carefully applied lipstick off her lips. Task done, she wadded the napkin into a tight ball and crushed it in her palm.

The masked stranger appeared to be studying her. When he eyed her fist, she made an effort to relax her grip. And when he slanted his gaze at Brian, doing a perfect impression of someone who didn't give a damn that his girlfriend was sitting by herself in a den of hot-blooded, hard-up males, she wished she could curl up and disappear. Humiliation ran rampant through her veins.

The stranger faced her. "You get off on jealousy, is that it?"

That took her off guard for a moment. "Do you always ask strangers such inappropriate questions?"

He gestured around the room as if to remind her where they were. "Ain't nothing inappropriate here."

Touché. She blew out a long breath. She'd likely never

see this man again, so what did it matter if she opened up to him. "Brian and I don't usually come to places like this."

"*You* don't, maybe. But I've seen him here on occasion."

Say what now? Surely not recently.

"Mind you, Ever Nights offers a variety of entertainment, not all as extreme as tonight."

Yes, Ever Nights played host to everything from wholesome weddings to nights of kinky debauchery. "So then *you* must come here a lot?" she countered.

One side of his mouth curled up.

He looked too handsome when he did that. Mischievous and mysterious. She heard herself ask, "So what's your *kink*?"

That half grin widened into a full grin and she was suddenly enthralled by the perfect way it displayed his straight white teeth...and *fangs*?

Vampire!

Her heart thundered. Her instincts told her the predator in him could sense the change in her pulse. She struggled to squash her anxiety, failing miserably.

With a challenge in his tone, he asked, "Do you really want to know my kink?" He leaned in to whisper near her ear, his hot breath kissing her skin and causing shivers to dance along her shoulders. "It's not something I can just explain. I'd be better if I showed you."

Drumsticks played a hard beat against her rib cage. A full-body blush warmed her skin. She glanced at Brian. Would he notice her alarm? But he was too busy burying his face in the peacock's cleavage!

Bastard!

The vampire followed her gaze, noticing that particular disgrace too, making it all the worse.

"You don't like vampires?" The vampire didn't sound offended by his own question, merely curious.

"I—uh" she clamored for words. Her newspaper had done a few articles on vampires. Some were PR puff pieces largely revolving around vampire-owned businesses like Ever Nights. Others had been reports on crimes in the city involving vampires who'd been unable, or unwilling, to curtail their appetites. She'd edited many of them. One bit of trivia she recalled about his kind: This vampire could sense her unease as easily as her furious heartbeat. Which meant trying to deny his question would be pointless. Her heart was fluttering like a hummingbird's.

"It's not that. I just...I'm not used to being around, um, vampires, is all." Though the town's population was largely vampires, she'd never held a full-blown conversation with one...over drinks...at a party meant for torrid liaisons.

"Well, don't worry. I won't bite." Again that half grin displayed his fangs.

She laughed in spite of herself. A little of her anxiety waned at his lighthearted attempt at humor.

"So you don't seem to be interested in participating in anything offered here tonight."

She shrugged.

"Was it your man's idea to come here?"

She sighed. "He thought we should get some stuff out of our systems before...well, things are getting serious." Yet she wondered if after tonight she would still want that.

The vampire muttered, "Things are getting serious with Blondie over there too."

She frowned. She didn't think he'd meant it as a jab, but it stung all the same.

His expression turned apologetic. "Sorry." He snapped his fingers at the bartender, and gestured to her glass. Seconds later her drink was refilled and so was his.

She took a small sip and set the glass down, feeling the sudden need to save face in front of this vampire. Striving for nonchalance, she said, "We've discussed it, he and I, and it makes sense. We're both young." *Relatively.* Brian was in his early thirties. She was twenty six. "We don't want any regrets later in life. We don't want to feel like we missed out on anything." If she sounded rehearsed, it was because she was repeating Brian's words verbatim.

"Sowing of the wild oats, as it were?"

"Precisely."

"Okay. Well, I see *him* working that needle, but I'm getting the sense you don't even plan to knit. Do you really think you're going to be okay sitting here all night while he's playing hide the salami?"

She raised her wine glass. "That's what this is for."

He gave her a whiskey salute. "Then cheers."

He faced the bar and checked his watch again. Someone on the other side of the room giggled and a couple darted out of the room, hand-in-hand, their eyes lit with excitement. The music shifted to a rhythmic melody that made her want to dance, but she dared not. Not on a night like tonight. She'd only end up inviting more unwanted suitors.

The vampire was looking away, so she took the chance to study him more closely. He wore a sharp charcoal tailored suit, high-end by the looks of it, and held himself with the air of someone perfectly at ease with all that was going on around him. Yet here he was, in this relatively quiet room. A jaded member of the club, perhaps?

His eyes wandered the room, his gaze not landing on any one person for too long. When he finished his scan, he faced her.

She sipped her drink, hoping he hadn't noticed her watching him.

"May I ask you just one more thing?" the vampire said, facing her.

"Sure."

"Aren't you worried about what happens tomorrow?"

"Huh?"

He swiveled her way and rested his arm on the bar. Without thinking, she mirrored his action, accidently bumping their legs together. At the touch, a jolt danced through her bones. She crossed her legs to one side, butting space between them. He followed the movement with his gaze.

She cleared her throat.

When he met her gaze again, she was once more drawn in by his vibrant green eyes. "Say he gets busy with that blonde over there, or even that whole table of ladies, while you dutifully sit here all night, chaste. Aren't you afraid you'll resent your fiancé later?"

Yes! "He's not my fiancé," she said, trying not to crumble under the oration of her very real fears. She recalled asking Brian the exact same thing, in so many words. He'd merely waved her worry away. *If we both agree that it won't be a problem, then it won't be, right?*

When she relayed that to the vampire, his expression turned disbelieving.

"What's that look for?" she said.

"Sorry, it really isn't my place to get involved."

"No, go on and say it. You don't think I'll be able to get past it? One pre-planned, pre-approved and agreed upon by all parties night? I'll remind you that you don't even know me." She feared this stranger could see through her even now.

22

He shrugged. "Maybe you can. Maybe this is just a tiny hitch in your happily ever after. But..."

Arms crossed, she prompted him to continue.

"More likely you won't be able to, but you won't tell him that. Not for years at least. Instead, you'll do everything in your power to convince yourself otherwise. You'll bottle it up and pretend you're not secretly resenting him this one night of passion that didn't involve you. You'll try to convince yourself that everything is fine, that what happened tonight is in the past and doesn't matter, but like a weed, that resentment might grow, day by day. Till one day, without you having realized it, it has become this monstrous thing that has consumed you body and soul."

He leaned back in his chair.

She opened her mouth to argue, but for the life of her, no sound came out. He'd hit on every one of her reservations, every worrisome point Brian had dismissed and downplayed and balked at. And he was one hundred percent right. What Brian wanted, what he was asking of her? It could destroy them before they even had a chance to get started.

"He told me I should find a partner." *Just call me Blurty McBableson.* There was no recalling the hastily spoken words. She wasn't even sure whether they were meant as a defense or an invitation to a door she'd intended to leave closed. Would he step through? Was she mad for even contemplating this?

"That would be one solution. It would keep you both on even ground. In fact, ten to one says he gets jealous." His eyes turned teasing. "I could call our lion friend back over if you like."

She cringed. "Please no. Anyone but him."

He flipped around on the stool and leaned his elbows

on the bar, taking in the rest of the room with a lively scan. "Then let's see. Who should it be? You could have your pick, you know? Most of these fools are just sitting around waiting for a wink and a nod from a pretty dove like you."

She followed his gaze, playing along. "Alright. How about that one?" she pointed to a spikey haired man dressed all in faux leather who couldn't be more than a couple years over twenty."

The vampire shook his head. "The pup? You'd break him like a dried twig."

"You think?"

He scrutinized her up and down. His slow perusal of her body left her skin heated. "No doubt," he said confidently.

Moving on, she jerked her chin toward a taller gentleman dressed in a suit and tie. "Him then?"

"Are we preparing taxes or having a last fling?"

She laughed. "Very well, who would you pick?"

As though taking the task very seriously, he rubbed his chin and considered the selection at hand. "That gruff fellow in the corner might be able to handle you."

She wrinkled her nose. "He looks like he smells of tomato sauce and garlic. What makes you think I'm a lot to handle?"

Again he took her in from head to toe. "Trust me, Little Dove, you're a pill. I can already tell."

The moniker sounded sweeter coming from his lips than it had from the Lion King.

The vampire continued scanning the room. "That willowy chap over there looks like he might be able to pull out at least *one* good night."

"Only one?"

"Mm. Any more than that and he'll be ready to introduce you to the parents."

"And that's a bad thing?"

"Hey, I thought we were trying to save your *current* relationship here." Something she was starting to question. "Come now, you're going to have to take this a little more seriously."

In any case, she was finally starting to have fun. "Serious. Got it."

One by one, they ticked off every guy in the room, she or the vampire invariably finding one flaw or the other with each of them.

"Looks like there's no one left," she concluded. "Any suggestions? Or am I SOL." She could see where this was going...and she was wildly intrigued.

"Huh. You're right," he said, feigning surprise. "We've gone through our entire supply. I guess there's only one thing left for you to do."

"And what's that?"

Swirling the whiskey in his glass, he met her gaze. "Me."

A spark of lust sizzled through her as she tried to keep her cool. "Oh, what a surprise." *Oh, how tempting.*

"I don't do this lightly, mind you. In our short time together I feel we've become like this"—he twined his middle and index fingers together—"I dare say I'd call you one of my closest friends."

She laughed, enchanted by his natural charm and easy humor.

"So if I must, I'll take one for the team. I'll step in front of the bullet. I'll sacrifice myself for the greater good."

"Sacrifice?!" She feigned an insulted expression.

"For you, Little Dove, I'll land on the grenade."

"I'm a grenade now?"

"Oh yes. Any second now you're going to go off. I think it would be best if you were in my bed when you do."

"Do you really think I'm going to give in just like that?" Tempting as it was.

He shook his head, losing some of his humor. "No. I think you're set on turning me down. But before you do, let me tell you how I see this going for you. You'll probably spend the next hour or so thinking about me, what I can do to you, how I can pleasure you, no strings attached. You'll debate the pros and cons and you might even realize one night with me really is the perfect solution to your dilemma.

"Sadly, you're going to talk yourself out of it. You'll go home and tell yourself you did the right thing. You were a good girl. Except now you'll have a heavy dose of regret to keep your resentment of Brian company, and after a few years, you'll begin to think of me, this night, what could have been, and the pleasure I could have brought you. It very well might haunt you for years to come."

She didn't respond. How could she when she couldn't even swallow? Couldn't catch her breath. Really, what could someone say to that? Instead, she finished off her wine.

He sighed and took a long pull of his drink. "Still, I understand your reservations. I see only one way to decide the right course of action."

"And that is?" she murmured, setting down her glass.

"As I see it, it's a matter of chemistry."

She cocked her head.

He placed his drink on the bar. "We should see if we have any." He stood and closed the space between them, inserting himself between her legs, his eyes bearing down on her as she stared up at him. She was all but too stunned to react.

"I'm going to kiss you now. If you feel nothing, then there will be no reason to continue. Moreover, as your self-appointed protector for the night, if you want, I will sit here with you, chatting innocently while keeping the wolves at bay." He leaned closer till their lips were inches apart. His breath caressed her face. "But if you do feel something, I'm going to take you to my private room and make love to your body until we're both too exhausted to move."

She gulped, heart thundering in her chest. Her gaze slipped to his lips. They looked soft and firm at the same time. Would they feel warm?

He leaned in and slanted his mouth over hers. The touch was feather light, a tease, a forbidden temptation. It fired her blood as desire shanghaied her every nerve.

She slanted her head, deepening the kiss.

His lips slowly swept along hers, stoking a spark that was quickly building into a blaze. She slid her hands through his dark hair and swept her tongue out to taste him. He groaned, following her lead. His big hand clamped the back of her neck, keeping her in place as he plunged, taking her mouth with carnal hunger. Her breath came in erratic gasps, making her lightheaded. Caught up in the moment, she fisted his hair and dragged him closer. In response, he pressed his big body deeper into the crevice of her legs. Her skirt rode high on her hips, but she couldn't bring herself to care. All that mattered was his delicious, devouring kiss. The way his tongue caressed hers like she was the answer to a prayer.

This was madness.

This was a terrible idea.

Brian was still sitting but a few tables away. Any minute now he'd notice what she was doing. Any minute he'd realize his mistake and tell her he was wrong for ever bringing her here. Would he become jealous as the vampire had predicted?

The vampire palmed the small of her back and jerked her body closer still. Her ass hung on the edge of the stool, the line of his zipper teased her core. She rolled her hips. He let out a rough sound that buried her in purified want.

Her legs wrapped around him, her heels digging into his calves. At the same time, her hands grasped his hair, their tongues dancing a furious tango. He gripped her exposed thigh, running his hand over her overheated flesh. The tantalizing sensation tore a small whimper from her.

Breaking their kiss, he pulled back with a bewildered expression. They were both panting, staring at each other like they'd just experienced something miraculous.

Expression turning fierce, he snatched her hand and pulled her to stand. "Come."

As he led her through the club like a man on a mission, embarrassment caught up with her. She worked to right her skirt, which was slightly askew, as her legs struggled to keep up with his long, purposeful stride.

It wasn't till her outfit was finally in order that she realized he'd escorted her into an elevator. In an instant, her mind diagnosed her situation. She was about to be alone with a strange vampire who was preparing to have sex with her in an undisclosed location. She should be frightened. She should be protesting. She should stop this before this went any further.

Or she could...not.

Her body thrummed with excitement and desire, the likes of which she had never experienced before. It was like she'd just taken a hit of the most addictive drug known to mankind, and was promised more.

Before the elevator doors closed, she glanced at where Brian was seated, fawning over the peacock.

He never once looked her way.

CHAPTER 2

The vampire's private room was more like a posh apartment. Well-lit and decorated in a clean, modern style, it had high ceilings, beige carpeting, and a large open floor plan. Soft music played from a stereo as she sat on a comfortable couch in the seating area.

He stood behind a built-in bar, busy making their drinks. They had removed their masks and she allowed herself to take him in fully. He was gorgeous, but not in a classically handsome kind of way. His jaw was just a bit too large and pronounced for that, and there was a bump in the bridge of his nose that made her wonder if it had once been broken, though it didn't diminish his looks.

And, oh, those eyes.

Captivating and lively iridescent pools. She could dive into those exotic depths and swim around for days. She'd heard vampires could hypnotize humans with either their voice or their eyes. So why did she feel no fear of him? Was she already under his spell?

He met her gaze, and though her heart skipped, she refused to look away. She felt in control of herself, but how would she know?

He crossed toward her and offered a flute of white wine. She accepted it, pretty impressed by the lack of tremor in her hand when their skin touched.

She took a quick sip. It tasted wonderful. "Thank you."

As he sat on the couch beside her, his gaze swept over her face, as if *she* fascinated *him*. For some reason, he wanted her, though there'd been plenty of other available, easier, more beautiful women for him to select. She wasn't a fool. He'd picked her out of the crowd. Focused all that considerable charm on her. Maybe he craved the challenge she appeared to pose back up in the club. Not that she'd been all that hard to get in the end.

Finally she took her gaze back and sent it around the room. "So this is an Ever Nights' private room?"

"Not exactly. This is my apartment."

Her eyes snapped back around. "You *live* here?"

He nodded.

"As in permanently?" The place didn't exactly appear lived in. There was some art on the walls, a couple ocean landscapes and a sparkling lake at sunset. There was a rubber tree plant in the corner next to a full-length mirror, and a large thin vase by the front door that housed an array of tall dried twigs. That was as far as the decor went.

"It's just one of my residences. I only stay here on occasion." Translation: when he wanted to be secluded in the company of vulnerable human women?

The full weight of her situation slammed down on her. She'd allowed herself to become totally alone with a strange vampire.

Even the friendly ones could be deadly.

So how could it be that she felt no danger from him?

It helped that Ever Nights had an exemplary reputation for keeping the peace within its walls. They had very strict rules geared toward safety. Just to attend tonight's function she'd had to read over them. Number one rule? Consent was a must for any extracurricular activities on the property.

Over the last ten years there had been little to no violence reported, save for a single gruesome incident several weeks ago that had plastered front page news. But that had been an attempt at sabotage by a jealous, vindictive competitor. Justice had been swift and severe, dealt out by none other than the VEA (Vampire Enforcement Agency).

"Are you nervous?"

She jumped at his voice and then blushed at her reaction. She might be nervous, but there was excitement too. She attempted a smile. It felt thin. "I've never done anything like this before."

"Never would have guessed that." There was a light-hearted teasing to his tone, but then he grew serious. "Look. If you want to go back up to the party, we will. Just say the word."

She could tell he wasn't giving her lip service. If she wanted, she could return to her seat at the bar and try not to notice Brian working his charms on other women while she sipped wine all night.

Like Hell.

A better idea? Experiencing a single unfettered night of wild passion with a sexy stranger who she'd likely never see again.

The vampire waited patiently for her answer, giving her time to back out. There was no chance of that happening, as long as they could agree to a few rules of their own...

After taking another taste of wine, she asked, "Do you

mind not...you know...." She curled her index and forefinger in front of her mouth, miming fangs.

He laughed before giving her another sexy half grin. "Only if you want me to."

"Would it hurt?"

He shook his head. "Just the opposite."

She'd heard as much through a couple of adventurous women in the office. She'd also heard how addictive such a thing could be. Had seen some of the dens where humans lined up to offer themselves up as a snack just for the erotic high.

"I don't think I want that."

He shrugged. "Then it won't happen." His thumb curled under her chin as he met her gaze. "Why don't you tell me what you *do* want?"

She hesitated, opening her mouth to speak.

Nothing came out.

What did she want? She didn't exactly know. She'd never had a casual one-night stand before. She didn't even know where to start. Should they kiss again? Should she just start stripping down to her undies? She glanced around, trying to decipher where they'd do it. The couch? The floor? She supposed one of the closed doors led to a bedroom....

Seeming to understand her indecision, he took the lead. Closing the distance between them, he put his arms around her.

"Is this alright?"

She nodded.

Slowly, as if not to frighten her, he lowered his lips to hers. Connection. This kiss was different than the previous ones. There was less fire, sure, but so much more steam. His hard, demanding lips swept over hers with an intensity that was contagious. It infected her heart first, making the organ thump, thump, thump, then her nerves, making them sizzle, and finally her skin, brushing every inch with a tingling fever.

Then he turned up the heat, applying more pressure and flicking his tongue over her lips. She gasped. He plunged, and their tongues met, clashing and twining together. After a moment, he laid her back against the couch, his palm leaving a hot trail down her side, over her hip. She became acutely aware of how high up her skirt had ridden when his strong grip found her backside, easily slipping past the fabric and kneading her there with a light pressure.

Her ribs worked to hold back the explosion of her pulse.

As if unconsciously drawn to it, his lips traveled to her neck where he lightly sucked on her flesh.

Her heart nearly broke free of her chest; desire now a wild unquenchable beast within her.

He pulled back as if to gauge her response. Whatever he saw in her expression encouraged him to take her lips once more with carnal excitement. This kiss was passion ignited; fire and heat and sizzle come together for a maelstrom of chaotic lust.

His rough palm returned to her ass where he squeezed her flesh with a delicious pressure. At the same time he groaned, sucking her bottom lip between his teeth.

Her body shook with ferocious need. She never knew she could be so mindlessly turned on.

Then his seeking fingers inched along the cleft of her rear toward her center. Continuing past the paltry fabric of her panties where he met her heat directly.

"So wet for me." His voice broke low and rumbled along her every nerve. "You'd come in a heartbeat if I kept this up, wouldn't you?"

Her body was already quivering with the promise of release. The forbidden nature of this liaison was heightening her arousal by delirious degrees.

He broke contact, stepping back with a sexy smirk. That roguish expression sent her heart into barrel rolls. He may have stopped touching her for the moment, but things were about to get intense. If that look had anything to say about it, this was panning out to be a night she'd never forget. Hopefully one she didn't regret.

He held out his hand to her. "Come."

She took his hand and stood, a bit flummoxed by his commanding tone, but also eager to see what he had planned.

He led her toward the full-length mirror. He stood behind her as she faced it. "I want you to watch me make you come." He found the zipper at her hip and unzipped her skirt. The fabric piled around her heels. He helped her out of her blouse next.

Now bared to his gaze but for her undergarments, her nerves returned.

"Mmm. Black silk," he said in a gruff tone, running the back of his finger over the strap on her shoulder blade. "This is gorgeous on you."

She shivered, those nerves dimming for him once more.

"You have a beautiful body," he told her as his hands traveled over her exposed flesh: her sides, her stomach, her hips. He kissed her lightly on the shoulder, his talented hands trailing up her torso to cup her breasts. The action brought her flush against him, and she could feel his power all around her. Thick cords of muscle flexed deliciously as he coiled one arm around her body as if to hold her in place while his free hand explored breasts, lightly pinching one nipple till she whimpered, then the other.

"You like what I do to you."

It wasn't a question. She met his gaze in the mirror, then her own. Cheeks flush, eyes hooded, she appeared drunk...lust drunk.

"The things I want to do to you. For you. Are you ready, Little Dove?" The gleam in his eyes promised nothing but pleasure.

Her breath caught with a zing of sizzling anticipation.

"You need me to make you come."

At length, she nodded.

He dipped his head and grinned, his lips softly brushing her shoulder. "I need you to say it, beautiful girl."

"Please," she muttered. "I need you to make me come."

Something like a groan rumbled out of him. He slipped his fingers past the fabric of her panties and found her core; hot, swollen, needy. Her head lulled as she moaned at the initial sensation of his foreign touch.

"Christ, you're so ready," he muttered with wonder, expertly stroking her sensitive folds.

"Oh, god!" she cried, shards of bliss assaulting her senses.

"How long can you hold out, I wonder?"

Already her body shook, bombarded by dizzying pleasure, primed to shatter. Waves of ecstasy pounded the walls of her resistance.

Then his wicked fingers found a rhythm that had her eyes rolling back in her head. Her head fell back against him.

"Mm, so close. Let me hear you scream." His thick finger circled her clitoris.

She did scream then. Wild, white-hot, bliss surged

in her veins. Blinding ecstasy took root at the base of her brain, building, growing, and finally exploding through her entire body. She tossed her head back and cried out to the ceiling as assaulting pleasure lashed her over and over, mercilessly, rendering her a mass of pure, erotic, quivering, sensation.

Her knees buckled under the weight of nirvana. The vampire hooked his free arm around her torso and held her upright against his body.

Slowly, breath by breath, she came back down. Her chest thundered, skin warm and feverish. Yet she felt refreshed. Desired.

And hungry for more.

CHAPTER 3

"Are you enthralling me?" She turned to face the vampire.

"Even if it wasn't prohibited in the club, I've no need for that sort of trickery." His sexy grin transformed into a sexy smirk.

Somebody was certainly pleased with himself.

For good reason. He brought out something wild in her. Tonight she could be anyone she wanted. She could become a more confident version of herself, a more desirable version. She could get what she wanted without feeling judged. Tonight was about freedom, excitement, exploration. She was utterly free to express herself in ways she never had before. Plotting to unravel him as thoroughly he'd shattered her, she mirrored his expression. He blinked, a crease forming between his brows.

With the drug of passion still galloping through her bloodstream, she fisted his shirt with both hands and ripped it open. Buttons flew in all directions, bouncing off the walls and furniture.

"Shit!" he exclaimed on an exuberant laugh. He gazed

down at her with a mixture of excitement and disbelief.

Her palms explored his hard torso. She guided him backwards, pushing him toward one of the armchairs. Seemingly interested in what she had in mind, he allowed her to take control. She worked to remove his belt and undo his slacks. When his knees hit the chair, he obediently sat.

Going to her knees, she freed his shaft and then immediately swallowed him down.

"Fuck!" His hips jerked, sending his cock deeper into her throat. Using her tongue to massage his length, she slowly retreated before plunging down once more. He jerked again, almost as if he couldn't help it, but he seemed to be putting in an effort to keep still, letting her do what she pleased. His skin on her tongue was like silk grazing steel. When she drew him deeper still, a rough, wild sound rippled through his chest.

"You are a bit of a surprise, Little Dove."

When she swirled her tongue around his tip, his fingers dug into the arms of the chair while another groaned expletive sailed out of him.

"Holy fuck, woman. As much as I love what you're doing to me, I need to fuck you."

She wasn't ready to stop. She liked the power of rendering him mindless with lust. Taking him to the root, she sucked hard.

"Ugh." His muscles coiled like a spring under stress. "Vixen." He gripped her by the shoulders and pried her off him.

Her mouth left him with a resounding *pop*. She licked her lips, all but ready to devourer him again.

"Christ have mercy," he breathed. With a swift motion, he brought them both to stand and then lifted her over his shoulder. "I can see I'm going to have to take control of this situation lest you unman me right here in my own living room."

She laughed as he carried her to the bedroom and then dropped her lightly on the mattress. Looming over her, he shrugged out of his tattered shirt, revealing a masterpiece of rock-hard abs and thick corded muscles. He shoved his pants down, displacing that gorgeous cock she wanted more of.

"If I didn't need to fuck you so hard right now, I'd let you have your fill," he said, catching her eyeing his shaft.

She grinned. "So then what are you waiting for?"

His eyes narrowed at the challenge. His hands hooked the backs of her knees and yanked her toward him, her body gliding easily over the soft sheets. That was all the warning she received as he slammed inside her.

Though she was slick and ready, he was a large man, and there was the barest twinge of pain at his invasion. She grimaced slightly.

"God you're tight." He froze, fear flashing in his eyes. "You're not.... You can't be a virgin."

"'Course not," she assured him. "You're just a big guy, if you hadn't noticed."

His body practically sank in relief. Then his hips rocked forward.

She gasped.

"Sorry," he said, his arms shaking with the effort to keep still as he held himself over her. "Does it hurt?"

"No," she sighed. "That was good. Do it again."

He did. Pleasure tumbled through her. She rolled her hips with him and let out a sound of contentment. "You feel good, vampire."

"You feel incredible, Little Dove." He pressed further

inside her, filling her to the brim.

"Oh!" she moaned. At the same time, he groaned and set into a slow pace that carried her closer to the edge with each measured thrust. As her moans grew longer, his breaths grew heavier.

"Are you good?" he asked.

"Yes. Don't stop."

His movements found a frantic pace that hammered her into a pinpoint focus toward reaching that invisible realm of ecstasy and bliss. With his thrusts, the bed *thunked* against the wall, marking their tempo and adding another layer to the sounds of their passion. Together they found that perfect rhythm.

"Oh, god! Yes. Don't stop!"

He grunted out something unintelligible and continued to piston his hips. His fingers threaded through her hair and he guided her to his lips. This kiss was a million times sexier than the other two combined. This kiss was not just hot. It was wild and out of control. It was hard and demanding, and profound. It was consuming.

A branding.

With this kiss he'd be taking part of her with him forever. A part she didn't even know existed, let alone could be claimed so thoroughly.

He broke the kiss and gazed at her like he'd just been gut-punched. Hand still tangled in her hair, grunted through harsh breaths, "You will return to me."

"Huh?" His hips were still rocking into her with perfect friction, making her mind nothing but a haze of unintelligible pleasure.

"Here. Tomorrow night. You will come to me again."

There was no way that was happening, this was a one-time-event, but he didn't give her time to formulate a response. As his cock slammed home again and again, he kissed her with a carnal intensity that she was helpless against. White-hot pleasure scored every nerve in her body, burning her from the inside out with pure, concentrated nirvana. She threw her head back and screamed.

His already furious pace doubled, flinging her pleasure to new, impossible heights. His thrusts turned into something unnatural, yet were pure heaven-made. Gripping her waist, he slammed her down on his cock, harder, faster, deeper. It was almost too much to bear. She prayed it never ended.

Once more, she screamed in delighted rapture. He roared, his release telegraphed in the straining of his muscles. The tendons in his neck were so tight they looked as if they could pop free.

She kissed his neck.

He groaned against her shoulder.

With a final, blissful thrust, his movements slowed. After a moment, he lethargically crumbled over her. She cradled him in her arms, working to breathe evenly and draw her mind back to the realm of reality.

She wasn't sure how long they laid there, his face buried in her neck as they both turned to mush. As her eyes drifted closed, she mused that she wasn't even worried about his fangs being so close to her carotid.

CHAPTER 4

"Little Dove," a soft voice cooed.

She curled into the soft sheets and grumbled, wanting nothing more than to stay in her cozy cocoon of slumber. But that voice? That sultry baritone was strange and unknown to her. Little Dove? No one called her that except—

She shot upright. The bed sheet nearly slid down her torso. She caught it against her chest.

I am butt-ass naked.

Oh, that's right. Because I just banged a stranger, and then passed out from bliss.

The vampire stood at the end of the bed, gazing down at her. He was fully dressed in his previous clothes but for a new shirt, buttons intact. How could he look even sexier? Even after the mind-bending orgasm he'd given her, her body stirred for more of his touch. She couldn't recall ever reacting to a man so strongly.

Guild fell upon her like a pall. "What time is it? Did I seriously fall asleep?" Wrapping the sheet more tightly around her, she scooted off the bed and searched the floor for her clothes, which were probably still strewn all over the living room.

How long had she been here? Was Brian worried? Looking for her even now?

"Only about twenty minutes," said the vampire.

"Huh?"

"You look a little alarmed. Don't worry. You've only been asleep for about twenty minutes."

"Oh. Alright. Thanks." Brian might not have even noticed her missing.

The vampire plucked her clothes off an armchair where they'd been folded and handed them to her.

"Thank you."

"You're welcome." He nodded and walked out of the room, giving her privacy.

As she dressed, slipping her blouse and skirt on, she discovered her panties were curiously missing. She searched through the sheets, around the bed, then all around the room. By the time the vampire returned, she was bent over on all fours, ass high in the air as she squinted through the darkness underneath the bed.

He cleared his throat. "What are you doing?"

She bolted upright, her cheeks flaming. "I was just looking for..." She broke off, spotting a familiar scrap of black fabric peeking out of his pocket. Was that...?

He followed her gaze. Swiftly, his thumb shoved the fabric deeper into his pocket. She blinked up at him.

Innocent look in place, he said. "Don't forget this." He held out her white feathered mask.

Still a bit stunned, she slipped it over her face and stood. Their gazes linked for a long moment. She was unsure what to do next. Should they kiss or something? Was he hoping for a round two? Should she demand her undies back? Or was she meant to bid him farewell and leave quietly?

The thought depressed her.

"Shall I show you the way back?" he offered.

She nodded, feeling...she didn't know what she was feeling. Her body was well loved, practically glowing from satisfaction. The things they had done. Naughty things. Wondrous and intoxicating. She felt...different. Danger and excitement had drugged her mind, but now she was coming down. Her fling was over.

So soon?

The way back. Back to her spot at the bar. Back to her old life. Back to Brian.

She followed him into the living room, a hard ball forming in the pit of her stomach. The vampire had given her exactly what she'd come for: one hell of an amazing night. Too amazing.

How could she go on knowing such passion existed in the world? Passion she had never before experienced? What if she never did again?

Ignorant to her unhappy musings, he walked her down the hall, stopping at the elevator. He didn't join her inside.

That heavy ball gained mass. "Well," she said. "Thank you for an unforgettable evening."

He inclined his head, and the elevator doors closed, leaving her with the image of his burning gaze.

Yet his silent goodbye poked at her self-esteem. She almost had to wonder if she'd been somehow inadequate. Disappointing even? Had she done something wrong? Been too eager? Not eager enough? Stayed too long? Damn it! Why had she fallen asleep? Talk about a faux pas.

Would she be as memorable to him in his endless nights of one-night stands as he undoubtedly would be to her? Was she just another notch on his bedpost? Easily forgotten?

Why was she even thinking this way? It was a single night of anonymous sex. Nothing more. It didn't matter if he remembered her or not....

Although, he had kept her underwear. Though maybe that was more of a habit. A trophy? Maybe he did that every time he was with a female. Perhaps he had an entire drawer filled with women's undergarments.

The idea made her giggle, and she latched onto it, dubbing him a compulsive panty hoarder. She laughed out loud, the sound bouncing off the elevator walls, reflecting her blurry visage. Her hair was a mess. Why, she almost looked like she'd been fucked out of her wits. Though she was alone in the elevator, she covered her mouth to hold back a cackle, one that would not be tamed. On and on she laughed. By the time the elevator doors opened, and music once more blasted her ears, she was sucking back air to laugh even harder.

She felt like a lunatic. Maybe she'd been fucked past the line of insanity.

Taking in several deep breaths, she wrangled control of herself. When she felt semi-normal again, she crossed toward a dark corner where a table sat unoccupied. Couples were still dancing and flirting, but a bout of paranoia made her worry they were secretly staring at her, knowing where she'd been. What she'd done.

When she took her seat, her heart was hammering behind her ribcage, as though she'd run a ten-K, and she was slightly out of breath.

Her first one-night stand had been a heady experience, and as conflicted as she was about it, she had to admit she was a little sad that it was over. In the span of a few hours, her world had been rearranged, like a toppled game board, but she no longer recognized where the pieces fit.

Her eyes darted back to the empty elevator. It was early

yet, by club standards. Would the vampire return to the party tonight? Seek out another partner?

A pang stabbed her chest, and confusion skated along her subconscious. She'd felt this way before, when her very first long-term relationship had ended. But that didn't make any sense. Why should it feel as if her heart was breaking all over again?

Clearly her wayward emotions were taking her for a ride. She wasn't cut out for casual sex and one-night stands. How did others do it and keep their hearts out of the mix?

"Any luck?" Brian bellied up to her table.

She gazed at him blankly for a moment, her mind stuttering before a thousand more emotions bombarded her so fast she could only register a scant few: Guilt, regret, defiance, righteousness. Nothing made sense.

"Hello?" He waved a hand in front of her face. "You have too much to drink or something?"

At length, she shook her head. "Sorry, I couldn't hear."

"I asked if you had any luck."

As if on autopilot, she shook her head again. When she registered her own movement, she rushed to correct herself, but Brian said, "Yeah, me neither. There's nothing but teases here tonight. Look, maybe you were right. Maybe this was a bad idea."

Her jaw dropped open.

"You want to just head back to my place?" He tilted his head, studying her expression. "You okay? You're looking a little pale."

Her fingers lightly trailed over her cheekbone. "I...yeah, I'm not feeling too well. Can you just take me home?"

Looking disappointed, he nodded. "Sure, let's go." He added in a derisive tone, "This night was a complete bust, wasn't it?"

CHAPTER 5

The following week, Kasima still battled her guilt. She hadn't meant to lie to Brian. Everything had happened so fast that night. After they'd left the club, he'd dropped her off at her place with a sullen, "You sure you don't want me to come inside?"

To have Brian in her home, in her bed, after what she'd just experienced? The idea had rustled her riotous emotions. "I'm really not feeling well," she'd told him, then speed-walked to her front door. She hadn't wanted to confess that night, worried about his reaction. Although the whole thing had been his idea, she didn't believe for a second he'd be cool with how things had turned out. In fact, he might just lose his shit when he learned the truth.

And still she hadn't been able to come clean.

Not because she didn't want to, but what should she bring up first? His alleged visits to Ever Nights or her sexcapades?

She didn't want to accuse him of anything when the vampire had shrewdly pointed out that Ever Nights offered an array of non-sexualized entertainment. It was an all-in-one kind of establishment—her coworkers talked of going there for Friday night drinks and dinner. So if she asked him about that before revealing her truth, it could make everything worse. Brian always hated it when she showed any kind of jealousy. It was the reason he'd split with women in the past, and the reason they'd been non-exclusive for so long.

If she brought up the masquerade first, it might appear as if she'd slept with the vampire out of spite. She wasn't entirely sure she hadn't.

Secretly she was passively avoiding the whole situation.

She reminded herself that if he could have, he'd have slept with someone too. With lots of someone's, probably. Truth be told, the peacock had looked like a sure thing. As Kasima had sat at that bar, she'd had no doubt they'd be engaging in the horizontal mambo shortly. After all that flirting and heavy petting? Who would have guessed she'd turn him down?

How ironic that Brian had been seeking a free pass and hadn't used it, while she'd resented hers, yet had turned it in like a kid at a candy store.

She thought of the vampire—which she found herself doing a lot these days. A problem she'd have to overcome if she was going to try to make it work with Brian. *Is that even what I want anymore?*

She'd replayed that fateful night in her mind a thousand times. She was still surprised at how easily he had seduced her. He'd been an expert at mowing down her defenses with that sexy grin, cool confidence, and fun banter. As if she was a vault, and he knew all the codes.

With seemingly little effort, he'd rendered her the definition of *easy*.

In an attempt to shake him, she painted him a villain, her subconscious desperately trying to find something sinister about the whole situation. She pictured him regaling his club buddies with his conquering story over their bellows of laughter.

So why couldn't she get him out of her head?

And what was the deal with him asking her to return? As if she would rush right back there the next night, like some wonton female looking to beg for more of his cock.

God, how she wanted more.

She hadn't gone, of course. It had all been a part of his seduction. He was a self-proclaimed regular at Ever Nights. He even had his own private apartment there. No. He didn't really want to see her again. Would probably laugh in her face if she shown up looking for him. Obviously he was a playboy bachelor—with a possible panty problem.

She didn't need that kind of mind-fuckary.

Even if he did want her to return, she'd decided she shouldn't. No. She *couldn't* see him again. Instinctively she understood there was something addictive about him, and it had nothing to do with his vamp status—he hadn't even bitten her, and still she felt like a junkie. Not to mention it had been a pre-approved, agreed upon by all parties, one night only, free pass....

So why was she having such a hard time coming clean to Brian?

She wrung her fingers together. He was going to be here any minute to pick her up for a dinner date. She promised herself that today would be the day she told him the truth. Omission was the same thing as lying when someone's heart was on the line.

Tonight would be their first date since the masquerade. Hoping to lessen the blow of her admission, she'd dressed up. The spaghetti-strap dress with a plunging neckline was cut just above the knee and cinched at the waist. Her heels were simple, black and short. She'd piled her hair over her head with a few curled flyaways, exposing the sleek column of her long neck—one of her better features.

The ensemble was enhanced by a simple necklace with a heart charm that fell perfectly into the hollow of her clavicle.

Brian should be blown away.

With a little added charm, her confession should go over without a hitch. She just wasn't sure if she should tell him now, or at dinner, or after they returned to her place for a nightcap. For some reason she wasn't anticipating the last. Probably because of her guilt.

When she heard a car door slam, she snatched her purse and headed out the door, not waiting for Brian to walk the short path to her door.

His brows shot up when he saw her. "Wow." His smile gutted her.

"Thanks." She hastily kissed him hello and hurried past him. "Shall we go? I'm starving."

"'Course," he said, returning to the driver seat.

She slid into the passenger seat, working hard not to fidget. He pulled away from the curb and took a right turn at the first intersection that led out of her cozy neighborhood, situated in a pocket of Riverstone that many would dub the rich side of town, which wasn't saying much. It was a single street of well-maintained houses. Most of her neighbors were small business owners or held upper management positions at the local casinos, where the real money was made. She was the odd one out, having inherited her two-story home from her parents who had inherited it from her very savvy and shrewd grandmother.

The economy had yet to bounce back after vampires had revealed their existence, resulting in a great civil war that had devastated not only America, but almost every nation worldwide.

Was now a good time? Maybe she should get it over with like a ripped bandage. "Brian...." she started.

"Can you believe this guy?" he snapped when another car pulled out in front of him. He blasted his horn, slammed his foot down on the gas and, pulled onto the shoulder to gun it past the offending car.

Used to Brian's aggressive driving, she held onto her seatbelt with a death grip.

"Some people shouldn't even be allowed to get a driver's license," he grumbled.

Reaching their destination, Brian pulled into an open parking spot and jerked the car into park. He grinned down at her. "Look at that. Record time."

She weakly smiled back. He didn't seem to notice her pensiveness. He shut off the engine, exited the vehicle, and waited by the bumper for her to join him. Her heels crunched on the gravel on her way to the restaurant's big double doors, her heart rate kicking up with each step.

The hostess showed them to a booth and handed them each a menu. Once they were alone, Kasima took in a fortifying breath. "Brian, there's something I need to tell you." Maybe it was better to do it now. He'd be less likely to make a scene in public. Always concerned for his professional reputation.

"Mm?" He scanned the menu.

"That night at the masquerade—"

The server, a balding male with a slim frame, sidled up to their table. "How are you this evening? Can I start you off with something to drink?"

"Anything new on tap?" Brian asked.

After reciting a few beers, Brian ordered his usual.

She asked for a white wine.

Brian went back to his menu. "I was thinking of getting the chicken. If you get the beef we can share. How's that sound?"

She hadn't even picked up her menu. "That's fine. Listen, I wasn't exactly...I mean that night when you asked if I'd had any luck I..."

He glanced up from the menu. "Sorry, what night are you referring to?"

"The masquerade." Her voice had gone low, embarrassed for anyone else to hear. "When you asked me if I'd had any luck...well, I was caught a little off guard and I wasn't exactly honest."

His expression was mildly amused. "What did you do? Kiss someone? Please say it was a girl."

She shook her head.

"Don't tell me you slept with someone?" He laughed as if that were preposterous.

She met his gaze and nodded guiltily.

He paused for a long moment. Then his menu flopped to the table. "For real?"

"When you asked me, well, at the time, I was feeling a little overwhelmed. And I didn't know you weren't going to go through with it. I guess it felt a little weird that I... had."

"You *slept* with someone?" His tone was disbelieving, and the level of his voice had risen slightly.

"Shh. Yes. That was the plan, wasn't it? You told me to."

"I didn't think you'd actually do it!" Underlining his words was something she'd never heard from Brian before:

revulsion.

Her hackles rose at that. "What do you mean you didn't think I'd actually do it? That was the whole point of going, wasn't it? Or did you just hope to get off with other women while I sat alone on a shelf till you returned to dust me off?"

"That's not what I meant. You just...you're not the type to..."

"To what? Go along with my boyfriend's stupid plan to *sow our wild oats* before we take our relationship to the next level?"

"To be so *easy*."

Her spine met the booth's cushioned back, air gushing out of her lungs as though she'd been kicked in the gut. People were starting to stare. Her flush had to be as vibrant as it felt. "You're going to want to apologize to me. Right now."

He pushed to a stand. "What I want to do is fix this."

She cocked her head.

"It's not fair. You got to sleep with someone else, and I didn't."

Her mouth dropped open. She'd feared that would be his main concern, not that his girlfriend had slept with someone else. It was possible their relationship held no meaning for him at all. She waited for a pang to hit her; it was curiously absent. Was she numb?

"We're going back to the club," he announced, stabbing his pointer finger into the table. "Tonight."

Back to the club? He shot out of his seat and started walking away. She scurried out of the booth to follow him. "Are you being serious right now?"

"Yes. This isn't something I can get past. Not unless I get my free pass too."

She wasn't sure if she should be insulted or disgusted. Both emotions swirled in her gut.

Outside, her heels rapped against the concrete. "This isn't a game, Brian. It was a one-night thing, whether one of us *got lucky* or not. Those were your rules. We agreed on that. It's over now."

He folded himself in the driver seat and wrenched the key in the ignition, starting the engine. Without thinking, she jumped into the passenger seat and closed the door just as he took off.

"Brian, I'm not okay with this." She strapped the seatbelt around herself. The wheels screeched as he pulled onto the main road.

"Well I'm not okay with my woman cheating on me."

"Cheating? You're being ridiculous. Did you forget the whole free pass thing? It was your idea in the first place." Why was he acting like this was all coming as a surprise? "I didn't even want the free pass, and I don't want to go to the club *now*." The vampire's gorgeous features flashed in her mind. What were the odds he'd even be there tonight? A flitter of something danced in her chest.

"Yeah, and you got to have your fun. I didn't." His face was a deep shade of red, his tone resolute. The last shreds of her feelings for him circled the drain.

She faced the road, grudgingly accepting she wasn't going to talk him out of this, yet she had one last thing to say. "If you go through with this, we're finished."

"Don't be so dramatic." He kept driving.

CHAPTER 6

Kasima entered the club behind Brian, seeking a phone to call a cab. Stupidly, she'd forgotten to charge her cell, and the battery was depleted.

Tonight, the club's decor was understated compared to that of the masquerade. The dramatic drapery had been removed, and all those previously darkened alcoves were now brightly lit by what she assumed was the club's typical soft lighting. A few small touches and the place was worlds away from where it had been. Why, it practically looked normal.

Only a few things went unchanged: Ever Nights was every bit as packed, the hidden speakers drummed out a hypnotically rhythmic beat, and people were still bumping and grinding on the dance floor. But the energy was different. This was just a bunch of people out for a night of dancing and socializing at their local watering hole. An innocent affair.

One marked difference: Brian didn't kiss her on the top of the head before tearing off into the crowd, which was a relief.

Good riddance.

She headed for the bar.

Once back home, she'd spend the rest of the night packing Brian's things, not that he'd left a lot at her house, but still, she wanted it gone as soon as possible—she'd given Brian the chance to grow up, but he'd proven that was impossible, and she'd meant it when she said she was done. She realized she might have seen something in him that wasn't really there, deluding herself.

After his belongings were sequestered in a convenient to-go box, she planned to take a seriously long, hot bubble bath. With that promising future, she sidled up to the bar.

"What can I get you?" the bartender asked. This bartender was slightly taller than the one who had served her the night of the masquerade, but was just as muscular and equally handsome. Did they manufacture beef-cakes in the back?

He waited for her order.

Oh, what the hell. "A shot of tequila, please, and a phone if you don't mind. I need to call a cab."

"Not having a good night?" he observed with a tell-me-all-about-it smile.

"Bad date." She left it at that.

When he served her the shot, she tossed it back, feeling the harsh burn of alcohol.

He immediately refilled it. "On the house."

"Thanks," she said, downing this one just as swiftly.

"There's a phone at the back where it's quieter." He pointed to a pay phone that hung on the wall by the restrooms. It was currently in use by a seedy looking fellow.

She pointed to the empty shot glass. "I guess I'll have one mo—"

"—and I want Dane at the entrance tonight."

That voice...

She spun around on her stool.

He looked bigger than she recalled. Even more muscular. She'd convinced herself she'd imagined his killer gorgeous features. Her appreciative gaze roamed his square jaw darkened by a hint of scruff that hadn't been there last week, the wide berth of his powerful shoulders, his muscle-packed arms poking out of his black t-shirt with the word STAFF written in thick bold lettering.

She wanted to slap her forehead. Staff? Had his job been to make sure everyone got lucky? If so, job well done. The man deserved a raise.

The second he noticed her, he did a double take and halted in his tracks, his gaze boring into hers. The employee next to him tripped to a stop an instant later, confused.

She swallowed, and suddenly her eyes couldn't decide what they should look at—him? The floor? The exit? The muddled employee who was now glancing back and forth between the two of them?

Meanwhile, the vampire was steadily taking her in, eyes so intense she could almost feel his gaze like a caress.

Then, without a word, he closed the distance between them. Her heart thumped heavily in her chest. Could he hear it? As they stared at one another, neither spoke. It might appear as though they were basking in each other's presence. Truth was she wasn't sure what to say. Finally his hand came up to cup her cheek. Warmth penetrated her skin, and she unconsciously leaned into his touch. Something palpable passed through their connection.

"Why didn't you return to me sooner?" he asked.

"I didn't think you were serious about that," she admitted sheepishly.

His brows drew together, a little crease formed between them. Was he hurt by that? Surely not.

He inched closer. "Then why are you here now?"

She dropped her gaze, embarrassed by the answer.

"Is this him?" Brian's accusing voice shot from behind the vampire. "Is this the guy you cheated on me with?"

A mental groan echoed through her nerves.

The vampire retracted his hand to face Brian. The bartender and the other employee watched the scene with amused interest. Her cheeks burned at their scrutiny.

"You must be Brian," the vampire said.

"How'd you know that? She talked about me while you two were f—"

"She told me about your night of unencumbered freedom. I believe you called it a free pass? Brilliant idea, by the way." Did Brian register the sarcasm? "But from what I understand, you couldn't close the deal."

She blinked up at the vampire. Where had he heard that?

Brian balked and then blustered for a moment. His eyes narrowed on her as if in the short time she'd been here she'd managed to relay his failure. "That wasn't my fault," he hissed.

"'Course not," the vampire conceded. "Nothing but teases here that night."

Kasima blinked as the vampire recited Brian's words. Could he have somehow heard their conversation? She glanced back at the bartender, who was now blatantly ignoring other customers in favor of the tense scene. At first, his expression was unreadable, then he offered her a shrug and a placid smile. Her gaze zeroed in on his fangs. Something told her the other employee was a vampire as well. They had extraordinary hearing. Perhaps her and Brian's conversation that night hadn't been as private as she'd assumed. And whatever was said had gotten back to her vampire.

"Teases, yeah," Brian concurred, not making the connection. "Except for my own girlfriend, apparently."

Her body went tense at the verbal blow. "*Ex*-girlfriend," she snapped.

Feeling all eyes on her now, she fought a blush, determined to retain some dignity in this very undignified exchange.

"We'll discuss that later," Brian replied dismissively, as if she were merely throwing a fit.

She shook her head, ready to inform him there wouldn't be a later when the vampire interjected. "Brian, I appreciate your situation, and I think I can help." He raised his hand and gestured to someone across the room.

Brian scoffed. "That so?"

Moments later, a dark-haired beauty stepped out from the crowd. "Rita, this is Brian. Would you mind keeping him company tonight?"

Rita gave Brian a flirty grin, then practically purred, "I'd love to."

Slack jawed, Brian's gaze raked over Rita's generous figure, from her crazy tall heels, shorter-than-short skirt, and boisterous cleavage. He glanced at Kasima fleetingly—who tried to convey with a look that she didn't give a good goddamn what he did—then back to Rita. "Alright then."

Rita led Brian back into the throng of guests with a practiced giggle.

As far as coffins go, this wasn't just the last nail, this was an air-tight seal that had been riveted shut and welded for good measure. He couldn't have fought for her less if he'd been saddled with the fortitude of a one-toed sloth.

Her embarrassment wouldn't have been so sharp if all

this hadn't been witnessed by her vampire. Her ego was taking its lumps tonight.

Turning to face the bar, she found the bartender had graciously refilled her tequila. She snatched the shot and brought it to her lips, practically inhaling the liquid. Time for a graceful escape. If that was even possible at this point. "Well, if you'll excuse me gentlemen, I see the phone is free now."

She edged around the bar, heading for the back.

The vampire was right behind her. "Where are you going?"

"To call a cab. I've had my fill of humiliation this evening." She picked up the receiver and dialed zero for information.

The vampire pressed down on the phone's lever, disconnecting the line.

She pivoted around. "Hey."

"You going to play hard to get now?"

"I'm going to play not available?" Giving him her back, she swatted his hand away from the phone.

He immediately returned it to the lever. "Why?"

She sighed. "I'm feeling a little battered and bruised at the moment."

With a gentle nudge, he maneuvered her to face him. Those intense green eyes of his captured her gaze. "Then let me kiss your wounds and make it better."

At the low rumble of his voice, she had to stifle a shiver.

"Tell me what has you feeling humiliated?"

"You mean aside from my very public breakup with my boyfriend, who thereafter happily skipped off with another woman under your command? You had someone spy on me after I left your room that night, didn't you."

He scraped a palm down the back of his neck. "Spy on you? No."

She gave him a don't-lie-to-me glare.

He shrugged. "When you didn't come back as I'd requested, I *might* have gone over the surveillance video from that evening."

Her eyes widened in horror. "Surveillance?"

"It's only set up in the public areas," he rushed out.

The terror of what else might have been caught on tape dissipated, and she slumped in relief. "What did you expect to find?"

"I was looking to see if I'd done something to scare you off."

"Huh." The answer was unexpected. "So, you really did want me to come back?"

"I wouldn't have said so otherwise."

She pointed at his shirt. "You work here."

He nodded.

"You might have mentioned that before."

Leaning his forearm against the wall beside her, he brought his big body closer to hers. "It wasn't as if we were exchanging detailed information about ourselves. I still don't even know your name, by the way."

"Kasima Wilder. You could have mentioned you were on the clock that night. Is it always your job to seduce the cold fish?"

"Lex Stirling. You were hardly a cold fish. Far from it, in fact. And would it have made a difference if I mentioned being an employee?"

"Maybe. I wasn't looking for a professional. Actually, I wasn't looking for anything at all. You can't deny you seduced me."

He chuckled. "Keep telling yourself that. From my perspective, *you* seduced *me*."

She snorted, rolled her eyes, and then gave a clipped laugh because that was just the most ridiculous thing she had ever heard. Though, hadn't she been unusually aggressive with him?

"My job was to preserve civility on a night when people often feel entitled and emboldened. I was instructed to step in when I see a guest growing increasingly uncomfortable by an overly aggressive individual. I had every intention of moving on once you felt comfortable again."

But he hadn't. He'd engaged her, flirted shamelessly, and had taken her to his private room where he'd made her body sing. Her cheeks grew warm at the remembrance.

Needing somewhere else to put her eyes, she glanced behind him where guests danced and mingled. The staff was no longer hidden in the background, but dressed to stand out in typical uniforms that telegraphed their employment; waitresses with aprons and pads for taking notes, security in black shirts and slacks. All were physically stunning.

"Is everyone who works here a vampire?"

"Is that a problem?"

She lifted one shoulder. "Well, we humans are basically your food. I've always wondered if it's difficult being around us without losing control."

"Do you find it difficult being around human food without losing control?"

"I do if it's pasta."

He laughed. "You have nothing to worry about. If it helps, I'm not hungry."

Because he'd fed already? Her mind conjured an image of him sucking neck, the expression of the woman in his arms was blissfully euphoric. Kasima mentally shook the picture away, as well as the stab of jealousy that had crawled in behind it.

"The club's owner is a vampire," he continued. "But not all the staff is. Like Rita. She's human."

Rita's pretty face was suddenly superimposed over the blissed-out woman, and before she could stop herself, she asked, "Is she who you fed from?"

He eyed her for a moment, one corner of his mouth curling up. "I don't mess around with coworkers if I can help it." He must have sensed her relief because he teased, "Are you going to be less prickly now? Can I kiss you without risking castration?"

She shrugged. "You could try. I guarantee nothing."

He gave her a full grin, which nearly stole her breath, then dipped his head to take her mouth in a soft kiss. His lips were warm and firm as they molded against hers. His spicy clean scent infiltrated her nostrils and flooded her brain with what had to be straight-up crack. Flutters ignited in her chest, sanity went out the window, and she was instantly lost for him. And maybe he was too, because when her hands came up to grip his dark hair, he looped an arm around her waist and pulled her flush against him, groaning into a kiss that was quickly devolving into something too hot for public consumption.

He pulled back, eyes lit with excitement. "I knew I couldn't have imagined how good you taste on my lips."

He tasted good as well. Too good.

There was a reason vampires were dubbed the perfect predator. Everything about them made you want them: they were naturally gorgeous—totally unfair—and for years, scientists have been attempting to synthesize their pheromones to be bottled and sold as a high-end perfume. Their bite was dubbed the greatest aphrodisiac known to mankind, and they could literally hypnotize humans with their gaze. She was the fly to his spider, the mouse to his cat. She knew all this, yet it changed nothing. She was caught.

A small growl emanated from her stomach, reminding her that she hadn't eaten since lunch.

He cocked his head. "You are hungry."

"I'm fine."

"Let me get someone to cover the rest of my shift and I'll take you out." Not giving her time to refuse—or, for that matter, accept—he darted off.

Alone and overheated, her body propped up by the wall, she heard the urgent beeping from the payphone's dangling receiver. As she hung it up, the music seemed to bump louder through the speakers than before, the vibration finding its way to her bones. A nearby group deep in conversation grew more boisterous.

She took in a breath. Was she really about to go on a date with a vampire?

Out of morbid curiosity, she scanned the room for Brian and Rita, but she didn't recognize any of the faces in the crowd. She tried not to think of what the two might be doing at the moment—it no longer concerned her—or how easily Brian had set her aside, as though he could pick her back up when he was done playing with his new toy.

The gall.

She deserved better.

She ran her fingers through her hair. It would be foolish to get carried away with this vampire—Lex. She recognized she was in a vulnerable state. The full weight of her break up couldn't have set in yet. Maybe that was why she wasn't feeling bad about it. It stung, sure, but not as much as she thought it would. Surely tomorrow the situation would settle in and she'd have a good cry about it. Till then, why not have a little fun? A real fling? She'd see where the night took her. Lex was clearly looking for a good time; she certainly needed one. She just needed to make sure to keep things between them simple.

Lex reappeared, sexy smile in place. "Are you ready?"

"Definitely."

CHAPTER 7

There were about ten cars scattered throughout the club's underground employee parking deck, most of them new and shiny and expensive looking, but for one shabby paint-chipped vintage pickup truck in a dark corner. Business was booming, apparently.

Lex fished a set of keys from his pocket and an eggshell BMW beeped, headlights flashing. She took an appreciative lap around the vehicle and whistled. "You own this beautiful machine?"

His shoulders went back a little. "I don't often indulge, but as you can see, we all seem to be competing for the nicest ride." He shrugged as if everybody had that problem.

"How many people work at the club?"

He turned thoughtful? "Cortez employs about a hundred people, give or take."

There were only about twenty people at the Tribune where she worked.

"Why?" he asked moving to the driver's side. "Are you looking for a job?"

She smiled over the hood of his car. "I've got one, but

heck, if your salary affords you this? Maybe I should consider a career shift." She slipped into the passenger seat, he claimed the wheel and pressed a button on the console. The engine purred to life. She had the urge to pet the dash.

"What do you do?"

"I work at the Tribune."

"Are you a reporter?"

She laughed. "No. Brian's the reporter." He was good, too. Next month, he was getting honored at an annual award ceremony. "I'm just an assistant to the editor. I do grunt work like schedule meetings and get coffee. You know, very important stuff." She wouldn't be doing it forever, though. Her real dream was getting a position as an editorial photographer. The Tribune would be the perfect stepping stone. As soon as a position opened up, you'd better believe she was jumping all over it.

"Oh, you must work for Mr. Dixon."

Her lips parted at hearing her boss's name. "You know Mr. Dixon?"

Lex gave her a conspiratorial smile. "He comes in at least once a month. Orders a shot, a beer, and a cocktease."

She blinked. Mr. Dixon was a kindly older man with salt and pepper hair, a paunch, and suspenders to hold up his slacks. She always saw him as a straight-laced, by the book, and even a little prudish. Her mind traded that wholesome image with one of Mr. Dixon salivating over Ever Nights' dancers. Could she ever look at him the same?

As they pulled out of the parking deck, moonlight glinted off the hood and bathed them in a dim navy hue.

"What do you like to eat?" he asked.

"I'm not picky," she replied. "Something quick will be fine." Her tummy growled again as if to concur.

"Kasima, I'm not taking you for fast food."

She stifled a shiver at her name rumbling from his lips.

"How about Le Petit Bistro?"

Le Petit Bistro was pricey, and usually booked out the wazoo. "We don't have to do anything so lavish. Besides, don't you need reservations for that place?"

"Cortez has a standing reservation. It's not a problem."

"He'll be okay with you using his name?"

"If he's not, he can take it up with me later."

She suddenly worried she was causing him trouble—during the masquerade, he'd ditched work to be with her. Was he ditching again tonight? Casually she asked, "Will you be missed back at the club?"

"They can handle tonight without me."

They drove in silence for a moment. She gazed out the window, watching the scenery roll by. The darkened sky was clear, and the stars were particularly bright as they winked for her.

From the corner of her eye, she noticed the vampire glance from her legs to the road and back.

Her body grew warm, and her mind drifted back to their night of passion, the way his kiss had burned so sweetly, how his muscles had toiled over her. He hadn't held back, neither had she, and she'd reveled in it. Wanted more.

He white-knuckled the steering wheel, a rumbling sound reverberating from deep in his chest. "Dinner or my place?"

"Huh?" She squirmed in her seat. Had he followed the trail of her thoughts? Or were her pheromones giving off signals that his keen vampire senses had caught on to? She gulped, a steady *thrum, thrum, thrum* drummed through her nerves. "How close is your place?" She could have him naked in a matter of minutes, feasting on his rock-hard flesh—

Her stomach chose that moment to growl once more.

"Not as close as Le Petits. Dinner it is." He sighed and scrubbed a hand down his face.

Arriving moments later, he pulled into a parking spot. Before she could unbuckle her belt, he was already out of the car and heading around to her side to open her door. Inside the restaurant, Lex only had to mention Cortez and they were immediately seated.

Kasima glanced around. The restaurant was lavishly decorated in a bygone French style with glittering crystal chandeliers, artwork outlined by ornate gilded frames, and massive floral bouquets in every corner that reached well above her modest five foot four inches. Several uniformed waiters lined the walls like statues, waiting to be called upon, while more servers scurried throughout, refilling glasses and checking on guests. Nearly every table was in use.

She picked up her menus, plural—she'd been given three in total. A dinner menu, a drinks menu, and the specials of the day. Most everything was labeled in elegant French script. Glancing from one menu to the next, she must have looked overwhelmed, because Lex muttered, "Tell me what you like and I'll order."

"You speak French?"

"I know enough to be dangerous." He winked.

She smiled. "Well, like I said, I'm not too picky. I'll eat just about anything as long as it's cooked properly, but better keep it simple to be safe."

When the waiter came by, Lex ordered a bottle of white

wine with a long tongue-twisted name, and then muttered a few words in French. The waiter nodded once, and then hurried away.

"Very impressive," she said.

"I ordered you the roasted chicken breast with lemon cream sauce."

"Sounds good. What did you get? Oh...sorry." She blushed. "I guess you won't be eating."

"Of course I will. I ordered the scallops in a caramel-ized onion sauce."

She blinked up at him. "And you'll actually eat it?"

His lips curled at the edges. "You haven't been around vampires too much, have you?"

"Not really."

"Human food is pleasant to eat on occasion, though it does nothing for us on a nutritional level."

Interesting. "So what about the having no reflection thing?" If she took his picture, would he show up on film?

"A ridiculous myth. So many of the myths are bogus. Such as the belief that we can't go out in the sun."

She knew that from seeing them out and about town at all hours.

"I love garlic. Crucifixes don't burn us. Neither will holy water. A stake through the heart wouldn't kill us. It would hurt like hell though."

"So are any of the myths true?"

"Beheading could kill us, but let's be honest, that'll kill anything."

The waiter returned with their wine and filled their glasses.

She took a ginger sip. "This is a very lovely place. Thank you for bringing me here."

"You're very welcome."

Another server floated by, dropping a steaming basket of bread on the table between them. Perfect timing. She needed something to do with her hands. Plucking up a roll, she pinched off a piece to nibble.

His tone dipped an octave. "So, how are you doing?"

"Good," she rushed out, her voice a little off. "I mean, I'm okay. A little nervous, I guess. Which is silly if you think about it because I've already seen you naked, and you me, so what more is there to be embarrassed by? Uh, not that it was embarrassing seeing you naked. Er, I mean, your nakedness was fine. Better than fine." *OMG, stop talking!* She pinched her thumb and forefinger together, making a circle. "It was A-okay." *What is wrong with me?* She shoved the roll in her mouth.

He stared at her for a beat before his grin turned amused. "I meant how are you doing with your breakup. Were you serious about that? I didn't get the impression Brian thought so."

Chewing slowly, she replayed Brian's dismissive tone as he'd told her they'd talk later. He probably thought they could patch things up after a long boring conversation about how he was right and she was wrong. Before this fiasco, she had thought Brian was going to ask her to move in with him soon, maybe even for her hand in marriage, given time. But tonight proved he wasn't ready for that kind of relationship. He wasn't ready to be exclusive with anyone. She just wished she'd recognized that sooner.

"Brian and I never would have worked out," she finally supplied.

"Oh?"

"I was trying too hard to make things work. To be what he wanted. I let a lot of stuff slide that I shouldn't have, and I kind of lost myself."

"It's good to figure these things out before you're in too deep."

She nodded stonily, but she wasn't sure she had anything really figured out. Had she made the right decision? She and Brian had so much in common. From the outside, it looked as though they were the perfect couple. The *exclusive* part of their relationship had really just been in its infancy. It may have just taken Brian a bit more time than her to get on board. Secretly she had dreamed of them working together; her doing the photographs for his top stories. They'd have made a great team. Still might, despite their breakup.

"Will it be a clean break then?"

Crumbs of bread had gathered on her plate from the fresh roll she was idly fiddling with. "Yes and no. We don't live together, but we do both work at the Tribune. It might be a little awkward for a while."

Lex pursed his lips and nodded. "Do you work closely together?"

"Not really. We bump into each other on occasion when he's not out investigating a story. We'd gotten in the habit of meeting for lunch a few times a week, but that will stop now, and he's often out on assignment."

"So it won't be too difficult for you to see him in passing after tonight?"

She shrugged. "Honestly, I'm not sure. Maybe I haven't fully processed everything yet. But he has dated a couple other women in the office before me, and they seemed to have gotten along fine for the most part."

"Seemed to?"

"Most of them had moved on to other ventures shortly after their breakup." Now she wondered if some of them had left for more personal reasons. Had the relationships ended mutually? Or had Brian broken their hearts?

"I'm sorry he was so easily swayed by Rita tonight." Lex paused. "Actually, if I'm being honest, I'm not sorry at all. But I am sorry if it hurt you."

She sighed. "I won't lie. It was...rough." A blow to the ego if there ever was one. Brian had acted as if her feelings were completely irrelevant. She squared her shoulders. "I think everything turned out for the best."

There was something like respect in Lex's small grin.

Their food came moments later. A delicious mixture of fragrances dancing in her nose. The first bite had her eyes rolling back in her head. *So good.*

When she gave him a thumbs up, he dug into his own dish.

"This is amazing," she murmured after several more bites.

He nodded in agreement. "When I'm of a mind to eat human food, this is my favorite restaurant."

"Well, for a vampire, you have surprisingly excellent taste."

He gave a wry scowl. "For a vampire, huh."

Her cheeks heated. "You know what I mean. The last thing I'd expect is for a vampire to have a Michelin-star pallet."

He leaned in, capturing her gaze. "If I'm being honest, I could take it or leave it. What I'm really craving is more of what we did the other night."

The bite of food she'd been about to eat fell from her fork and plopped on the plate.

"I'm fighting the urge to rush you out of here so I can have you all to myself again."

A rogue shiver charged through her body. She pushed her plate away. "Look at that! I'm full. Now, where is that waiter?" She scanned the room, signing for the check.

Lex purred a dark chuckle. "Please finish eating. I would feel bad if you left here still hungry." He forked more food into his mouth and so did she, both of them eating with marked efficiency.

When the check came, he slipped several bills into the sleeve without glancing at it, and they headed back to the car, her nerves taking the reins in her gut. Was she really about to go home with a vampire? She scanned his powerful body as he walked ahead of her to open the passenger-side door. There was something animalistic in the way he moved, like a sleek panther, sure of every step. When she stood in front of him, he reached out to cup her cheek, running his thumb lightly across her lips, his gaze riveted.

"We don't have to go to my place. We don't have to do anything. I can take you home if that's what you want. I'd understand."

The offer was so unexpected, so sweet, and so not what she wanted. She smiled, looking up at him from under her lashes. "I've always been curious to know what a vampire's home looks like."

He grinned back, giving her a flash of one sleek fang, which she found far too sexy. "You're about to find out."

CHAPTER 8

Turned out vampires lived like ballers.

Well, this one did, anyway.

Mechanized wrought iron gates opened to an expansive manicured yard that coiled smoothly around the sides of the house, lined with flourishing square-trimmed bushes. An army of trees with trunks three times her width stood bastion on either side of the driveway, their branches arching overhead, blotting out the moonlit sky. The house wasn't a mansion, per se, but her little two-story townhome was a glorified shack by comparison. Its contemporary style, red and brown tiled roof, and delicate mixture of stone and stucco siding, made it both sleek and natural looking, melding nicely with its environment.

The three-car garage opened as he pulled up. She spotted a tarped vehicle, and a monster of a motorcycle.

"Do you ride?" he asked, noticing her staring.

She shook her head. "I've never been on one."

"Maybe I'll take you out sometime."

"I think my grandmother would turn over in her grave." As well as both her parents.

The inside of his home was equally amazing, with high vaulted ceilings and accent lighting over abstract artwork. Dark painted walls matched the deep grey furniture, contrasting beautifully against the ivory carpet. A huge entertainment system recessed into one wall, facing a luxe leather reclining couch with built-in cup holders in the arm rests. A fully stocked wet bar took up the entire far wall. Through a wide archway to her right, she spotted a pool table displayed proudly at the center of a small room with cue sticks mounted beside it.

"You have a nice home." Or would *bachelor pad* be a more appropriate moniker?

"I rarely stay here," he confessed.

"Why not?"

"I work so much, it's easier sometimes to just stay at the club."

"So you don't often bring women here?" Why did that sound like she was fishing?

His lips curled into a wry grin. "Would you like a drink?"

"Please," she said, allowing the evasion. Once more she felt very unsure of what to do or say. What was expected of her? Was she supposed to act casual, funny and amusing, or alluring and sensual? She seemed to have done well for herself at the masquerade, but that had been wholly accidental.

At the bar, he uncorked a bottle of white wine, found two glasses, and filled them generously. "I think we should get something out of the way before this goes any further."

"Oh? What's that?"

He returned to where she stood and handed her a glass. "You should understand that I'm not boyfriend material."

She sipped her wine, not sure how to respond to that.

"What I mean is, I can give you a fun time, but..." He rolled his hand in the air.

Ah. "But I shouldn't expect anything more than that," she finished for him.

"I wouldn't want you getting the wrong idea about what this is."

"So you're like the eternal bachelor."

He smiled. "Something like that."

"And this is just a one-night stand?" Or rather, a second night stand. Did she want more of what he offered? That would be a *hell yes* to the second power.

"Well, I'm hoping for more than one night..."

Her pulse leapt. *More?*

"...but a commitment is something I can never offer you."

Her heart sank, and she wasn't sure why. It wasn't as if a relationship with a vampire could ever work out in the long term. Could it?

At the same time, she felt just a little sorry for him, because it meant he might never experience a deep, long lasting connection that came with loving, *truly loving*, another person.

As long as she'd known them, she recalled her parents being so desperately in love with one another. If soulmates really existed, then they surely had been. Their love had been wonderful to behold, glorious and pure, and had shaped her very concept of the idea of love in general. She naturally longed for the same ironclad connection. The same indestructible link. Since they'd passed away, she felt bereft without it.

She wasn't going to find it here. Not that she was surprised by the fact. Far from it. He was an unnaturally strong, long-living creature who had forever to waste. And she was essentially his lunch. She didn't figure love mixed well in such an uneven food-chain relationship. Little bunnies didn't fall for big bad wolves—not smart bunnies, anyway. Of course, nor did they hop willingly into the wolves' den—

"Is that going to be okay?" he said, pulling her from her thoughts. "Considering your breakup, well, I'd feel like a shit if I didn't make my intentions clear."

She took another sip of wine. "So, you're not looking for a relationship, I appreciate your candor, but then what do you mean by *hoping for more than one night*? What does that look like to you?"

"I'd call you if I'm feeling...lonely."

She ran her finger along the rim of her glass. "Do vampires such as yourself get lonely?"

His eyes narrowed slightly on her movement, as though he couldn't figure out if she was teasing him. "I was lonely this past week, thinking of you."

Her heart tripped. "And what if *I* get lonely?"

"I'd give you my private number." No hesitation. "We'd meet here, or at your place, if you're comfortable with that, or at the club. Spend the evening together."

She dipped a finger in her wine and then sucked the liquid off her finger. He audibly swallowed, the reaction giving her a thrill. "And what if I say no?"

"I'd take you home, no more said."

She strolled around the room, pretending to take in the artwork. He was offering her great sex for as long as it amused him. It sounded so crass, so...intriguing.

"So we'd be like FWBs?" When he arched a brow, she clarified, "Friends with benefits."

His smile was downright wolfish. So why didn't she feel like the little bunny?

"You could call it that," he said. "Or you could say I'm offering myself as your temporary rebound."

Could she let him use her like that? She'd be using him too. They'd be using each other. Could that be so terribly wrong? Actually, there was something liberating in the idea. They'd have their fun, and when it ended, there'd be none of the customary scars.

The alternative? Go home alone, sulk over yet another failed relationship, beat herself up over her terrible taste in men. Instead, Lex would make for one hell of a distraction.

Moreover, she wouldn't have to try so hard to be what he wanted. She wouldn't have to worry if he'd be the man she needed him to be, because this was a temporary arrangement with a defined end. Heck, they wouldn't even have to talk if they didn't want to.

She sent him a coy smile. "So when do we start?"

He grinned devilishly. She shivered at the wicked promise in his eyes. Her body reacted with a powerful surge of lust, heat radiating through her core. Her nipples budded under the fabric of her dress.

As if attuned to her body, his gaze dipped to her breasts. He stalked forward and brushed his knuckle over one tender mound. "I too am eager to get to the *benefits* part."

She sucked in a breath at the shocking pleasure. "That so?"

"Mm," he replied, watching as his own actions caused a flush to spread along her skin and listening as each exhalation kicked her lungs into gear. "You were a wild thing that night," he muttered. "Do you always make love with such abandon?"

She'd like to have blamed the alcohol for her behavior, but she hadn't been more than buzzed, and something told her it was this vampire who brought it out in her. "Try me and see."

She wasn't sure if she'd moved, or if he had, but in a heartbeat, their lips crashed together in a hungry kiss filled with carnal urgency. Fingers coiling through her nape, he clamped her in place while he expertly invaded her mouth. His kiss was hard, demanding, and filled with sublime heat.

He clutched the hem of her dress and dragged it just above her waist. Then his hands dove to mold around her exposed cheeks, squeezing with a pressure that tore a moan from her.

"Wait, I don't want to spill my drink on your carpet." Amazingly, she'd retained her grip on her wine, just barely.

He took the glass and carelessly set it on a nearby sideboard. The liquid sloshed. Then there was no space between them. Skirt bunched at her waist, tongues dancing together, her hands fluttered over his massive body, noting how fluidly his muscles moved under her touch. While she appraised his sculpted figure, he kneaded her backside. With a firm grip, he yanked her to him, making a low growling sound. The move forced her to her tiptoes. As if to take her even more off balance, he snatched one leg and hooked it around his waist, then ground his crotch against her core. His actions were surprising, and so damn hot. She could tell how aroused he was. Sweltering heat bloomed inside her, unfurling. His body danced against hers. He could make her come like this. She was already so close.

Her hips rolled, begging for more, her body close to combusting. His strong fingers squeezed her ass even harder, and he let out a low growl in response.

Going a bit mad, she fisted the hair at his nape and

demanded, "Don't you dare stop until I scream."

"Wouldn't dream of it." His voice was that of a beasts—deep and rough and hungry. It would have been a bit terrifying if she wasn't soaring on a current of blistering pleasure. His hips ground faster, his big body looming over her. His thick fingers dug into her rear almost to the point of pain, but it felt oddly rapturous, like the harder he squeezed the better it felt and the higher she soared.

He buried his face in her neck and lightly nipped her tender flesh.

She screamed as a scorching-hot orgasm ripped through her. "Yes!"

"Fuck," he groaned as if he were about to follow with his own release, but then suddenly they were on the move. Her back found the wall. Lex set in with a fever, kissing a hot line down her jaw, over the side of her neck, to her shoulder and back again. The sensation had unrecognizable sounds erupting from her.

Why was he still dressed? She needed her flesh against his.

As she did the night of the masquerade, she gripped each side of his shirt and ripped his glorious chest free.

"I can see I'm going to have to invest in some new shirts with you around," he said, but didn't sound put out at all. He sounded turned on.

She fisted a hunk of his hair and placed her lips next to his ear. In a sex-kitten voice, told him, "I need you to fuck me, Lex. Right now."

Groaning, he twirled their bodies away from the wall. For a moment the world was a blur. Then she was falling. Soft cushions broke her fall. The couch. He knelt over her, grappling with his belt and zipper. She shoved down her panties before helping him remove his ruined shirt. His hands returned to rid himself of his pants, and her dress found the floor next.

Then at last, blessed skin on skin! He felt amazing, strong, out of control. Perfect.

Not yet entering her, he slid his erection over her heated sex, driving her wild with desperation. He felt so good, but she wanted so much more. Cupping his neck, she dragged his mouth toward her breast. Obeying her directive, he took one straining nipple between his lips and sucked. She cried out, arching her back.

"Fuck," he exclaimed again. "You're going to make me come before I even enter you. Are you ready for me?" As if to check, his hand dipped between her legs, his thumb circling her swollen clitoris. She let out another ragged moan, her hips undulating with his movements. "You're so wet, beautiful girl. But I think I want to see you come again before I take you."

She was almost there. Already she cried out with each clipped exhalation. "Lex...oh, God. Don't stop."

"That's it, baby, let go. When I fuck you, I want to hear you roar."

His naughty words drove her over the edge. Her body tightened as pleasure speared her, her lungs working out a scream.

"There it is," he said, his talented thumb continuing its ruthless assault. And just when she was about to descend from the height of her pleasure, he entered her. A deep, roughened groan rippled from his chest. *Perfection.* Another scream tore out of her. She'd gone from empty to feeling so filled up, it was almost too much. And yet, not nearly enough.

"Are you alright?" he asked. "Did I hurt you?" Even as he spoke, he pumped his hips, as if he couldn't help himself. His size was a lot to take, but she'd been more than ready.

"No," she panted. "You feel so good." Her hips rolled for more.

With that, he surged forward, setting into a steady rhythm. She threw her head back, her nails digging into flesh, scoring her pleasure in red, raw lines along his shoulder blades. He grunted out a heavy exhalation as if he loved it. His pace increased, and she could only hang on as her body tripped toward another release.

As his hips pistoned, he buried his face in the crook of her neck, snarling against her flesh. The sound was a shot of pure aphrodisiac. She screamed as another, more intense orgasm raked her.

"Yes! Yes! Yes!" She cried his name again, pleasure erupting, washing over her every nerve. Wonderful, agonizing ecstasy taking over, ravaging her lungs and scrambling her brain. It was too much; it wasn't enough.

His orgasm followed directly after. His grip on her tightened, one more pump, then another. His muscles stilled, then shuddered. His warm breath fanned out along her skin as he relaxed atop her and caught his breath. She loved the weight, her body wrapped around his.

She ran the tips of her fingers along his back, over the scratches she'd carelessly made in the heat of their lovemaking. Vampires healed unnaturally fast. The marks would soon be gone.

Finally, he rolled off her and lumbered to his feet. Still drunk on her back-to-back orgasms, she sat up on the couch and swayed slightly. As he headed away, she took in the glorious view of his ass with what had to be a goofy smile. There wasn't any part of him that wasn't magnificent.

A few seconds after he disappeared, she heard the sound of a shower running, and again, that feeling of uncertainty returned. What was she supposed to do now? Stay here till he returned? Would it be weird to join him? Would it be weird *not to*?

The door was ajar. If he didn't want her in there, he would have closed it, right?

Decided, she padded through the door after him. Already steam was filling the small space...yet the shower stall was empty. Lex was gone.

He reappeared through a second door that connected another room, carrying a set of towels. He placed them on the sink counter and then tested the temperature of the water before stepping under the spray. All that tanned skin and corded muscle turned glossy under steaming rivulets. It didn't matter that she'd just orgasmed like seventy-billion times, lust returned to her in full force.

He met her gaze and, with a half-grin, held his hand out to her. She took it, and he lightly tugged her under the warm stream, kissing her under the water, his roaming hands mapping out his intent. By the time they got around to actually washing themselves, he'd gotten her off two more times.

She was almost delirious from the overload of pleasure and understandably exhausted when Lex shut off the shower. Yet, amazingly she grew aroused once more watching him towel off, terry cloth brushing all that hard damp skin.

As suspected, he could tell.

"You're trying to kill me," he teased.

She flushed. Damn vampire senses.

He closed the space between them, head dipping to claim her lips. This kiss was soft and slow, tender, but it revved her libido all the same.

He pulled back. "If we don't stop, you'll be sore."

She thought about what happened next. He'd take her home, or maybe call her a cab. She wasn't ready for this to end.

"If we stop now, I'll die."

His lips twitched. "Well, we can't have that." When he took her lips this time, there was nothing slow about it.

CHAPTER 9

A vengeful slice of light assaulted her eyelids, the morning sun breaching the cracks in the blinds. She turned her head seeking refuge behind her pillow. Just another few minutes of rest—

Reality whipped her awake. Her eyes snapped open.

She was still in Lex's bed.

She'd stayed the whole night!

That wasn't supposed to happen with a one-night stand. Though they were a bit more than that, weren't they? FWBs. Friends could spend the night together, couldn't they?

Soft sheets tangled all around her body—sore, just as Lex had predicted. Yet she felt great. She'd just experienced the best sex of her life...was there more to come? She smiled and stretched, wondering if vampires got morning wood like human males did.

She frowned when she found the other half of the bed empty.

Her bleary gaze took in the clock on the nightstand. It was nearly eight in the morning. Oh, shit. She didn't have a change of clothes with her, and she couldn't walk into the office wearing her dress from the night before. She was going to be so late!

She shot upright. What if Lex had already left for *his* job? That'd mean she was without a ride...

And her phone was still dead.

Only now did she realize the dangerous predicament she'd put herself in. Alone in a vampire's home with no car and no phone and no one knowing where she was. "I'm such an idiot." She never took risks like that.

So why had she with Lex?

She recalled how safe she'd felt with him. How kind and chivalrous he'd been. He'd offered to take her home even though he'd clearly wanted her to stay. It had been impossible not to trust him after all that. But would she feel the same today?

Slipping out of bed, she entered the bathroom and found a tube of toothpaste. After finger-brushing her teeth she battled the rat's nest that was her hair till it was somewhat tamed. Then she returned to the bedroom and donned her dress, which had been left neatly folded on top of his dresser.

Once again, her underwear was mysteriously missing. *The man has a problem.*

As she exited the room, the scent of food met her. She found Lex in the kitchen, frying something. *For me?*

"Morning," he said without looking. "I hope you like eggs."

She sidled up to the breakfast bar, taking a seat on a stool. She couldn't help but mirror his words from last night. "I can see I'm going to have to invest in new underwear with you around."

"I don't know what you mean." His lips curled at the

corners. "How are you feeling this morning?"

"Good. How about you?"

"I think you very nearly broke me." He sent her a heart-stopping grin.

She pretended to examine her nails. "You've got to be fit to keep up with me."

"I'll have to work on my endurance." That familiar hunger lit his expression.

"Now hold up. Don't start looking at me like that or we'll never leave this house."

"Hmm, that doesn't sound like a bad idea." He chuckled, returning his attention to the eggs just as the sharp scent of something burning invaded her nostrils. "Dammit."

Carrying the hot pan to the trash, he dumped the batch in the bin, where several eggshells resided, and then returned it to the stove. After adding a little more oil, he retrieved two eggs from the almost-empty carton next to him and cracked them into the pan. They sizzled on contact. As the shells joined their fallen comrades, he muttered, "I figured eggs would have been easy."

"Uh, have you gone through all of those?"

With the spatula, he poked at the yolks. "Don't worry, I have a backup plan."

Other groceries were spread out over the counter: milk, orange juice, bread, butter. Next to that, a still full grocery bag. "Did you...did you go to the store?"

"I realized we didn't have anything for human consumption here. It never occurred to any of us. There's a small market nearby. It was a quick trip."

"We?"

"I share this house with a couple coworkers."

"Oh? And where are they this morning?"

"Double shifts, I think."

"You didn't have to do all this. I normally just have a bagel and coffee or something simple like that. "

"It's my pleasure. This is the first time I've had a reason to use this stove. As you might have guessed, I don't ordinarily have mortals over for breakfast."

She tried not to let that delight her. He could mean that he usually sent them home before the sun came up.

While the eggs cooked, he set a plate of blackened bacon in front of her. "I, uh, hope you like them extra crispy." Next he poured her some orange juice. Dutifully she took a sip, which made him smile.

It was as if he looked up *well-balanced breakfast* in an encyclopedia.

There was something extraordinarily heartwarming about that.

"Thanks." She bit into a piece of bacon. *Ca-runch.* "Mmm," she lied, grinding the leathery meat between her molars.

He cringed at her expression and turned back the stove. After a few minutes, he scooped something that resembled eggs, which were oddly browned, onto a plate and handed it to her. Picking up her fork, she tentatively took a bite, chewed, and then...ugh...swallowed. "Yum."

Easily seeing through her, he threw his hands in the air. "Well, I tried. Just because I still consume human food doesn't mean I can cook it."

"It's fine, really. See?" She shoved another bite into her mouth, chewed, and chewed and...gulped.

He shook his head and sighed. "I'll just have to take you out for a proper breakfast."

She did a double take. He wanted to spend even more time with her? The most she'd expected from him this morning was a "*Hey, thanks for a great night. How about I call you next time I want to get it on?*" Or maybe even a grunted "*Return to me tomorrow night.*"

And she would.

Already she craved more of this strange erotic man.

"I can't," she told him. "I have to get to work. I'll have to call in late as it is. I can't exactly go to work looking like this."

He tilted his head, eyeing her with steamy intent.

Stifling a shiver, she cleared her throat and pointed at her face. "Eyes up here, buddy. I'd love nothing more than to ditch work and spend all day translating that look, but—"

"Then do."

"Sorry, what?"

"Call in sick. Hang out with me today."

"Seriously?"

"Life is short," he said. "Let's have some fun. You only live once."

"Or in your case, forever."

"We all have an expiration date. Even vampires. We can be killed. Sure it's not super easy, but nothing lasts forever." A shadow of sorrow crossed his expression, gone so fast she wondered if she'd imagined it. "My motto is live every day to the fullest, because it might be your last. Besides, I just promised you breakfast, and I'm not about to let you finish that." He snatched her plate and dumped the contents in the trash.

"I'm a little overdressed for a restaurant at eight in the morning."

"Nonsense. You look lovely."

"For visiting a club, maybe."

"How about if we stop somewhere and get you some

more appropriate attire?" He retrieved his cell phone from his pocket and held it out to her.

Taking it, she tapped the device with her forefinger, contemplating. She couldn't recall the last time she'd taken a sick day. Or a vacation, for that matter. There was never a good enough reason, and keeping up with her bills was top priority, but spending more time with Lex was so enticing, and if she called out, she wouldn't have to see Brian today. It would be nice not to have to deal with that situation so soon after their breakup. They could certainly use the time apart.

Who was she kidding? Her decision had been made the second Lex placed the phone in her hand.

Her call to the office was a mini trial in self-control. The second Mr. Dixon picked up, Lex crossed his eyes and stuck his tongue out. She'd nearly choked on a laugh. It was a miracle she'd held it together, pretending to be ill for her boss. Luckily he seemed to have bought it.

After hanging up, she chastised, "You. Are. Terrible."

"You mean terribly cute and adorable?"

"Ha! More like ridiculous."

"*Ridiculously* adorable?"

"Only half that statement is spot on."

He polished his nails on his chest. "It's the adorable part, isn't it?"

CHAPTER 10

Ten minutes later, they pulled in a parking lot banked by a set of apparel shops.

"Uh, these stores might be a little out of my price range," she told him.

"No worries. Pick out whatever you like. I'm paying."

She shook her head. "No, I couldn't. Look, I think we passed a couple more reasonably priced stores back there. I'm a great bargain hunter."

He parked and shut off the engine. "Well, we're already here. Might as well take a look around. If you can't find anything you like, we'll check out your bargain stores."

The first shop was brightly lit with chic mannequins displaying tasteful ensembles. She glanced over a line of blouses while he sifted through a nearby rack of men's shirts. Looking to replace the one she'd ruined? When she started to feel bad about that, she reminded herself he'd confiscated her panties.

When Lex wasn't looking, the pretty attendant behind the counter followed him with her eyes, then met Kasima's gaze. The girl smiled guiltily and then fanned herself in an exaggerated manner. Kasima grinned in return. Yes, he was fan-worthy.

"What's funny?" Lex asked.

"It's nothing."

He shrugged. "My sire is getting married in a few weeks. I could use a date to the wedding. You interested?"

"Oh? Um, okay."

He selected a finely pressed white button-down and draped it over his arm. "Good. Then pick out something formal to wear as well, if you like."

She glanced at the price tag attached to the sleeve of the blouse she was considering. Her blood pressure spiked. That was roughly half a month's salary. She dropped the sleeve and backed away, scanning the rest of the displays for—Ah, there. She migrated to a clearance section in the back, but the prices were still pretty high.

Lex joined her then, having dropped his selections off at the register. "Find anything?"

She shook her head. "The prices here are...well, I just don't usually splurge on these kinds of clothes."

He checked the tag of a wool coat she'd been admiring. "Tell you what. Go get settled in a changing room and I'll bring you a few items to try on."

She raised a dubious brow. "You're going to pick out clothes for me?"

"With the attendant's help, yes."

She glanced at the attendant behind Lex who was busy folding the shirts he'd handed her.

"Only a couple of outfits," he insisted, sensing her hesitance. "Just to see how they look."

She sighed. It wouldn't hurt to indulge him.

In the dressing room, Kasima sat on the bench, peeking out at Lex and the suddenly all-smiles attendant rifling through racks and holding up items against her own body for Lex's approval.

Kasima sat back on the bench and waited. A few minutes later, the girl presented her with a pile of elegant clothes...no tags in sight.

"Hi there," the woman said kindly. "My name is Avery. Let me know if you need anything in a different size."

"Thanks."

Before leaving, Avery peeked behind her, making sure Lex was nowhere near, then whispered, "Tell me he's available."

Kasima shook her head, smiling at the girls flushed cheeks. "He's with me." *For now.*

She stuck out her bottom lip. "I was afraid of that. You caught yourself a drop-dead hottie-pitotty. Does he have any brothers?"

"Not exactly. Ever been to Ever Nights? I'm pretty sure they manufacture beef-cakes like him in the back."

"Oh, yeah? I've never been, but I'll have to check it out." Avery winked and then left her in private to try on the clothes.

She donned a wide-strapped floral sundress first, twirling in the mirror to make the bottom flare. The fabric was soft and lightweight, the fit perfect. She opened the curtain to ask Avery for the price, but Lex was there.

"Wow," he said. "You look great."

"Thanks, but I don't see a price tag."

"Huh," he said, curiously unsurprised. "That's weird. Hand it to me and I'll check with Avery when she comes back."

"Already on a first name basis, are you?" She'd meant it as a joke, but a spark of jealousy had slipped into her tone. Which was irrational since they weren't really together like that.

His lips twitched. "Show me the next one."

She closed the certain and then slipped the sundress

off before passing it to Lex.

Her next outfit was a plum skirt. She matched it with a thin white blouse that had crisscrossing ties in the front that kept the v-neck from opening too wide. Provocative without being too revealing. When she stepped out, it wasn't Lex who waited for her this time.

"That looks sick!" Avery chirped.

"Thanks. Where did—" she saw him then, across the store...in the lingerie section. She cleared her throat and fought a blush.

Returning, he handed Avery his lacy selections. "Ring these up, too." His tone had become rough.

"Those aren't for me, are they?"

"I'm certainly not going to wear them." He turned to her with a wide grin, but then his expression went slack as he took her in. His tone dropped an octave. "We'll take what she's wearing as well."

Returning to the register, Avery gave her a quick thumbs up behind Lex's back.

Stepping closer to Kasima, Lex muttered in a husky tone, "If I thought you'd let me, I'd take you right here in this dressing stall."

Her breath caught. Fiery heat seared her blood.

Seemingly debating, he looked over his shoulder at Avery, busily ringing tabs, then back at Kasima, back at Avery, Kasima.

"Don't even think about it." Why did she sound so breathy?

At length, he grunted, "I can wait."

That she was inspiring such lust in a man like him gave her a heady hit of confidence that she didn't normally feel.

"You should wear this out to breakfast. Later, you will try the rest on for me."

"The rest?"

He stepped past her and collected all the clothes she had yet to try on, taking them to the register. "Ring all this up."

Kasima slipped her heels back on and rushed after him. "But...Lex...wait a minute."

Avery was already ringing up the new items. When she finished, the total made Kasima go pale. Lex didn't even flinch. He fished out his credit card and handed it over.

"I can't let you buy all this, Lex."

"Why not?"

"Because, it's too much. I wouldn't be able to pay you back for some time."

"I don't expect you to pay me back at all."

"Will there be anything else?" Avery asked sweetly, as if it wasn't enough Lex had just dropped damn near a G in her store.

"We're good for now," Lex replied, reaching over to take the bag now stuffed with overpriced garments.

In a daze, she followed him out to the car. He stored the bag in the trunk and then came around to open the door for her.

Before she got in, however, he wrapped his arm around her waist and stared down at her with a hungry expression. Her entire body sizzled under that gaze. He bent to take her lips in a tender kiss. She got the impression he was holding back, trying to be careful with her. He'd have to be with his supernatural strength. Still she didn't fear him.

Her own body hummed with desire.

He broke the kiss to mutter in her ear, "Woman, you have me so keyed up I can barely think straight."

At that, her mind went on a complete hiatus. She nipped his ear. "You turn me on like crazy." She reached down to palm his crotch, fondling his length through his jeans.

He let out a smothered groan. "If I wasn't such a gentleman, I'd take you in that alley over there."

If he tried, she might just let him.

At breakfast, he sat patiently while she ate her blueberry waffles, not ordering anything for himself.

She wiped her mouth. "So, this event you spoke of? You say it's your sire who's getting married?"

He nodded. "The whole thing's a bit sudden."

"Oh? You think he's jumping in too fast?"

Hands steepled in front him, he shook his head. "If you saw him and Naia together, you'd know it was inevitable. Pretty sure she had him by the balls on day one."

Kasima smiled at the notion of a fated romance. How fanciful. "You said it was happening in a few weeks. Would that be on a weekend?"

"It's on a Friday."

"Hmm. I work on Fridays. After calling out today, I wouldn't be able to take another day off for a while."

"Why not?"

"I have bills to pay."

He waved an unconcerned hand. "No worries. I'll send someone over to speak with your boss. I have a very strong feeling you're do for a paid vacation."

She blinked at him, speechless for a moment. He could send any one of his clan to *compel* her boss into thinking a paid vacation was just the ticket. "You're used to getting whatever you want, aren't you?"

He grinned devilishly, displaying those fangs that she was finding sexier by the moment.

"Are you finished eating?"

She nodded, pushing her plate away.

On their way out of the diner, Lex asked, "What do

you want to do now?"

"I'm not sure. I don't often play hooky like this."

He opened the car door for her. "I'm a bad influence on you, aren't I?"

"The worst." She slipped inside. It felt like she'd had more fun with him in the last twenty-four hours than she had in the last three years of her life.

He folded his big frame into the driver seat and then started the vehicle. "Have you been to Adventure Land? I hear they just opened a couple new rides. The Brain Scrambler and something else."

"The Tower of Terror," she supplied. "I edited an article about the new additions a few weeks ago. They're supposed to be two of the largest attractions built since the end of the war." Most of the amusement parks had been decimated from the fighting, along with much of everything else. Riverstone was one of the fastest-growing cities, having bounced back quickly after the depression, and was one of the few cities that were economically stable—largely in part due to the vampire population, and the businesses they'd built. Her Grandmother often dubbed it New Las Vegas, which apparently had been a bustling mecca of casinos and entertainment, but was little more than a desert wasteland now.

Lex eyed her with renewed interest. "Have you ridden them yet?"

She shook her head. "My parents took me to Adventure Land a couple of times when I was younger. I was always too small to ride the big rides, but I always wanted to."

"Why didn't they bring you back when you were older?"

"They'd always planned to, but they both worked full time to pay off the mortgage and make sure I got an education."

His brows rose at that. The government had been weakened by the long war on American soil, to the point of nearly crumbling entirely. Those in office were still struggling to regain power and stability. Education was the last on a long list of priorities. Almost every educational facility, but for those backed by wealthy benefactors, such as ivy-league schools, had long been closed, the buildings in ruins or repurposed. As a result, the responsibility of education landed on parents and, sadly, required a lot of money. At best, lower-income families focused on trade skills.

Lex asked, "What kind of education did you receive?"

Though her education was far from ivy-league, it was well rounded, thanks to her parents' efforts. "They hired tutors for me, making sure I could not only read and write, but knew math and history as well." When she'd shown interest in photography, they'd done everything to cultivate it, only wanting her happy. Damn, she missed them.

"Their efforts paid off. You're the assistant to the editor at the Tribune. They must be very proud."

"I'm sure they would be. They passed away a few years before I got the job."

"Oh, sorry." He pulled the car onto the road and brought it up to speed. "Do you think they would have liked me?"

She glanced at him. "My mother would have adored you. My dad? Let's just say, if he were alive, he'd be dusting off my grandfather's old rifle. He warned me to steer clear of the vampires in town."

"Yet here you are."

"Here I am."

After a while, he asked, "So, you never wanted to visit

Adventure Land on your own?"

She shrugged. "Just been too busy."

He appeared appalled, yet teasing at the same time. "You should always make time for fun. Otherwise, why is life even worth living?"

"I do make time for fun, but my financial responsibilities take precedence. My parents left me their house and a modest inheritance, but I promised myself I'd keep up with the bills and save for retirement."

"Tell me what you do for fun."

She grew a little self-conscious, fidgeting with her nails. "It's nothing really. A hobby. I just like to take a few photos here and there." God how she wished she had her camera on her right now. The way the morning light illuminated Lex's features and gorgeous green eyes made her itch to photograph him.

"You're a photographer." He pulled onto the highway, and she could already spot the sun glinting off the tall roller coasters in the distance.

"I'm not a professional or anything, though that's the goal."

"Have you thought about taking snapshots for The Tribune?"

"I've asked my boss about it," she replied, brightening. "He said he'd keep me in mind if any positions open up. It would be ideal."

"I'd love to see some of your stuff. Maybe you could show me later?"

"Uh, sure. Maybe." Her gut twisted in a tangle of nerves. The last person who'd seen her work had been Brian, and he hadn't exactly been wowed.

What if Lex glanced over her work and his response was a resounding "meh"?

It would be crushing.

CHAPTER 11

Adventure Land was pretty packed for a weekday. Lex was right about making time for fun. She was lucky enough to live so close to one of the few amusement parks to have been completely restored after the devastation of war and turmoil. While others traveled miles to enjoy the thrilling rides and adjoining water park, it was practically in her own backyard.

As she and Lex cleared the brightly flourished entrance and traveled closer to their destination, the smell of sugar and fried food spiked her senses. She was reminded of her parents' smiling faces as they'd indulged her excitement as she eagerly flitted from one sight to another. Her father had carried her on his shoulders when she'd grown tired, while her mother had passed her cotton candy. Such a happy memory.

She took Lex's hand, suddenly overwhelmed with gratitude that he'd brought her here.

He glanced down and smiled at her, weaving his fingers through hers.

The Tower of Terror grew by increments, taller and

taller, till she was craning her neck to find the top. She could see the train filled with people being chain-lifted up the vertical incline higher, higher. Next came the desperate screams as the coaster rolled into a freefall, riding the rail down, down, down, along a small curve at the bottom and then up and around an insanely large loop only to fly up another near-vertical incline.

The anticipation made her flush as a low wave of adrenaline coursed through her. The closer they got to the front of the line, the faster her heartbeat, and suddenly a bit of dread crept in. She'd never been on such a ride. What if she got sick? Oh God, what if she got sick all over Lex?

The line moved faster than she'd anticipated, and too soon someone was lifting the bar to an empty car and gesturing for her to take a seat.

"Um," her voice shook. "I don't know. Maybe I should just stay down here and watch."

Lex gave her hand a squeeze. "Remember, you only live once, dove. I promise you'll have fun." The confidence in his voice shattered her resolve while the look he gave her made the rest of the world go fuzzy. That was a straight-up bedroom look.

She allowed him to guide her into the seat before sidling up beside her. The attendant locked them in. The click of the bar over her front brought things back into sharp focus. "I can't do this. What was I thinking? Stupid, stupid. I don't even really like heights." When the cars started to slowly move, she felt faint. Panicked. "Lex! Get me off! Get me off!"

"Shh." He placed his hand on her knee. "Love, calm down. Breath. It's just your adrenaline spiking. You're safe with me."

She glanced at his hand, then at him, her heart rate

paining her with each new thump. "I think I'm going to have a heart attack."

"Shall I distract you?" With a wolfish grin, his hand moved to her inner thigh. She jerked, reminded of her lack of panties.

"Lex," she warned, looking around self-consciously even as white-hot lust bolted through her. He was turning her into a beast of pure animal cravings. They had already left the station and begun crawling up the incline. The people in front and behind were blocked by the bulky seats, so no one could see where his hand was headed.

The incline shifted upward and gravity pushed her back into her seat, the tick tick tick of the gears guiding them skyward like a timer set to the beat of her heart. As they inched higher, he inched closer. Yet then he hesitated, and she thought she'd go mad.

Her hips rocked with need, and he took the hint. "Lex, please," she moaned.

With that, his fingers delved between her legs. He let out a solid oath when he discovered how wet she was. Satisfied expression on his face, he lightly glided his finger along her core. She closed her eyes, sinking into the sensation. As the coaster continued to rise, so did her blood pressure. She gulped in air as the first hint of orgasm touched her nerves, building, building.

Then he slipped his finger inside. "Are you ready?"

Her eyes flashed open at the sound of a loud click.

The coaster dropped. And then she was flying, weightless, wind rushing past her ears as ecstasy so sharp and so hot seared her from the inside out. Her scream was lost to the wind, riding away on a wave of exhilaration. The first sharp turn brought a second layer of excitement to her scream. Adrenaline compounded on top of her unending orgasm, making her delirious with pleasure. At some point, she registered being upside down as another orgasm hit her like a freight train. As they descended at breakneck speeds, the intensity increased and the pleasure turned euphoric, exquisite, and unmerciful.

As the coaster halted for a moment at the top of the second incline, she gasped for breath and fought to orient herself. She locked eyes with Lex. His gaze was hot and hungry, piercing and intense. He smiled his wicked smile for her as he teased her sensitive flesh once more, bringing forth a new wave of pleasure just as gravity took them back down and through a second loop.

She was a thousand shards of ecstasy in a body ready to explode. She was upside down and inside out and turned around. She was out of body, flying free. Dying from pleasure and so damn alive.

She barely registered Lex righting her skirt, the coaster slowing, the bar being lifted. She leaned on him down the short set of stairs and out to a bench where she crumbled, dizzy and smiling like a dope. He knelt in front of her, rubbing her arms as though he feared she might be cold, though the sun was blazing down on them.

"Are you okay? Are you going to be sick?" His words filtered through her muddled mind.

"I think you made me drunk." She laughed, swaying. Her body still hummed. "I just need a second."

"Should I get you something to drink?" He rushed away before she could answer. Soon enough he returned with water. "Here sip it slowly."

She did, letting the chill cool her.

"Better?"

She nodded. "Thank you. I'll never look at a roller coaster the same way again."

He laughed. "Ditto."

"So, what's next?"

"How about we find a ride that's a little less exciting."

She wasn't sure it that was possible with him around. "If I remember correctly, there's a slow-passed water ride around here somewhere. Used to be one of my favorites."

"Lead the way."

As they strolled through the park, he gave her his arm, which was the sweetest thing ever. "There!" She pointed to a two-seater boat carved into the shape of a swan disappearing through a darkened heart-shaped entrance.

"A lover's ride," he intoned.

She halted at his tone. "I guess it is."

There was something wary in his gaze.

"Are you about to get squeamish on me after what we just did?"

"I'm just making an observation. This is a ride for *serious* couples, committed couples...who are in love." He gave her a look that, if translated correctly, meant he feared she was getting a little too attached.

"Look, I'm not about to ask you to marry me or anything. And love is *way* off the table." She grinned, hoping to defuse the tension she felt coming off him. She was beginning to suspect he was a commitment-phobe, just like Brian. Perhaps she attracted them like fire ants to a rotting carcass. "We're just having fun, right?"

"Right," he confirmed slowly, then let out a relieved sigh.

Well, that smarted a bit. Not that she had any intention of dating him long term. Dating wasn't even the right word for what they were doing. Farthest thing from it. They were a convenience to each other. Nothing more. She wasn't sure which one of them she needed to make that more clear to.

"You have nothing to worry about." She swiped her hand through the air. "You're a rebound, plain and simple. Besides, getting serious with someone like you...after Brian...that'd make me a first rate idiot."

"Ouch."

"Oh, stop. You know what I mean. Sure, I want what every girl wants: love, family, security, maybe kids someday, but right now I just need to have a little fun, and that's what you're all about: spontaneity and living for the moment and awesome orgasms on coasters."

He chuckled, giving her a half grin.

"So if at any time you or I feel like this gets too serious, we should end it. No muss, no fuss."

At length he replied, "Agreed."

"Good. Because tomorrow I have to go back to work where my ex-lover will likely hound me for the whole day, so you're going to take me on this stupid lover's ride and then maybe another roller coaster, and we're going to have fun, got it?"

His grin turned full-watt. "Yes, ma'am."

When they got in the boat, they both became a bit awkward as it rocked lightly and coasted down the skinny canal, as if they were both suddenly unsure how to proceed. Maybe insisting on this ride hadn't been the best idea.

She surveyed Lex from the corner of her eye. He had that air about him. That air guys get when they were grudgingly humoring the girl even though they'd rather be doing anything else, anywhere else. "Fun fact, I used to always get so scared just before the boat entered the tunnel."

Just as they crossed beyond the threshold, Lex surprised her by hooking her waist and drawing her near. "Well, don't worry, dove. I'll keep you safe from the giant heart of doom."

The tunnel closed in around them, the light at their backs. "But who will protect me from you?"

"Fun fact: I only bite a little."

She snickered, glad to have returned to a place of teasing. "Hold on, the good part's coming up."

"Mmm, is that so? Oh...you mean the ride. Don't tell me a bunch of mechanical dolls are going to spring out of the walls and start singing."

Her laughter echoed off the cavern-esque tunnel. They'd just entered the main chamber, stopping at the center. "Prepare to be amazed."

He shifted in his seat. "Optimal position for amazement acquired."

Under them, an ethereal blue light illuminated the water. To the right, an orange light flashed, followed in a circle by a yellow, pink, green, and finally purple. The walls sparkled with faucets of color.

"Hey," Lex said, gazing around, "that's pretty cool. I wouldn't go so far as amazing."

"Just wait."

From seemingly nowhere, a crescendo of percussion instruments began to play. The subterranean lights began to move and swirl like living creatures. Light danced off the cavern in a glorious rainbow of color, vibrant and stunning. The bass moved in, hitting its stride just as countless smaller lights flashed below, joining in the ballet of movement and transforming the ceiling into a starry display that shimmered and danced in coordination to the music. When the cymbals crashed and the composition reached a climax, the refracting light morphed into a set of star systems in motion, little suns orbited by little planets. When the lights shifted again it felt as though they were sitting at the center of a traveling galaxy, beautiful and awe-inspiring.

As the music faded, she noticed Lex peering down at her. Wiping her stupid grin away, she tucked her hair behind her ear. "Pretty lame, I know."

"No," he replied, his expression a mix between amusement and something she couldn't decipher. "That was really...something."

When they drifted out into the sun, he leaned down and kissed her. Her heart did a flip. Then he pointed in the distance. "We're riding that next."

She squinted to see a tethered round cage rocketing hundreds of feet into the sky. Finding the tether's limit, the sphere snapped back toward the earth, only to halt seconds before hitting the ground and slinging vertical again.

The Brain Scrambler.

She gave Lex a wide grin. "Let's do this."

CHAPTER 12

When Lex pulled up to her house, she didn't think anything could dampen her good mood—even though Lex had gone quiet throughout the ride, as though he suddenly had a lot on his mind. The day had been packed with fun, adventure, and stolen kisses. The best day she'd had in a long time. She had hoped it would continue long into the night...but Brian was sitting on her front porch, openly scowling as she and Lex stepped out of the car.

"I think this is where we say goodnight," Lex said, glaring at Brian.

Her gut sank. "What? No. You can, uh, stay if you want. I'll get rid of him."

Lex hesitated, and for a moment, she thought he would stay, but then he shook his head. "It looks like your boyfriend wants to talk. I don't wish to get in the middle."

Was he subtly reminding her that they weren't a couple?

"Ex-boyfriend," she countered, trying to shrug off the disappointment that Lex didn't seem terribly bothered by Brian's appearance. Was he getting worried about their closeness today, worried she was growing attached?

"Right. *Ex*." For a moment, she saw something dark in his expression. When she blinked, it was gone. "You might want to make sure *he's* aware of that."

She glanced back at Brian, who was waiting on the porch with his arms crossed, face stern. What was he thinking coming here tonight, looking as though he had a reason to be mad? He'd be even madder when she sent him away, but that was his problem.

In an attempt to salvage the night, she muttered to Lex, "Really. You don't have to go. I've no interest in sorting things out with Brian tonight. Besides, you said you wanted to see my photography." She was reaching and she knew it.

"Another time, maybe. I should go anyway. I was supposed to be at the club for a late shift."

"Oh. Okay then." He hadn't mentioned that earlier. She'd figured they were *both* taking the day off. She got the feeling he was using Brian as an excuse to leave.

Growing impatient, Brian descended the porch and took a few paces toward them. "I thought you were sick." There was a clear accusation in his tone. "I came to see how you were."

"You shouldn't have," she called back to him.

"Clearly." There was venom in his tone. She didn't care.

She faced Lex. "Will I see you tomorrow?"

He shook his head. "No can do. Maybe this weekend. If not, I'll pick you up for the wedding in a few of weeks. Sound good?"

Another sting of disappointment pierced her. "Oh. Okay, sure."

He returned to his car without even a kiss goodbye.

She waved weakly as he drove away, a strange gully of emptiness overtaking her.

She realized at some point during the day her heart had grown a little too fond of him. He probably sensed that. Was that why he'd shifted from her sexy, sweet, attentive Lex to *Lex: the escape artist*?

Obviously he didn't like her as much as she liked him. Not if he so easily handed her over to a rival without even an argument. At the very least, he could have acted bothered. What if she and Brian got back together this night? It wasn't going to happen, but Lex didn't know that.

She just realized he'd been in such a rush to get away from her, she hadn't gathered her prize from the back seat, the plush teddy bear he'd won for her...after roughly twenty attempts to toss a tiny ring onto the slender neck of a glass bottle. That might have been when he'd stolen a large chunk of her heart, which currently felt like it was being torn to shreds.

Brian pulled her from the memory. "What the hell, Kas? You're ditching work to hang out with vampires now?"

She took in a fortifying breath and headed toward her front door, bypassing him. "It's none of your business who I hang out with."

"Of course it is. Vampires are dangerous."

"Oh really?" She marched up the stairs and fished her keys out of her purse. "Is that why you took me to their *dangerous* den and then left me alone to go hook up with other women?" Yeah, she wasn't getting over that any time soon. How could she have even gone along with such a stupid plan? Brian had worn her down for months, that was how. But if he really cared about her, he wouldn't have put her in such a situation.

He paddled right past that. "And you never call in sick. Even when you *are* feeling under the weather."

"Right. So I was due for a personal day." She opened her door and then blocked the threshold with her arm when Brian tried to enter. "Brian, I don't want to talk right now. I'll see you at work tomorrow. Okay?" She shut the door with him still blustering. Then she plopped on her couch, listening to him rant at the door for another minute or two. Finally his footsteps trailed down the stairs. The engine of his car sounded just before tires peeled away.

Alone and a bit bummed by the way the night had ended, she played the day over in her head. He'd been having as much fun as she'd been having. Or so she'd thought. They'd gone through most of the rides, though he hadn't been naughty with her again. They'd eaten junk food. Played games. Their last activity had been the ring toss. She'd admitted to Lex she'd always coveted the cute stuffed bears hanging off the booths, teasing everyone who passed.

He'd planted himself in front of the ring toss, determined to win her a prize.

He must have played twenty rounds, till he finally slipped that little plastic ring around the lip of a bottle. But by then, she hadn't even really cared about the bear, but that he had tried so hard to get it for her. It had touched her heart in a way that was dangerous to them both, and he must have seen that on her face.

Since then, there had been shadows behind his smile. More than once, she'd caught a frown on his face when he thought she wasn't looking.

Whatever she'd done wrong, it must have made him desire distance between them. Maybe he feared he was misleading her, that she was becoming attached to him. If so, she'd have to reassure him otherwise.

The next day, Kasima sat at her desk, diligently checking the seating chart for the upcoming award ceremony—Tanya from human resources was head of the party planning committee and had asked her to check it and make sure everything was in order. Tanya was generally meticulous when it came to these kinds of things, so Kasima didn't expect to find any issues, but this year's ceremony was going to be a huge event with several neighboring news organizations joining the fun, and rumor had it Tanya was going through a rough breakup. *Preaching to the choir, sister.*

She glared up at the delicate vase on her desk with three red roses sticking out of the mouth, wondering if it would be cruel to get rid of it. It had been sitting there when she'd arrived to work this morning. At first, a thrill had danced through her, thinking it was from Lex.

Then she'd read the card.

Brian wasn't ready to take no for an answer.

Mr. Dixon's voice echoed through the intercom. "Ms. Wilder. Can you come in here, please? I need to dictate a letter."

"Sure thing, Mr. Dixon." She grabbed her company-issued laptop and joined her boss in his office, taking the seat across from him. As Mr. Dixon spoke, she typed, not missing a beat. When they were finished, she asked, "Have you given any thought to me taking a few photos for the paper?"

"So eager to move on to a different department and be rid of me?" His plump face stretched into a teasing smile.

"Of course not," she reassured. "You know I love being your assistant."

"Yes, I'm sure it's exciting taking notes and answering

calls. Well, as you know, we already have enough photographers, but if anything opens up, I'll let you know."

"I appreciate that, Mr. Dixon."

He nodded and shifted his attention to his computer screen, effectively dismissing her. Before she closed the door behind her he called, "Oh, Kasima?"

"Yes?"

"A coffee would be great."

"Sure. Coming right up."

By the time she finished going over the seating chart and a few other minor tasks, it was a little after eleven, and the office was bustling with employees going about their business.

Her phone rang, and she answered it with her practiced greeting, "You've reached the office of Roger Dixon, this is Kasima speaking."

A deep, smooth voice resonated through the receiver. "It looks like I accidently took your bear hostage."

Her heart jumped into her throat. "Hi," she squeaked, a little too eager. She tamped it down a little when she added jokingly, "Are you calling to demand a ransom?"

"That depends on what you're willing to do for his safe return."

Her mind took a nosedive into the gutter. "I'm sure we can come up with something that will satisfy both parties."

His smooth chuckle rippled through her, and there she went again, smiling like an idiot. Thank the heavens he couldn't see how easily he affected her. Unfortunately, Brian chose that moment to appear. He cocked his head at her expression. She sat up straight and wiped her features clear.

Brian checked his watch. "Hey, Kas."

"I'm sorry," she said to Lex. "Can you hold a sec?" Then she pressed the receiver to her chest. "Is there something you need, Brian?"

His grin faltered slightly at her businesslike tone. "I was wondering if you'd join me for lunch today."

She sighed and shook her head. "I don't think that's a good idea."

"Come on. It's just lunch. I'd really like to talk to you about everything."

She paused for a moment, wondering if she should just get it over with. It seemed breaking it off with him was going to take a little more effort. Maybe if he got some solid closure....

"Do you like the flowers I got you?" he asked suddenly.

She lightly pinched the bridge of her nose. "They're nice, but you shouldn't have. I—"

"They were delivered yesterday, but you didn't come into work. I was afraid they would wilt, but they held up pretty good, didn't they?"

"Uh, yeah. Brian, could you give me a minute?" She put the phone back to her ear and said to Lex, "Sorry, can I call you back?"

"Sounds like he's not giving up," Lex muttered. He must have been able to hear her and Brian's conversation. "I wouldn't have taken him for the persistent type. Tell me, yes or no, would you like me to come rescue you from getting browbeaten into having lunch with your relentless ex?"

She smiled. "Yes, that would be fantastic."

"Very well. I'll be there at noon."

"Sounds great."

"And Kasima?"

"Yes?"

His tone dipped. "I can't stop thinking about what we did on that roller coaster."

She swallowed, feeling a blush creep into her cheeks. Brian's eyes narrowed.

Ignoring him, she muttered to Lex, "Me too."

"And I can't stop picturing what I'm going to do with you next."

She shivered, trying to come up with a response that wouldn't make her sound like the puddle of lust he'd just turned her into.

"See you soon," he said, and hung up. She covered the receiver as if he was still on the line, and glanced up at Brian. "This is going take a while."

Pressing his lips together, Brian stomped away.

CHAPTER 13

After submitting an order for ink cartridges, she glanced at the clock on her computer. A few minutes till twelve. They hadn't discussed where to meet. It might be best for her to make her way to the parking lot and wait for him there.

She bent in her seat to retrieve her purse from the bottom drawer of her desk. When she straightened, she was staring into the adorable glossy black eyes of a fluffy teddy bear. Lex was holding it out to her, grinning. Grinning, she reached for it, but he snatched it away.

"Ah, ah. There's still the ransom to discuss."

She walked around her desk, all innocence and sweetness. Then she grabbed for the bear, but Lex was too fast. Wearing an amused smirk, he now held it over his head.

She sighed. "Well, what are your demands?"

"Let's start with a kiss."

She glanced around, disheartened to see Brian frowning at them from the break room doorway.

"Um, maybe not here," she whispered. Though they were no longer together, she didn't want to flaunt her new relationship—or whatever it was—in front of Brian.

Lex followed her gaze and then let out a barely perceptible growl that was borderline hostile. Where was this reaction last night?

Brian speared Lex with a piercing glare, and both men locked gazes.

She got the sense that this little faceoff could get out of hand fast. Lex might not want her for the long-term, but his body language said for the time being, she was his and Brian had better back the fuck off, or else.

She tugged on Lex's arm. "Come on. I'm hungry."

After another tense moment, he allowed her to drag him out into the parking lot where he commented, "Those flowers he got you are practically comical." At his car, he opened the door for her.

"They aren't that bad," she lightly defended, then regretted the statement.

Lex's face went hard. As soon as she settled in the car, he shut the door and then made his way around the front to take his seat behind the wheel. "Three measly roses? Not much of a gesture after the shit he pulled." Then he plopped the bear into her lap. "This at least took skill."

She laughed. "So it did." Was Lex jealous of Brian? No. That would be beyond ridiculous. She scooped the bear up for a hug. "And I *wuv* my wittle Fluffy Wumpkins."

That pushed Lex out of his grumpy mood and into one that appeared slightly disgusted. "You can't name him that!"

"Why not?"

"Because it's cruel, that's why."

"Cruel? How could it possibly be cruel to call a teddy bear fluffy?"

"His little bear friends would tease him relentlessly,

and he would never develop the confidence needed to grow into a well-rounded adult. He'd grow up with a complex that would turn into some kind of personality disorder that we, his well-meaning parents, wouldn't catch until it was far too late. By then he'd have already turned to self-medicating with drugs and alcohol."

"Is that so?" She wagged her finger at the bear. Bad Fluffy Wumpkins."

Lex shook his head. "No. It's going to stick. And we refuse to support his drug habit, he'd start a life of crime, robbing stores and such. Sure, he might get away with it once or twice, but eventually he'd get pinched, because, let's face it, he's never been all that bright, brain full of cotton, that one. Do you know what they'd do to a guy named Fluffy Wumpkins in prison? It's not pretty. Anyway, before you know it, he's living in a cardboard box, reeking of gin and piss, performing seedy favors in back alleys for his next fix. No. I won't allow it."

She shook her head, laughing. "You're right. That would be a terrible fate. So then what should we call him to avoid a life of teddy bear crime, addiction, and prostitution?"

"It should be something masculine, like Spike or Beast."

She squeezed the bear again. "My little Beastie."

Lex groaned through a smile. "You just ruined it, woman."

She giggled. "Spike it is then. Little Spiky Wumpkins."

Lex chuckled. "It's the best I could do for you, Spike."

After a moment, Kasima cleared her throat. "I suppose it's time to settle our account. I believe you're owed a kiss." She bit her lip, surprised by her own lascivious intent.

"Oh, no you don't," he grumbled. "You're not getting

away with a little peck on the cheek while I'm driving."

"I wasn't talking about kissing you above the waist."

His jaw dropped, and his gaze darted between the road and her and back again.

She tossed the bear in the back seat and reached out to pop open the button of his jeans. He swallowed audibly as she undid the zipper, freeing him. He stiffened before her eyes. When she took him in her hand, he groaned, "Shit, woman. You're full of surprises today."

She stroked his length. "I trust you can drive while I suck your cock?"

Muscles straining, he said, "I could fly an f-15 while you suck my cock."

"Good to know." She leaned over and teased him with her tongue. The gruff sound that filtered through his lungs sent a shiver down her spine. Already she was aroused beyond belief. When she sucked him fully into her mouth, he let out a harsh oath. The smoothness of him glided easily over her tongue to the back of her throat where she manipulated his member in a way that had him nearly snarling with pleasure.

"Fuck me, where did you learn to do that?"

She did it again and he cursed once more, his hips bucking for more. As she slowly pulled back, her cheeks hollowed from the suction and his shaft jerked in protest. Then she drove him to the back of her throat again, and he muttered something unintelligible. She worked him this way a few more times, bringing him to the brink of coming before changing it up and twirling her tongue around his sensitive tip.

"Jesus, fuck, girl, you're going to make me explode."

At that, she cupped his balls and took him as deep as she could. His euphoric groan stretched the span of his orgasm, which she drew out with each swallow, licking him clean.

When he was finished, she sat up, a little smug and satisfied with her work. His dumbstruck expression nearly made her laugh.

He adjusted his features and focused on the road. "You know we just scarred Spike for life, right?"

She settled back into her seat. "Guess we'll just have to put some money away for bear therapy."

"Do you realize how expensive that is going to be?"

"Well, we could always forego blowjobs in the future."

Feigning a horrified expression, he said, "Get ready for extensive therapy, Spike."

She laughed again, feeling so at ease with him like this.

Moments later they were seated outside a little deli. She'd ordered a pastrami on rye; Lex, a meatball sandwich—she suspected he'd only ordered so she wouldn't feel awkward eating alone.

She nibbled on her fries. "So you took off pretty quick last night."

He put his sandwich down and looked at her. "Yeah, I did. That was rude of me."

"Was it something I did?"

He hesitated. "Brian was at your place. I wasn't sure if you wanted to talk to him, and were too polite to ask me to leave. I didn't want you to feel obligated to do anything."

She got the impression there was more he wasn't saying. "I was afraid you were tired of me."

"Sorry. I didn't mean to make you feel that way."

A silence stretched between them that felt heavy. "Well, I just want you to know I'm cool with our arrangement."

He raised a brow.

"I mean, we're just having a good time, right? No strings. No emotions. Obviously one day I want the whole package: love, family, career. I just don't want you to worry that I might make this"—she gestured between the two of them—"into something it isn't."

He leaned back in his chair, not looking as appeased as she'd expected. "Sure. Right."

"Good. Okay. Just wanted to put that out there."

He leaned in and picked up his sandwich. Paused. "I guess I was getting a little worried about that. It's nice to know we're still on the same page."

"Right. Same page. Same sentence." So why did she suddenly feel ill?

With a little light conversation, they finished their meal, though the energy between them had abated a bit. And by the time Lex drove her back to work, she still felt a little out of sorts. It didn't help when Brian confronted her as she made her way to her desk.

"I'm worried about you, Kas," he said in a softened tone, as though she'd been out scoring crack.

She positioned Spike on her desk next her monitor. "Oh?"

"You're seeing this vampire too much."

"It's none of your business, Brian."

"What if he's compelling you? It's what his kind does."

She snorted. "He's not compelling me."

"Oh really? Because you'd know if he was? I wrote an article last year about this very topic. The subject of vampire compulsion never realizes they're under control unless the vampire allows it."

She blinked, recalling she had helped edit that particular piece before Brian had turned it in. The woman he'd interviewed had allegedly been compelled to sleep with a group of men, but for some sadistic reason, the vampire had made her recall her actions only after the fact. After the story came out, Cortez and his clan had coordinated with the VEA to investigate the claim, but she didn't know if anything had come of it.

"Lex isn't like that," she defended.

"Or so he's compelled you to believe."

Pinching the bridge of her nose, she said, "Brian, please don't make this break up harder than it has to be. I'd like to remain friends, if that's possible."

Just then, Mr. Dixon returned from his lunch break. "Oh, Ms. Wilder. I spoke with your new fella. Your request for paid time off is approved." He winked and then disappeared into this office, leaving her gaping.

Brian gave her a patronizing look. "He isn't like that, huh?"

CHAPTER 14

Kasima read the card again, half in a daze.

This is the kind of bouquet you deserve. —Lex.

She glanced up at the monstrosity that occupied a good portion of her desk. The floral arrangement stood roughly three feet high from base to top, and boasted at least three-dozen long-stem roses. It had arrived shortly after lunch, and nearly every woman in the office had since fluttered by to get a look at it and dig for information on the sender, offering little tidbits like, "Whoever he is, he's a keeper, honey."

They didn't know Lex didn't *want* to be kept. So then why did it suddenly seem like he was courting her? How was she supposed to keep her heart out of the mix when he kept tugging on it like this?

Maybe he just sent the flowers to mess with Brian, who had taken one look at the arrangement and stomped off in a huff. Or maybe Lex was more into her than she'd realized. Was she reading the signals wrong? It would help if his signals weren't so contrary. She tried to recall if he'd seemed disappointed by her words at lunch, or relieved.

She thought there had been relief, but maybe that was just what she'd expected to see.

One thing was certain. She wasn't about to leave the massive arrangement in the office for folks to gawk at all week. Thankfully her shift was over.

Transferring the arrangement to her car was a bit of a hassle. With Spike nestled under one arm, she cradled the vase in the other, having to peek through the forest of flowers to see her way. She exited the side door ass first, and then scuttled sideways down the steps very carefully to avoid face-planting. Yet she managed to trip over an uneven patch of sidewalk that she always tended to forget was there. Luckily she kept her footing. At her car, she balanced the vase on her hip while digging around in her purse for her keys and squishing Spike further into her armpit. Finally she managed to situate the arrangement in the back seat. Spike rode in style, sitting next to her in the passenger seat.

A mixture of floral fragrances saturated the interior of her car. By the time she pulled up to her house, she wasn't sure if she was flattered by Lex's stunt, or pissed. It had drawn a lot of unwanted attention to her and Brian's breakup. She was now fodder for the gossip mill. Some of her coworkers had even inquired oh-so-sweetly how she'd managed to land a new man *so soon*.

She stepped out of her car and began the arduous task of dragging the arrangement through her door, leaving it in a corner of the foyer. She grudgingly admitted it looked pretty good there. She shelved Spike on the hutch in the dining room, then stripped on the way up the stairs toward the shower. Tonight she planned to veg out on the couch, maybe read a book, and forget her worries.

Unfortunately her worries decided to follow her

home.

Not a minute after she'd soaped up her hair, her doorbell rang. She prayed it wasn't Brian, come to lecture her some more on the follies of dating a vampire.

Squeezing the excess water out of her hair, she slipped into her terry cloth robe and cinched the waist tight on her way to the door. Through the peephole, she spied Lex.

Her heart shimmied behind her ribs.

When she opened the door, he took in her damp hair, robe, and bare feet. The corners of his lips curled up. "I can see my timing is impeccable."

"Indeed," she replied derisively, and invited him in.

He closed the door behind him. The arrangement caught his attention and his grin turned wide. "Do you like them?"

"Yes," she replied, adding, "but I'm a little mad at you for sending them."

One of his dark brows curved up at that, even as his expression grew mischievous. He moved toward her, tone dipping an octave. "Why ever so?"

She stepped back, maintaining a few feet of distance between them. "Because I think you only sent them to irritate Brian." He came closer. She backed away, the blood in her veins rushing with excitement.

He shrugged still advancing. "That was just a convenient bonus. The main reason was to show you what a *serious* apology looks like."

She rounded the couch, but he cut off her path, cornering her. Her back found the wall. Smiling devilishly, he closed the space between her, caging her in. She gazed up at him, her skin growing warm. "Apology? For what?"

"For taking off last night like I did." He tugged at the knot of her terry cloth belt, and the loop slowly came undone. Her lungs shuddered, a wave of breath crashing in and out. Her robe fell open, revealing a thin line of damp skin down her front. His gaze was riveted. Now *his* breath had changed, becoming irregular. With slow, exacting movements, he brushed the robe off her shoulders. Terry cloth piled at her feet.

Her nipples budded against the cool air. She swallowed and licked her lips.

His knuckles feathered down the sides of her arms and his palms came to rest around her waist. "You look beautiful this evening."

"Thanks," she breathed. "You look overdressed."

"We can fix that." He dipped his head to her naked shoulder and lightly kissed her, lips lingering there. "I told you the reason I left was to give you and Brian space to talk, and that was true, but what I didn't say was thinking of you with him bothered me all night."

"It did?" Desire coated her voice.

He nodded. "More than I thought it would. I argued with myself all the way home, wondering if you might have preferred me there as a buffer." His lips trailed up her neck, lightly caressing the skin back and forth. "Then I worried you might be compelled to forgive him. Maybe invite him in." His grip on her hips tightened. "From there my thoughts only degraded."

"That never would have happened. He and I are over." After Lex, the thought of being with Brian again was repulsive. In fact, after Lex, the thought of being with any other man was repulsive, which was worrisome.

He trailed his lips along the line of her jaw, scrambling her thoughts. Then, finally, their lips met, and an electric heat crashed through her blood.

In that moment, he owned her lips, her body, hell her

soul might have even been up for grabs. Then he pulled back. "It shouldn't have mattered," he muttered, confusing her lust-drugged mind. "I shouldn't be worried about such things. It shouldn't bother me."

Reaching up, she swept her fingers along his cheek, and whispered, "I like that it bothered you."

Hands skating around her hips to cup her bare ass, he met her gaze, then sighed. "I know. And that's not good either."

In a move that almost seemed practiced, he reached down and hooked her leg behind the knee, brought it up around his waist, then hiked her up to straddle him. She crossed her legs at the ankle, loving being in his arms like this. Plastered perfectly between his rock-hard body and the wall, she took his mouth in a searing kiss meant to burn away his last comment. Not good? How could this passion be anything but?

She should have felt embarrassed being naked and clinging to him like a barnacle while he was still fully clothed, but it only heightened her lust.

Hips rolling against him, she muttered, "Bedroom's upstairs."

Needing no further instruction, he managed to effort-lessly balance her weight, taking the stairs two at a time. In her room, they landed on the bed, kissing more urgently as she helped him out of his shirt and pants. She was already dying to feel him, she moaned in bliss when he finally slipped inside her, both of them clawing and pawing, trying to get closer to one another as if neither couldn't get close enough, as if they were both lost or drowning and only pure, undiluted passion could save them. As they made love, pleasure took them beyond reason.

When she caught a glimpse of his fangs behind his lips,

she was so lust-drunk, she thought she heard herself beg for him to take her neck.

"Baby?" he grunted in question, driving between her legs. "You sure?"

She panted. "Yes. Please. I want to experience every part of you."

His gaze seemed to darken with unfettered desire, his fangs lengthening before her eyes, and she wondered where her sanity had run off to, because she was suddenly wild with impatience.

He let his mouth trail sensually down the sensitive slope of her neck. She shivered at the sensation. The hammering in her chest had to be distracting for him, either that or driving him mad. What would it be like to have one's food practically begging to be devoured? Was she really going to let him do this?

"You will feel nothing but pleasure," he said in a whiskey voice, as if he could sense her vacillating.

"O-okay." Her voice was hoarse and cracked.

His hot mouth came over the crook of her neck, his breath fanning along her skin. She shivered again, her pulse speeding up, animal heat flooding her body. He kissed her first, right along her pulse point. Then she felt the sensation of twin needles lightly grazing her flesh, like a dangerous caress, just before—"Oh!" She moaned. Stars danced in her vision. A hot blast of ecstasy erupted in her every cell, the pleasure mounting, growing, till—

She screamed, coming so hard and so fast the world spun around her. On and on it went, reality tilting on its side, and bending in on itself. He groaned against her flesh, pulling her atop him to straddle his lap, his back against the wall, as he greedily fed.

Their bodies toiled furiously, mindlessly seeking more.

More friction, more pleasure, more delirious bliss. It was almost too much to bear...and then he wrapped his palms around her hips and slammed her down on his cock. She screamed up at the ceiling, nirvana flooding her in the most potent orgasm of her life. His release followed. He threw his head back to bellow.

With a hand at the back of her neck, he brought their foreheads together, pleasure slowly ebbing. They sat like that for a while, breathing heavily, neither speaking. Something was happening. Something foolish. A small chunk of her heart slipped into his possession.

The thought sobered her.

Pulling back, she disentangled herself from him and then headed into the bathroom to finish her shower. She wondered what to expect from him now. Had this been a booty call? Would he be gone when she exited the bathroom? Or would he be waiting for her on the bed, ready for round two?

She told herself it wouldn't matter either way. It shouldn't.

When he joined her under the spray, a thrill shimmied through her.

Yet, as if his world hadn't just been shattered from a mind-bending experience, he dragged the soap along his toned chest, soaping up. She washed her hair, trying for nonchalance, when her mind was still reeling from his bite.

She might have thought he was entirely unaffected if he didn't continue to steal glances at her from the corner of his eye. "So...how did you, I mean...did you enjoy that? Or rather, how are you feeling about what we..."

Was he actually unsure? Could he be any sweeter?

She grabbed his hand and pulled him around to face

her, sliding her forefinger down his chest. "It was amazing. I can't believe I was so afraid to let you do that."

His lips parted in a wide grin, sporting fang. "Not so scary now?"

She lightly tapped one with her finger. "Not even close."

His grin turned sly. "Watch out. You could lose a finger that way."

"You wouldn't bite me...there."

He caught her hand and nibbled her finger, making her giggle. Then he kissed her knuckles before releasing her to continue washing. "So, what did you have planned for this evening?"

"I was just going to veg on the couch, read, or maybe watch a movie."

"May I join you?"

"Of course." She sounded far too delighted, but how could she not? He was delighting her in every way.

After drying off, she dressed in a cute pair of loose shorts and a tank top. Lex wore his jeans, and nothing else. Hello sexy, sexy man.

Downstairs, she asked, "So what type of movie are you in the mood for," sparking their first ever argument. He preferred something with action and explosions while she suggested something more romantic, which had led to their first ever compromise: a classic film with shootouts and car chases, but with an underlining romance between the two main characters.

Then they had snuggled up on the couch, like a real couple.

She froze at the thought, ice sneaking into her veins at the thought.

She had to stop doing that.

She couldn't allow this attachment to grow any more than it already had. They were FWBs. But how could she not when he was sweetly running his fingers through her damp hair, as if he didn't even realize he was doing it, while his clean scent invaded her senses?

At some point during the movie, she must have nodded off because the next thing she knew, Lex was tapping her on the shoulder. She opened her eyes. The credits were rolling. Sitting up, she covered her yawn.

"I supposed I should get going," he said.

Her heart lurched. She rushed out, "Or you could stay. I mean, it's pretty late. No need to drive home just to go to sleep." She shrugged, trying to dial it back. "Unless you'd rather not. No biggie."

He turned thoughtful. "Well alright then. I'll stay, if you don't mind."

She clicked off the television and then headed up the stairs, secretly celebrating when he followed.

He paused halfway up, admiring the photographs that lined the wall. "I didn't notice these on my first journey up. Though, admittedly, I was quite distracted at the time." He smirked up at her, then returned his attention to the photos. "Is this your work?"

She nodded, suddenly self-conscious. "Uh, yeah." They were some of her favorite shots. The first one he looked at was taken in a field during autumn. The grass was tall, yet yellowed from the changing of the seasons. The setting sun had helped to exaggerate the vibrant color of it. Far off in the distance was a woman in a pastel floral dress dancing in the light breeze—it had been her mother.

He moved on to study a dramatic black and white snapshot of a darkened street. Kasima had situated the shot so that the light of a streetlamp was at her back and her own shadow stretched out toward a brightly lit city along the horizon.

When he moved on to the next photo, her heart shuddered with a ghost of pain. It had been taken no more than a month after her parents had died. After a particularly stormy day, she'd found herself wandering a deserted meadow and found a tree that had been struck by lightning, ripped down the center and still smoldering, yet the trunk stayed rooted to the ground, almost defiantly. She hadn't thought much of photographing it at the time, and had set it aside. That day, she had just been going through the motions, still dealing with her grief. But as spring had rolled around, she'd gone back to that same location and snapped a second photo.

The last image Lex observed was of the same tree, the gaping wound in the trunk healing. The tree had not only remained upright, but was sprouting new growth.

"Very impressive," Lex said finally. "I like the symbolism here."

She blinked at him. "Thanks. One day I hope to travel the world and take photographs professionally."

"The world? Hmm. Sounds adventurous. Although, not a lot of paying jobs out there these days for world photographers, are there?"

No, there weren't. War had torn through every corner of the earth. The kinds of employers that would offer such a position were practically non-existent. Most photographers were either freelance, or working locally. "Honestly, I'd be happy just taking photos for the Tribune."

"You'd do a great job."

"You think?"

He nodded. "There's something evocative about these photographs. You're very talented."

When they continued up to her room and got under the covers, things between them seemed to grow a little awkward. The whole situation suddenly seemed too domestic. But if he felt the same, he didn't show it. He simply rolled onto his side, hooked her by the waist, and pulled her against him. His warmth was magnificent.

He murmured in her ear. "I think your bed is more comfortable than mine."

"Oh yeah?"

"Mmm. I might have to stay the night here more often."

She grinned in the dark. "We'll see. As long as you don't hog all the covers."

"And if I do?"

"Then we'll just have to get more covers, won't we?"

"Good thinking. Are you comfortable?"

Immensely. "For now." He had a unique musk that smelled far too good. "Do you mind if I ask a personal question?"

"Shoot," he said.

"Well, I was kind of wondering what makes someone decide to become a vampire."

He let out a soft chuckle as if he'd been expecting this line of questioning. "Different reasons, I suppose. Some want the power. Some want immortality. But you can't just decide to become a vampire. It doesn't work that way. You'd have to petition a known sire to change you, and ultimately, it is they who decide whether or not to change you."

"Oh. I didn't know that."

"Yes. You see, the method of changing a human is a closely guarded secret, only passed down to a very select few in the vampire community. Cortez believes that's the only reason why our kind hasn't overrun the planet entirely, and thereby threatening human existence."

"Then I'm very glad for that."

He chuckled. "As is the rest of humanity, and *most* of my kind."

"So why did Cortez decide to change you?"

"I didn't have any options left. It was either that, or death."

She gasped, turning over to face him. "What?"

"All throughout childhood I was in and out of the hospital, ill from one thing or another. My body just wasn't strong. While other kids were out running and playing, I was bedridden."

She leaned in and kissed the pulse point of his neck. "I'm so sorry you went through that."

"Thank you," he replied, but his voice sounded odd, like her tenderness was unexpected. He cleared his throat. "War was still raging, so we didn't have access to great healthcare, but finally doctors diagnosed me with terminal cancer. They gave me six months, but already I could feel my life draining away, and I was only sixteen."

She bit back emotion for the child he'd been. He didn't look anywhere near sixteen now. Since vampires didn't age, there was more to the story. By all appearances, he'd been somewhere in his late twenties when he'd been changed. "How long ago was this?"

"This was towards the end of the long war, about fifty years ago." His fingers combed through her hair as he continued. "I was so angry with the world. And tired of fighting. I think my parents could tell I was ready to give up. It was the reason they went to Cortez, desperate and pleading to save me. I had no idea what they'd planned till I was already being interviewed by the city's most notorious vampire. Somehow they'd managed to convince him to consider making me part of his clan."

"And he agreed, just like that?"

Lex snorted derisively. "Not in the least. He said I would need to prove myself first. And I do believe, in my adolescent rage, I scoffed in his face. I demanded to know how I could possibly prove myself when I could hardly stand under my own weight." Lex paused for a moment as if recalling the pivotal moment. "He'd coolly replied, 'You'll have to stay alive in order to find out.'"

Kasima's jaw dropped.

"Yeah, you're probably thinking the same thing I was: *What the fuck?* So, in my own teenage, smart-alecky way, I thanked him for coming and then dismissed him with the bird. He just laughed at me, pulled up a chair, and said, 'you want me gone, boy, then either prove yourself unworthy, or die. Nothing short of that is going to make me leave.' You can imagine I had some choice words for him after that. And with each one, the grin on his face only grew wider, which of course pissed me off even more.

"Once I grew too exhausted to rail at him, he questioned me extensively, asking me everything from what I would do with immortality to things I'd believed to be inconsequential and a waste of what precious little time I had left."

"Like what?"

"Like what my favorite color was, or if I preferred cats over dogs. I'd have sworn he was mental with that one. What I didn't know then was that Cortez had a way of... *seeing* what was in someone's heart."

"How so?"

Lex hesitated. "He just gets a really good sense about people."

She got the impression there was more to it than that, but didn't want to press. "Okay, so what did you say?"

"Though I didn't have one, I was just being snotty, I'd told him I'd be happy to feed either to my pet snake."

She thunked him on the chest. "And what was in your heart?"

He smirked. "I'm sure in my heart I had longed for a playful pup or a furry feline. I'd never had any kind of pet. Allergies."

"And Cortez could tell how you really felt about it?"

"Indeed."

"Remarkable. Okay, so what did you say when he asked you what you would do with immortality?"

"Since I had lived such an unfulfilled life, I said I would do only the things that brought me joy."

From what Kasima had observed thus far, he seemed to be on point.

"So anyway," he continued. "Years later, he finally changed me, and here we are."

"Years later? But, why wait so long. And how did you survive?"

"The blood of a sire vampire. It can't cure terminal diseases, but it did give me strength enough to combat the illness better on my own. Also, Cortez brought in specialists, just for me. The kind of doctors my family would never have been able to afford. After several surgeries and a boatload of chemo, I was declared cancer free seven years later. But Cortez made me wait yet another seven years before he changed me."

"Why?"

"I don't know, exactly. Perhaps I hadn't finished proving myself worthy."

"You never asked him?"

"I...no. I never did."

They went silent for a moment. "Do you mind one more question?"

"Not at all."

"You, um. You didn't compel Mr. Dixon, did you? You know, to let me have the day off for the wedding?"

"No."

"But he's giving me the day off *with* pay. He never does that if he doesn't have to."

Lex chuckled. "Oh, that. I simply offered him VIP tickets to next year's masquerade."

"That's it?"

"That's it. Folks would give their right arm for VIP access to an Ever Nights Masquerade Ball."

"Huh. And I barely even wanted to go."

He barked out a laugh. "I'm very glad you did, though. I'll have to send Brian a thank you card."

"Don't you dare! I thought he was going to blow his top when he saw that ridiculous arrangement."

Rich, dark laughter rumbled through his chest. She was about to scold him again, but he playfully rolled her over and took her lips with his. There would be no more talking tonight.

CHAPTER 15

Kasima padded carefully across the room, the wide strap of her weapon slung over her shoulder.

Lex slumbered peacefully, unaware of the danger. Soft morning light pierced the shutters and slashed across his beautiful face. Still he did not wake. Even as she slunk even closer, her toes sinking silently into the beige carpet. Closer. She raised her weapon to strike.

Click.

The sound of the camera's shutter caused Lex to stir. He scrunched his face up and squinted one eye open. "Hmm? What are you doing?"

Kasima gave a wide, sly smile, and then snapped another photo. She giggled at his perturbed expression.

His gaze narrowed. "You sneaky little minx." His arm shot out and snaked her waist. She squealed as her body tumbled over his onto the mattress. He took care as he maneuvered her onto her back with his big body pressing down on her, their faces inches apart. "Those pictures are going to cost you."

"Is that so?"

"Mmm," he murmured, focused on her lips. It seemed as though he was about to kiss her, but by the time she realized his true intent, he'd snatched her camera.

He went to his knees on the mattress, examining the buttons. "Now, how does this work?"

"Oh, be careful." She bit her lip.

"I'm not going to break it." He held it up as if to take a selfie, then with his free arm, positioned her in front of him. "Say cheese."

The flash nearly blinded her. Then his hand slipped down her belly and past the hem of her panties, and she was no longer concerned for her camera's safety.

* * *

Over the next three weeks, Kasima lived in a near-constant state of bliss. Even during work hours she could hardly keep from smiling—because she knew she'd soon be with Lex again. How long things could go on like this, she didn't know, but was happy just to live in the moment with him.

He'd taken to meeting her for lunch every day, which had caught Brian's notice. Only once more had he approached her to ask, "How long do you plan to punish me like this?" That wasn't her intention. She'd tried to explain that, but Brian had only left in a huff. They hadn't spoken since.

Lex stayed at her place most nights. When they weren't going at it like rabbits, they talked about everything and anything. He told her about all the adrenaline-junkie activities he'd done after his transition into a vampire. Skydiving was among his favorites. Followed by bungee jumping and swimming with great whites. He said jokingly that it was like visiting distant cousins, then he'd smiled in a way that bared his fangs.

She told him about her loving parents who tried to give her everything she wanted—or at least everything she needed. How they couldn't always afford trips to exotic destinations, but managed to make local spots magical and memorable for her. Like the time they all went camping near Big Bear Lake. At her young age, the name alone had invoked anxiety—she'd feared a bear would rip through their tent in the dead of night and drag her away.

She'd refused to sleep.

Then her father had told her that they were staying in a very special campground where fairies lived. He said they didn't like bears either because they ate all the tasty fruit, so the fairies used magic to keep them away. Kasima knew her father liked to make up stories, and said she didn't believe him. "But," she told Lex. "For the rest of the trip, I had secretly kept an eye out for little creatures with fluttering wings and human-like bodies." That had made Lex smile. Later he confided more about his cancer. How he'd spent his seventeenth birthday in the bathroom being sick due to the chemotherapy.

She'd spent her sixteenth birthday at the beach with her parents and a couple of friends. "I'm glad to know you have such happy memories," he'd said sincerely, then teased her by postulating if they were kids together, he'd have hounded her for a date. "I might have been ill, but I wasn't blind to attractive women. Especially ones in skimpy bathing suits, as I'm now imagining you in."

That prompted a midnight trip to the beach where they made love on the sand under the moonlight.

One evening at sunset, he'd had her collect her camera and drove her to a bluff overlooking the town. When she insisted on making him her subject, he'd grudgingly humored her. She'd captured him from every angle, and would forever cherish every shot.

She no longer feared his fangs. Instead, the sight of them aroused her, which he was very well aware of and used to his advantage at every opportunity. The man couldn't get enough of her. Or she him. A part of her realized she was falling for him...hardcore...but she convinced herself she'd be fine when they were over. She'd have to be. The end was looming. Whenever she erred and gazed at him with something too much like love, he'd grow uncomfortable for a time. He had to know he was enchanting her. He had to be worried about that.

So she devoured every moment with Lex like the last meal of a death row inmate, because one day it *would* be her last.

CHAPTER 16

Ever Nights was closed to the public for the first time in ages—only guests of the wedding were permitted—still, the place was packed and literally dripping with elegance; the entryway was newly bracketed by two massive wall fountains, and behind the water, tiny lights sparkled so that it looked as though the liquid was glistening with diamonds.

Hell, considering the source, maybe there really *were* diamonds back there.

Note to self: Check fountains for diamonds.

The lavish motif continued into the ceremony room with white floral arrangements three times larger than the one Lex had sent her posted along the walls every few yards. Strands of glittering lights hung everywhere, twinkling softly. Alabaster chairs, mostly filled with guests, had been set up on either side of a clear path that led to a beautiful blooming platform, which was situated under a silky plume of draped gossamer fabric.

The room was abuzz with conversation, everyone chatting with their neighbors as they waited for the ceremony to start. It was a diverse crowd. Both humans and vampires mixed throughout. Riverstone was a unique town in that the two lived together with reasonably few reports of incidents, but the people here tonight were close friends and family of the bride and groom, so there was a sense of acceptance and ease throughout.

After they took their seats, Kasima leaned in to ask Lex, "So, is the bride a vampire too?"

Lex hesitated. "No."

Kasima's head swung around. "She's human?"

"Mmm."

How...interesting. "How did the happy couple meet?"

The question caused a small grin to sweep over his lips. "Well, the short story is Naia was hired to spy on Cortez."

"Like a private investigator?"

He chuckled. "She's actually a singer by trade...or maybe it's more like by birth."

Performers often believed that of themselves. Kasima knew a girl who, in their teens, declared she was born for the stage. The girl had two left feet and couldn't hold a note. "So then why would she have been hired to spy on Cortez?"

Lex leaned closer and lowered his voice as if he didn't want anyone overhearing. "An old clan mate with a vendetta got it in his head that Naia had a special kind of...mystery about her that Cortez wouldn't be able to resist. It was just about the only thing the prick had been right about. The two have been nearly inseparable since."

"Aw. That's sweet. Well, except for that whole revenge bit."

"Some other shit went down, but I won't go into that. As you can see, it all worked out in the end."

"So what happened to your old clan mate?"

"Let just say he won't be bothering us anymore."

That sparked her curiosity, but just then soft processional music began to play. The guests grew quiet. A handsome man, the groom she surmised, strode down the aisle with purposeful steps. His dark suit was pressed neatly, his chin proud and high. He exuded a unique mixture of confidence, respect, authority, and even a bit of danger that others might like to claim but could rarely back up. Based on the way he met and held every eye in the crowd, Cortez could back that shit up. When his gaze found Lex, the two nodded silently to one another. A man with a wild mane of blond hair joined Cortez on the platform looking just as dapper, yet ten times more uncomfortable in his tailored suit. He hooked his finger in his collar and tugged lightly, then threw someone a thumbs-up.

"Who's that?"

"Ryder, the best man." There was something slightly resentful in his tone.

"Why aren't you up there as a groomsman?" she asked.

"Believe me, most of us wanted to be, but it would have looked a little uneven with a crowd of bachelors on the groom's side and only the two bridesmaids on the bride's side. So Cortez declared he would only have two groomsmen up there with him, and Cole, being the brother of the bride, was automatically allotted one of the slots. The rest of us had to fight it out amongst ourselves."

She digested that for a moment. "What do you mean by fight?"

"Not physically, though, many of us would have preferred that."

"You would have preferred to fight?"

He passed her a cocky grin. "Had fists been involved, I

would have won."

"Is that so?"

"Mmm," he grunted. The rest of the guests had restarted light conversation when it appeared the rest of the procession was not yet appearing.

"So what did you all do instead of bashing each other's brains in?"

He scratched the back of his neck and answered with slow reluctance. "We, uh, had to kiss a pig."

"Excuse me?"

"Victor, the club's head chef, owns a ranch just outside town. One night, after all of us had been drinking and arguing about who should be the best man, he suggested a contest. He'd grease up one of his piglets, and the first one of us to catch it and—" he cleared his throat "—kiss it on the rump would be the winner."

She gaped at him for a moment, then had to cover her mouth to keep her laughter from bursting out.

"I'll tell you what, that little bugger was fast."

"I'd love to have seen that."

Looking perturbed, he said, "I suspect Kenzi might have caught the spectacle on her camera phone."

"Oh, then you'll have to introduce me to her," she teased.

"I'm sure she'd make herself known soon enough."

The officiant took his place, and another shift in music declared the ceremony underway. For the first time, the groom's regal facade cracked slightly. His Adam's apple bobbed and his gaze had lasered in on the entryway.

A dark-haired bridesmaid appeared wearing a long, delicate wine-colored dress with a deep v-neck and lacy straps. Her face was bright and eager for the attention of the room, which had gone silent but for the soft music and sporadic sounds of delight here and there.

"That's Kenzi," Lex offered.

Suddenly, the music shuddered and scratched like a needle to a record, and Kasima worried the player was malfunctioning, but then the hard beat of electronica took over and Kenzi strut-danced down the aisle, pausing halfway to wave her arms in the air and energizing the crowd. Everyone laughed and cheered.

At the altar, she whirled and pointed to the entrance. A second bridesmaid danced down the aisle as Kenzi had, only her movements were a touch more risqué with a couple booty pops and a shimmy of her torso. Joining Kenzi, the two of them gestured back at the entrance.

"Please stand for the bride," the officiant said.

Everyone eagerly stood. The music changed again, remaining just as electric and punchy, but with a sweeter undertone.

Then the bride appeared in a glittering white gown that bloomed at the bottom like a thousand delicate petals, and everyone gasped. She was accompanied by a young man with short blond hair, the brother Lex had mentioned? The two marched to the beat of the music, not quite dancing, but with an elegant rhythm. At the halfway point, they paused and the man spun the bride in a circle while she rotated around him. The gown fluttered through the air, making her look like a music-box ballerina.

The bride faced her groom with a wide, infectious grin. The groom's returning gaze was smoldering, and Kasima could tell he deeply loved his bride. Happiness for the two plucked at her heartstrings, but then a tragic longing took over. Would she ever find a love like that? Her eyes began to sting with unshed tears.

The electric beat fell away from the music, leaving behind a soft fanciful melody. The bride's brother guided her the rest of the way down the aisle. Before they reached the end, he paused and gently pulled her around to face him. He whispered something in her ear, which made her bottom lip quiver and her eyes glisten. Then he kissed her gently on the forehead before handing her over to Cortez and taking his place next to the best man.

The guests sat. The officiant launched into his speech, and everything seemed to happen so fast. When he spoke of the love between the bride and groom, Kasima's throat grew thick. By the time the vows came about, she was swiping at her cheeks. Lex handed her a handkerchief.

After the officiant instructed the groom to kiss the bride, the room became a whirlwind of excitement. Deafening cheers erupted from the crowd, most jumping out of their seats and clapping. A few sharp whistles zinged through the air. Cortez kissed his new wife like the crowd didn't exist and only the wedding night occupied his mind.

The bride's hands ran wildly through his hair as if she couldn't get enough.

Then they faced the crowd, clasped hands, and raised them in triumph. More cheers and whistles rang out. Then they raced back up the aisle, smiling politely, yet dodging congratulations before disappearing through the entryway.

Kenzi clapped her hands once to get everyone's attention. "Alright, bitches! Who's ready to party? The reception hall is open and we have a full bar, great food, and some amazing performers. The lovebirds will rejoin us shortly after they've... ahem... changed."

"Come," Lex said, standing and offering her his hand. "We are seated near the newlywed's table."

CHAPTER 17

The reception hall was like entering the land of Oz. Glittering lights transformed the ceiling into a starlit sky. Wispy clouds of gauze draped down. White rose garlands climbed the walls and columns, floral scents permeating the air. A half-moon of cream-clothed tables surrounded an open dance floor and a stage where a live band lured people to their seats with one of Kasima's favorite hit songs—"

"Oh my God, is that Sugar Mouse on stage?"

Lex nodded. "You know their music?"

"Uh, duh. Doesn't everyone? I used to have the lead singer's poster hanging up in my room," she sighed. When the singer started in on the chorus, she suppressed a squeal, wanting to run up to the stage like a lovesick teenager. A few other guests were already there, starstruck.

Lex must have read her thoughts, because he said, "Go on. When you're done crushing on the band, I'll be over there." He pointed to their table across the room.

She grinned up at him, practically bouncing. "Okay, I won't be long."

He leaned down and pressed a hot kiss to her lips. "No rush. I'll have you all to myself for the rest of the evening."

Her blood suddenly rushed with lava, and she nearly suggested they start *the rest of the evening* now, but he turned to head toward their table and the band reached a thunderous crescendo, drawing her like a siren to the stage. For a few magical minutes, she danced and sang along, and even made contact with the lead singer's hand when he reached out for the crowd, then she glanced back at Lex who was watching her with a light kind of smile she couldn't decipher. It made her want to go to him.

So she did, crossing the room as he watched her with heavy lids.

He stood as she approached, and she went on tiptoes to kiss him.

"Have fun?"

"Immensely. This is like a wonderland," she said, admiring the room.

An unfamiliar male voice muttered from behind. "Yeah, it's like dining in a room for fairies and unicorns and everything else that spits love and craps rainbows."

She turned to see a stoic man with a square jaw and wide shoulders. Though he wore his suit well, she got the impression he'd be more comfortable in biker gear or fatigues or something with a gun holster.

"Dane," Lex greeted coolly. "This is Kasima. Kasima, this is Dane, one of my clan mates."

At her name, Dane did a double take, and his harsh face actually softened. "Ah, Kasima. Nice to meet you. I've heard...well, very little actually. Lex has been keeping you pretty well under wraps. But don't worry, vampires gossip like teenage girls, and we'll know all about you soon enough."

A woman around Kasima's age stood just behind Dane, sidling quite close to him as if for protection. She was glancing side to side like she expected an imminent attack. Dane sighed and glanced up at the ceiling, before slicing his gaze down at her. She didn't notice his look of annoyance, busy eyeing the room.

Planting a hand at the small of her back, Dane stepped aside and pushed her to the forefront. Her expression turned so stark, like she'd just been delivered to feasting sharks.

"This is Evie," Dane said.

Evie gave a weak smile and nodded in greeting. "Hello."

"Hi, Evie," Lex said in a voice you might use with a child. "It's great to see you again. How are you doing?"

"Good. Thanks," she muttered quietly, anxiously, then resumed her survey of the room.

Behind Evie's back, Dane lifted arms as if in exasperation, giving Lex a helpless look. Lex responded with a stern expression and seemed to be saying something with his eyes. A silent conversation was taking place and Kasima didn't have the key to decipher it.

"Yeah, yeah," Dane grumbled. Then he snapped to Evie, "Come on. We're going to the bar."

As soon as they'd gone, Kasima muttered, "What was that about?"

"It's a long story. Suffice it to say, Evie went through something...traumatic. Dane is...sort of helping her through it."

Huh. Kasima would have assumed Dane wanted nothing to do with the girl.

"Oh no." Lex scrubbed a hand down his face. "The vultures are descending."

Just then, Kenzi, the bride's maid, appeared. "Lex! Look at you. You actually showed up when you said you would. How novel."

"Kenzi," he greeted her with a warning in his tone.

As if on cue, Kenzi focused her shrewd eyes on Kasima. "And this must be the mysterious Kasima who's been stealing you away from us at every opportunity."

"Uh, yup. That's me," Kasima said, facing Lex with a raised brow. "Whom *everyone* seems to know about."

He shrugged. "Like Dane said, these people gossip worse than teenage girls."

Kenzi glanced down at one of the place settings and picked up the card with her name on it. "And what a fun surprise. You're both been seated at *my* table."

Lex snorted. "Shocking, since you helped Naia with the seating chart, and you are unfailingly nosy."

Kenzi took her seat with a smirk, and waved her empty champagne glass at a nearby waiter.

The waiter scurried over to fill it, along with the other glasses around the table, even those whose seats had yet to be claimed. Kasima peeked at the nametags of their missing tablemates: Goldie and Donovan.

"A toast to new friends," Kenzi said suddenly, raising her glass.

Lex picked up his champagne. "And to those friends minding their own business."

Kenzi countered brightly, "And to old dogs learning new tricks."

Lex gritted his teeth. "And to old dogs whose bite is worse than their bark if some people aren't careful."

Kasima rolled her eyes, gathering the gist. She lifted her glass, interrupting. "How about to the happy couple?"

They both blinked at her. Kenzi smiled and clinked

her glass to Kasima's "Oh sure. We can toast to that."

After they all took a sip, Kenzi held out her hand to Kasima. "So we weren't formally introduced. I'm Kenzi, and I'll be your BFF for the night and possibly the foreseeable future. What are you doing tomorrow? We should do lunch."

Lex shook his head. "Go easy, Kenzi."

"Don't worry. I'm not going to scare her away...yet. Why don't you go grab us a real drink while us girls chat. You know what I like, and if you don't know what she likes by now, then you are a bad boy toy."

Kenzi was something of a spitfire. Kasima liked her already.

The second Lex was halfway across the room, Kenzi leaned in and whispered, "So how is our little Lexington in the sack?"

But her voice wasn't quiet enough in a room full of vampires. Kasima saw Lex studderstep, but he continued toward the bar.

"I bet he's as magnificent as he is hot." Kenzi licked the pad of her forefinger and mimed scorching it in the air. "*Tsss.*"

Kasima laughed. "Let me put it to you this way. On a scale from one to ten, he's so off the charts, he doesn't even register." Had Lex heard that? He was at the bar now, engaging the bartender.

"I *knew* it!" Kenzi leaned back in her seat, body melting, and groaned, "Arrrrg, I need to get laid."

A balding man from a nearby table had overhead that and smiled her way.

Kenzi sat up. "Ew. Not you, perv."

The man didn't seem put off in the least. He merely smiled wider and wagged his bushy eyebrows.

Kenzi turned amused. "Alright, I like your style, I'll put you at the bottom of my list. My very *long* list."

Naia and Cortez entered the reception area. Cheers from the guests erupted. The newlyweds inched into the room as people crowded around to offer their congratulations. When they got near, Kenzi stood to hug Naia. Kasima politely rose as well.

"You look amazing," Kenzi said.

"Thanks to you," Naia replied, twirling and showing off a shorter, sexier version of her wedding dress. "Everything was perfect. You did such a wonderful job with the decorations and the dress and well, pretty much everything. Right, my love?"

Cortez offered Naia a pleasant smile. "As always, I'm finding it impossible to notice anything but you."

"Awww," Naia, Kenzi, and even Kasima sighed.

Naia rewarded her new husband with a quick peck on the cheek. He dragged her close and stole a full mouth kiss.

Kasima's skin could have turned the deepest shade of envy.

Cortez noticed her then. His unfathomable gaze caught hers, and held.

In that moment, she couldn't look away. Couldn't breathe. Not because he was doing anything vampiric, at least she didn't think so, but because of something else entirely. Something unfathomable. A baser instinct set off warning flares in her brain. There was something about his eyes boring into her that set her instantly on guard.

His gaze was like slowly being stripped to the bone.

He raised a brow.

Kenzi cleared her throat. "Cortez, Naia, meet Lex's date, Kasima."

Naia's lips rounded, and then transformed into an inviting smile. "Oh, *Kasima*. So nice to finally meet you."

Guess everyone really does know about me. But why should they? Why would Lex talk about her to anyone if things between them had an end date? Maybe he talked with his friends about all his lovers. Maybe, in his circle, that was normal.

Kasima put her hand out in front of her, intending to shake Naia's hand. Instead, Naia pulled her in for a full-on hug.

"Oh, okay," she said, a little stunned.

"Lex is a good guy," Naia muttered.

Kasima was learning that. Too bad he wasn't *her* good guy. Not like she wanted.

CHAPTER 18

Lex returned to the table, drinks in hand. "Ladies, let's try not to overwhelm her in one night."

Placing her at arm's length, Naia chirped, "I *must* hear the story of how you two met."

Kasima cocked her head. Maybe they didn't understand that she and Lex weren't a serious couple? Then Naia's words brought back the memory of that night; the masquerade ball, their first kiss, their bodies clashing...all the salacious things they'd done since then.

Cortez coughed into his hand. "A story for another time perhaps."

What had Lex said about Cortez? That he had a way of reading people? She wondered if he could somehow sense the direction of her thoughts. She blushed furiously.

Lex came to her rescue. "Yes, another time. We don't want to monopolize the two of you. People are waiting to offer their congratulations."

Sure enough, there was a crowd of people mingling by the table of honor.

"He's right," Cortez said. "There's no getting around it.

Even if they are more interested in schmoozing rather than celebrating our union. Best to just get it over with. Besides, I think Kasima could use a minute to settle in before we accost her."

She *was* feeling a bit overwhelmed.

As soon as they were gone, she accepted the drink from Lex and took her seat.

Kenzi finished off her champagne and was waving her glass for a refill while sucking on the straw of the tropical-umbrella drink Lex had sat in front of her.

Waiters buzzed around the room, dropping off mini rose-shaped puff pastries drizzled with sweet raspberry sauce. Kenzi plucked one from the tray and popped it into her mouth, chewing as she addressed Kasima. "So, Kas, can I call you Kas? Tell me about yourself."

"Uh, well," she began. "I work at the Tribune as the editor's assistant."

"You work with Mr. Dixon?"

"Yes. I hear he likes to visit the club."

"On occasion. Sweet old guy. Likes to chat. I think he's lonely, though. You have any siblings?"

Kasima shook her head.

"Pets?"

"Uh, no."

"Kids?"

"Not yet."

Kenzi's eyes darted to Lex and back. "Do you want them?"

Kasima felt like she was being quizzed. "I haven't really thought about it." Could vampires have kids?

Lex scraped a hand down his face. "Shall I get you a hot lamp, Kenzi? Cool it with the inquisition, would you?"

"Kasima doesn't mind a few questions. Right, Kas?"

Lex sighed. "She's too polite to say otherwise."

"How else do you expect her to get the Kenzi stamp of approval?"

"She doesn't need the Kenzi stamp of approval, do you, Kasima."

"I—"

"How would she know? You obviously haven't told her anything about us. Why is that? Hmmm?"

"She doesn't need to know about any of you."

Something sharp seared Kasima's chest.

Kenzi waved that away. "Don't be ridiculous. Of course she does. Right, Kasima?"

She didn't get a chance to reply. Lex said in a mitigated tone, "I'm sorry. If I knew you'd be turned into a spectacle, I never would have invited you."

Another slice to the chest. "It's fine, Lex. I'm having a great time. And I don't mind answering a few questions."

Kenzi affected a superior expression. "You see."

Lex sat back and swigged his drink. "Just say the word and we can duck out of here."

Kenzi's grin was both playful and threatening. "I would find you."

Naia plopped down at one of the empty seats, blissfully interrupting the squabble. "Someone should tell those stiffs over there this is a wedding, not a damn networking gig."

Lex glanced over to where Cortez was chatting with several professional-looking individuals. "You want me to bounce them for you, Naia?"

"Tempting, but no. Those are the guys from High Spirits Brewery and Wine. They've been wooing Cortez for the last year, hoping to get his business. I think Cortez is ready to make the deal, for the right price."

"Poor guys," Lex shook his head. "They don't even realize Cortez knows *exactly* how low they're willing to go."

Naia smirked. "He'll make sure the deal is fair." Then she turned to Kasima. "So, tell me about yourself."

"Ugh," Lex groaned. "Not you too."

Naia put her hands up. "Wha'd I say?"

"He thinks we're being nosy," Kenzi offered.

"*You're* being nosy. Naia, you get a pass because it's your wedding day."

"Well, how could we not be? All I hear about lately is how once again Lex has run off to be with his secret lover."

Kasima struggled to keep the shock off her face.

A male voice interjected from behind. "And how he's utterly whipped." It was the man who'd walked Naia down the aisle. He held out his arm to shake Kasima's hand. "I'm Cole, brother of the bride, newest member of the Cortez clan, and totally available when you get sick of Lex."

She laughed at his playful smile. Lex grumbled, shooting Cole a death stare.

Cole didn't seem bothered. He grabbed Naia's hand. "I hope you all don't mind if I steal the bride for a sister brother dance." There were already several people on the dance floor.

"Great idea, Cole." Kenzi chirped. "Kas and I will join you."

"Okay," Kasima said as Kenzi tugged her out of her seat.

"Perfect," Kenzi said, finding a space close to the far side of the stage, Kasima suspected, so their voices would be drowned out by the large speakers. "Now grumpy old Lex can't interrupt us. He never dances."

"Never?" Kasima decided to test that. She caught his

eye back at the table and crooked her finger. He crossed his arms and shook his head, ass planted firmly in his seat. She shot him a pouty frown. No go. Yet he seemed content to watch her dance, heat in his gaze. She made sure her movements were as sensual as possible.

"He did willingly set foot on a dance floor once, but that was to break up a fight. I'd like to say he threw elbows to the beat, but I can't be sure. Other than that, I've never seen him so much as tap a foot with enjoyment."

They lost themselves to the music for a moment. Kasima kept peeking at Lex, teasing him with her body. Lex never took his eyes off her, even as he had to shift in his seat.

Before long, Kenzi resumed her questions. "So, what are your intentions with our Sexy Lexy? Can I expect more wedding planning in my future?"

"I hate to disappoint you, but we're not serious. We're just having fun." She placed a hand over her chest where a pang zinged. Only she was starting to wonder if things between them had grown more serious than that. Or at least was starting to. It was clear Lex had spoken about her with at least a few of his friends. They were all very interested in her, acting like she was his girlfriend or something.

"Well, I guess that's *typical Lex.*"

Like ceramic to concrete, Kasima's hopes shattered. Of course this was his typical behavior.

"Honestly, we're all a little shocked you've held his attention for this long.

Or maybe not.

"It's got to be some kind of record for him. I must know the secret of your success."

Phenomenal sex? "I don't think there is a secret. Lex just needed a date for the wedding is all." Kasima glanced back at Lex. He was now leaning forward in his chair, still watching her, but with that bedroom expression that sent lusty chills over her skin.

"He's never ditched work for a girl before," Kenzi continued.

Kasima stopped dancing. "He's been ditching work?"

Kenzi nodded happily, still gyrating to the music. "Usually he's a workaholic, but ever since the masquerade, he's been cutting out early, coming in late, or strong-arming others to take his shifts."

From across the room, Lex cocked his head at her: *What's wrong?*

She gave him an *everything's fine* smile and resumed dancing, her mind drifting over the past week and how often she and Lex had been together, now realizing during some of that time, he'd been shirking his duties to be with her. That wasn't FWB, booty-call type behavior. Couple that with his winning her stuffed bears, buying her flowers, and the consistent sleepovers, an outsider looking in might see a couple in love, or headed that way.

Already she knew her feelings for him were beyond what they should be.

Was he on the same page? Or was she just a fool who had lost control of her heart.

She decided after the wedding was over, she would speak to him about her feelings. Better to get it out in the open. And if things had to end, better they ended before she fell even deeper for him.

If he didn't reciprocate her feelings, it was very possible that tonight was her last night with Lex, so she decided to make it a memorable one. She wanted to dance with Lex.

Breaking away from Kenzi, she faced Lex and rolled her hips enticingly.

Leaning forward in his chair, his gaze darkened.

Eyes locked, she crooked her finger at him.

Even though his eyes were hooded, as though he wanted to do as she bid, he shook his head.

"Hmm," Kenzi said, catching their interaction. Mischief lit her expression. "This ought to be interesting. Do you trust me, Kas?"

"Huh?"

Kenzi pointed to the eavesdropper from earlier. "You! Eyebrows. You're going to dance with us."

The man needed no more encouragement than that, jumping to his feet and placing himself between the two women. He was facing Kenzi to start, but Kenzi flipped him around and whispered in his ear, "I like to watch. You have till the end of this song to impress me." Then she shoved him at Kasima.

"Hi." The man smiled down at her, closing the space between them.

"Uh." She sent Kenzi a beseeching look.

"Just go with it," she muttered. "It's already working."

Working? She peeked at Lex, who was now frowning, on the edge of his seat. Kasima put her arms around the man's neck. *Dirty tricks.*

A couple heartbeats later, she heard Lex's voice just behind her and had to suppress a grin.

"What are you doing?" he asked darkly, grudgingly, as if he knew exactly what she was doing, and had come over here anyway. Because he couldn't stand it?

Mission accomplished, Kenzi tugged the balding man back toward her. "My turn, stud."

Kasima faced Lex, answering, "Trying to get you on the dance floor. And look at that. Here you are."

"I don't take pleasure in dancing," he grumbled, yet he

moved closer and hooked her waist.

"You will with me."

His lips twitching, "I'm finding that is true with everything."

He stared into her eyes as she peered up at him. Their bodies fell into a natural, sensual synchronicity, the heat between them turning electric. Could he hear how his words inspired a sudden change in her pulse? Her heart fluttered for him. Did he know he could easily command it? That it was very nearly his for the taking?

Was it written all over her face? She shifted in his arms, giving him her back as they danced. Palm sliding around her stomach, he clamped her close.

"You thought to make me jealous," he murmured in her ear.

"Mmm. Did it work?"

"More than I'd have liked." His tone was thick with a mixture of smooth desire and amused irritation.

"Oh?"

"I never believed I could be quick to jealousy. You have proven otherwise."

"Honestly, Lex. I only danced with him for a few seconds. It couldn't have made you *that* jealous."

"No?" His tone lowered several octaves. "I wanted to rip the poor man's throat out just for touching you."

She froze, blinked, and flipped around, eyeing him from under her lashes. "No you didn't. Don't exaggerate."

"Would that I were."

Such a declaration should read insane, psychotic, dangerous, and part of her *was* alarmed by it, but another darker, more primitive, hidden part of her reveled in the strength of his response.

Before she could say anything more, Kenzi and her possibly still-endangered dance partner sidled close to them. "Naia's getting ready to sing." She turned to Kasima. "Have you heard her voice? She sings like angels giving birth to baby unicorns."

As she walked across the stage to claim the mic, Naia's dress sparkled like a billion tiny suns. She cleared her throat. "First I want to thank everyone for coming, and everyone who helped make this day so magical for me and... my...uh...well, my *husband*." She smiled so brightly at that, like she couldn't believe the words.

The crowd's cheer was deafening. She was a simple human, married to a powerful vampire, and she had thoroughly been accepted by these people.

Naia continued. "I'd like to sing a song now that I wrote for my husband, to express just how much I love him." As if on cue, the band started up, and Naia started her ballad. The beautiful sounds that left Naia's lips made Kasima's heart swell.

Gently, Lex tugged her back around to face him, and they resumed their dance, albeit a bit slower now. Her arms slipped around his neck and she rested her head on his shoulder, letting Naia's beautiful song wash over her. She sang of destiny and love and losing oneself so entirely in another. Kasima had never heard a more beautiful voice. It vibrated in her bones, each note deeper than the last.

"I hope I didn't scare you just then," he said. "You looked startled. I realize now that was a very vampiric thing for me to say."

"It's fine," she sighed, feeling a bit dizzy and hot. "I kind of liked it." As if she hadn't touched him in ages, almost reverently, she ran her hands along his chest. She went slowly, memorizing every hard plain and valley.

He chuckled. "I should threaten more lives for you,

then?"

She ignored that, knowing he was teasing. As the music toiled, fiery lust kindled in her veins. "I wish it could be like this forever."

He sighed. "I know how you feel."

She pulled back. "Do you?" Could he truly feel the same? If so, why should they not scream it from the rafters? Love was not something to avoid. To run from.

His eyes were intense, lit by some emotion she couldn't decipher, and she knew she was right about him. He loved her, just as she did him. Maybe she just needed to be the first to admit it. Why ever had she feared this?

His head dipped, and he took her lips in a soft, slow kiss. Her heart went into overdrive, beating so fast it was almost painful. Was this his way of saying it? To show her just how he felt without words? She tilted her head to deepen the contact, darting her tongue out to taste him. He groaned and kissed her with more urgency. Her heart brimmed with so much emotion, she was sure it would burst at any moment.

Lex broke the kiss and rested his forehead against hers. "How do you make me want you this much?"

The simple statement set off a cache of fireworks in her chest. Little bursts that seemed perfectly synchronized with Naia's heartfelt music.

Kasima peered deep into Lex's eyes. "I love you."

CHAPTER 19

Several things happened at once.

Lex's eyes went shockingly wide. Naia's song cut off. And Kasima wanted to kill herself.

Like a lever had been pulled, all the happy feelings from a moment ago flushed away, leaving behind dark emptiness.

Somehow, she'd recklessly misjudged the situation.

"Oops," Naia muttered. She was cringing, looking over at Cortez, who stood by the stage holding the severed microphone cord. Tiny sparks shot from then ends. Why would he...?

Why would *I*...?

Kasima glanced back at Lex, who had taken a step away from her.

A pall of dread sank over her. "I mean...well...what I meant—" she cleared her throat. "—is that I love *dancing*, is what I meant to say. The dancing, with you, is what I love." Her stomach clenched.

Lex scratched the back of his neck, seemingly searching for a response. Which obviously wasn't going to be "I love you too, baby."

A stabbing pain shredded her chest, the sensation so sharp, it was a wonder she remained so still. No one else had noticed her inner destruction. Except Cortez was now studying her. She had to get out of here.

Yet she managed a laugh, fanning herself. "Whew, I think I had too much to drink. I'm not making any sense. Excuse me, I need to go find the little girl's room."

Amazed that her voice hadn't quaked, she scurried away. Each breath into her lungs sent a new set of knives through her heart, flaying it with fresh cuts. Her eyes burned. Yet she held it together, at least until she locked the bathroom door behind her.

Then a devastated sob gurgled up through her esophagus. Palms planted on the countertop, she polished the sink with her tears.

What the hell had she been thinking? What had possibly compelled her to admit something so...so...destructive? His expression couldn't lie. He'd been horrified. Recalling it thrashed her once more.

He doesn't feel the same about me as I feel about him. She'd been a fool to think she could keep herself detached. While she'd been falling for him, he'd only been having fun with her. He wanted her in his bed, but that was it. She realized now that, stupidly, she'd been holding out hope for more. And that would never happen.

Her half-hearted cover up on the dance floor hadn't fooled him. If he hadn't been before, he was now probably contemplating the best way to break things off.

Another gouge formed in her chest.

She hadn't reacted this strongly when things ended with Brian. Why did Lex have to go and be so goddamned wonderful?

Through a watery gaze, she looked at her reflection. The outward version of her wasn't as much of a mess as she felt on the inside. Her hair was still in place, ringlets curling down. Though her eyes were red-rimmed and her cheeks were damp, she'd had the foresight to tint her lashes with waterproof mascara in light of tonight's event.

She dabbed at her face with a paper towel as she worked to pull herself together. She couldn't hide in here forever. And now that this was likely her last night with Lex, she was desperate not to waste another moment away from him. She felt as though a timer had been set, counting down.

If things must end, at least she could keep her chin high, dignity intact, when they did. No need for him to know how broken she'd be once he was gone.

Eyes dried, she straightened, took in a fortifying breath, and smoothed out her hair before exiting the restroom. Lex was seated at their table with Kenzi and two others who must have just arrived in mid conversation: Goldie and Donovan. Goldie was the other bridesmaid. Donovan had officiated the wedding, and sometime between then and now, had changed his clothes.

Kasima pasted a smile on her face and scooted into her seat.

Lex leaned in. "The music was so loud before, I thought I heard you say something about drinking too much. Are you feeling alright?"

She offered him a smile and nodded, but her lips felt too tight. Was that how they were going to play this? Would they pretend nothing had happened?

"I ordered you some water." He gestured to the frosty glass in front of her.

"Thank you."

Kenzi craned her neck around. "Did I just hear the phrase *drink* and *too much* in the same sentence on the night of my girl's wedding? Blasphemy! I can see I'm going to have to teach you the sacred meaning of the word *party*, young grasshopper." She turned to the other two. "You two still haven't told us where you've been. You missed Naia's bang-worthy music. I almost lost my mind with my new bald-headed pervy friend over there."

Donovan and Lex both cleared their throats at the same time, and Kasima got the sense that she'd missed something.

Goldie huffed out a breath. "I had to go straighten something out at The Pit. Donovan was nice enough to drive me."

"Boomer's still being a dick?"

"Oh, only on the days that end in Y."

"Well, never fear, Kenzi is here. Shots all around! Then when we're good and toasted we'll discuss ways to dispose of his body."

"Ha! I wish," Goldie said.

A waiter brought over the shots. Three for each of them. One green, one blue and the last one deep orange. "Cortez calls this Oblivion's Descent." Her grin was laughably wide.

Following Kenzi's lead, Kasima went for the green one first.

"Is that wise?" Lex asked.

She downed the shot with the others. "We're here to have fun, right?"

Eyeing Kasima, Lex took his shot. What must be running through his head?

Kenzi raised her second shot. "To Kasima, who finally got our little Lexington out on the dance floor. Girl, you must be magic."

Her smile felt like plastic wrap stretched too thin. "For my next trick, watch me make this shot disappear." The alcohol burned on the way down.

Laughing, Donovan shook his head and pinned Lex with a look. "You *danced*? The devil must be freezing with all that new ice down there."

Once again Naia joined them. "You guys are taking shots without me?"

"Plenty to go around," Kenzi said. As if on cue, a waiter appeared with more rainbow-colored shots.

Cortez sidled up to his bride, and a small crowd gathered around.

"We should make toasts," Goldie said, giggling like a lightweight.

Cheers erupted as everyone clamored for their turn to toast to the happy couple.

Kenzi stood, raising her glass to Naia and Cortez. "Here's to you, here's to me, the best of friends we'll always be. But if we ever disagree...then fuck you, and here's to me!" Laughter rang out.

A man with a Russian accent chimed in, "To the new couple: Never sweat the petty things, but always pet the sweaty things." More laughter rang out.

The toasts only degraded from there, but Kasima was starting to have fun again.

"May all your ups and downs be between the sheets," someone called from behind. The crowd hooted and hollered.

Then Donovan stood and took on a more serious tone. "Cortez, I have always admired you like no one else, but never once have I been jealous of you. Not until tonight. Naia, you've found the luckiest man in the world, because he has you."

Emotions grew thick in Kasima's throat. She glanced at Lex. His eyes were on the table as though his mind was elsewhere.

Naia dabbed at her eyes, and Cortez kissed her on the cheek.

The whole room had gone silent with approval.

Donovan raised his glass. "So, may you love like you've never been hurt, dance like no one is watching....and screw like it's being filmed."

Once more the crowd turned rowdy.

"No problems in that department," Cortez boasted. Naia lightly slapped him on the chest with the back of her hand.

After another round of drinks and toasts, Cortez and Naia said their last goodbyes before heading out to wherever they planned to spend their honeymoon. Lex offered to take Kasima home. The car ride was awkward and layered in silence. She wasn't sure what to say; *sorry I said the L-word? It won't happen again? Don't leave me?*

That just sounded too pathetic. She said nothing.

He pulled up to her curb, and she debated trying for one last kiss.

"So, listen," he started, and immediately her heart sank at his tone. "With Cortez gone, I'm going to be a little busy over the next few weeks. With work and all. So I might not see you for a bit."

"Yeah, no, me too. Work's going to take up a lot of my time. There's this banquet I'm helping to plan, so I won't be very available." This was it. This was how they were going to say goodbye.

"Okay, good. So, we're okay then," he peered at her through the darkness. Was he worried she'd start blubbering? Begging?

"Yeah, we're great."

Silence stretched for a minute.

"Okay. Good." Then he leaned close to place a kiss on her lips. She blinked, a little surprised, but then she leaned into it, allowing herself to enjoy this final, warm moment. The perfect way to end it: with his drugging scent in her head and his soft lips molding to hers. A memory to cherish.

He pulled away too soon. "I'll call you, yeah?"

She nodded and scurried out of the car, not trusting her voice. Once inside, she closed her door, sank to the ground, and surrendered to heartache.

CHAPTER 20

Over the next couple of weeks, Kasima threw herself into work as never before. Like a carnivore on the hunt, busy work was her meat. When a file needed attention, it was handled with swift accord. If Mr. Dixon asked her to read over an article, she scoured each word three times for good measure. Emails didn't have a chance to pile up before she ripped through them. She didn't go out to lunch much. Just nibbled at her desk on whatever she could find in the break room's lone vending machine while she worked. Yet there never seemed to be enough tasks to keep her mind off the fact that Lex still hadn't called.

It wasn't the least bit surprising. He'd warned her not to get attached. It was her own damn fault. In a way, she appreciated his prudence, using his bosses' honeymoon as an excuse to create this distance between them.

She'd reached out a few times, calling his number. After the third time ringing through to his voicemail, she began to feel foolish. So she stopped.

It was for the best.

Falling for a vampire was the very last thing she needed right now. It was the very last thing she needed *ever*. There was no future with Lex. Even if they were still FWBs, their relationship had always been destined to end. Sooner was better than later. Less messy that way.

Didn't mean it doesn't hurt.

Assisting Tanya turned out to be a much-needed distraction. This year's awards ceremony was panning out to be bigger than ever. Poor girl was overwhelmed trying to accommodate all the different news outlets wishing to attend. *Meat.*

Kasima took over production of the program booklets that were to be mailed out. On the centerfold, she'd listed all the names of the awards to be handed out and nominees in each category, Brian's name among them.

After printing, folding, and stapling each one methodically, she slipped them into envelopes and piled them in the plastic bin on her desk labeled outbound.

When that was finished, she took it upon herself to organize her computer files, but it was so menial, her mind wandered once more.

What in the world had gotten into her that night for her to blurt out something so stupid? The atmosphere? Or the romance in the air? The alcohol?

Of course she wasn't *really* in love with Lex. The idea was borderline ridiculous. Laughable.

A delivery man entered the office, his arm wrapped around a delicate red vase with a gorgeous arrangement of tropical flowers.

Heart snapping into her throat, Kasima shot to her feet. The rusted wheels of her chair along the floor screeched in protest, catching the man's attention. He smiled and approached. "Are you Betsy Finkle," he asked kindly.

Kasima blinked. "Huh?"

He checked his notepad. "I'm looking for a Betsy Finkle."

"No. Uh. Betsy's right over there." Kasima pointed toward the cubicles that divided up the room where Betsy's nameplate was on display. But there was no need. Betsy had heard her name and poked her head out curiously. Seeing the bouquet, she visibly brightened and rushed over to accept the flowers.

"Oh! He shouldn't have done this." She giggled, claiming her prize.

"Sign here," the delivery man said indifferently, then he left without another word—as if the misunderstanding hadn't just sliced Kasima straight through, flaying the tender bullseye of her heart.

When Betsy's voice drifted in as if from a great distance, Kasima realized she was still standing, staring after the delivery man.

"...my favorite...so beautiful...don't you think?" Betsy beamed as the bleeding wound in Kasima's chest quaked.

She nodded, her throat too tight to speak. A couple of people had gathered around to admire Betsy's arrangement. Brian stood in his office doorway, keen eyes on Kasima.

Had any of them deciphered her assumption that the flowers were for her? Were her thoughts written plainly on her face? Was the useless hope that had sprung into her soul exposed?

Fire entered her cheeks.

"...he's such a sweetheart," Betsy continued, then seemed to notice Kasima's expression. "Though it's nothing compared to that marvelous bouquet you got the other day, Kasima."

The wilting display that still sat in her foyer? The one that she really should throw away, but hadn't been able to bring herself to do it yet?

"Albert must have been paying attention when I told him about it," Betsy added. "I went on and on about it. Must have given him a little incentive to step up his game. Yesterday, for the first time, he told me he loves me."

"That's great!" Kasima blurted a little too loudly. She cleared her throat. "So great, Betsy. They really are beautiful. Albert did good. I've got to..." Sitting back down, she grabbed the stapler and some nearby sheets of paper, stapling them together. "Sorry, I have to get back to work now. I'm swamped."

"Of course," Betsy said, still grinning from ear to ear. "Me too." She turned and practically glided back to her cubicle. Likely, she was too euphoric to have noticed Kasima's distress.

The papers she had stapled were for two unrelated accounts. As she pried the sheets apart, Brian gave her one last studying look before reentering his office.

After straightening a stack of files that had already been straightened, Kasima quietly resumed her tasks, all the while working to patch the drip, drip, drip of her freshly lacerated heart.

* * *

At the end of the day, when many of her coworkers had clocked out for the day, Brian approached her desk. "How are you doing?"

He'd been pleasant enough to work with over the last few days, seeming to have moved on. They'd been friends first. Perhaps their relationship could return to that state?

Already she'd spied him flirting with a couple of new hires. The same way he'd flirted with her, with that infectious smile and easy swagger. Maybe one of them would be the girl to tame his heart. Wouldn't *that* be ironic, if Brian found the love of his life before Kasima?

"I'm fine," she lied. "How are you? Working on any

juicy stories for the paper?"

"I've got something in the works. That's actually what I wanted to talk to you about."

"Oh?"

"I've been working on this story and I'm trying to find the right hook. Maybe you could help me? You were always so good at that stuff."

"Sure. What's the story about?"

He glanced down at his watch. "Well, if you're ready to go, we can talk about it on the way."

"Go? Go where?"

"Oh, uh..." he blinked, looking a little taken aback. "I thought Mr. Dixon would have talked to you about this by now."

"He's been out of the office. Talk to me about what?"

Brian grinned brightly. "I convinced him to let you be my photographer on this one."

Kasima sat speechless for a moment. "Seriously?"

He nodded.

Excitement fumbled in her chest. Why now? She'd offered to be his photographer before, but his responses had always centered around being a one-man show.

When she asked him this, he replied, "I've always admired your talents, and I know you want this more than anything. Kas, I just want you to be happy."

He appeared so sincere and earnest. It reminded her why she'd been attracted to him in the first place. That Brian would do this for her, even after everything that had happened? She didn't know what to say.

He checked his watch." But we've got to get going. Don't want to lose the light."

"I don't have my camera. It's at my house."

"We'll pick it up on the way."

CHAPTER 21

When Brian parked his Bentley in her driveway, Kasima told him, "I'll just be a minute."

Instead of waiting, he got out of the car. "What do you say to a quick cup of coffee before we head out? I've been dragging all day."

She considered him for a moment, wondering if this was a ploy. She kept expecting him to bring up Lex or their relationship, but he hadn't yet, and he did look tired. Honestly, she wouldn't mind a caffeine injection herself.

"You've yet to tell me where we're going." In the living room, she stutter stepped, having completely forgotten about her little obsession.

Pictures of Lex littered her dining room table—him slumbering so beautifully in her bed just before she'd woken him from the noise of her camera; the two of them together in bed when he'd wrestled away her camera to take a photo of his own, him on the bluff at sunset smiling at her like she was the greatest thing since apple pie, and a thousand others over the course of their affair. She'd been developing them every night, trying to create the one perfect print that she could treasure always.

Like a junkie caught with his stash, she rushed to scoop them up before Brian saw. She wasn't quick enough. He snatched one that had fallen from her grip, frowning. "Well, I can't say I'm not jealous. You used to photograph me like that."

She wanted to tell him he was wrong—that she'd never been so captivated by another individual, so consumed and enamored and haunted—but that would only hurt him. Instead, she muttered, "I'm sorry. I didn't mean for you to see these."

She retrieved the photo from Brian and inserted the stack into the hutch drawer where Spike was shelved, watching her with judgy black eyes. Kasima couldn't decide whether it would be healthier to get rid of the thing. Truth was, her gaze drifted toward it more often than she'd like to admit, especially when she was missing Lex. Which was always.

On impulse, she grabbed the bear. *Into the drawer you go, Spike. Tell your bear therapists about this.*

Stuffed full of her scars, she shoved the drawer closed and faced Brian with a benign expression. "You start the coffee, I'll gather my things for the shoot."

"Sounds like a plan."

Upstairs, she changed out of her confining office clothes, mulling over what Brian had revealed about his story. He thought he had a lead on the recent influx of a dangerous new drug being trafficked around town. Many people have already overdosed.

At first she'd worried that this assignment might be dangerous, and had voiced those concerns, but Brian assured her he only wanted a few shots of him interviewing a couple vagrants who had recently come in contact with the drug. They'd already agreed to have their picture in the paper for a "nice fee."

She stepped into her most comfortable jeans, and donned a simple black tank top, then traded her heels for a pair of worn in running shoes. After tying up her hair, she grabbed her camera case and headed back down the stairs to the kitchen. "How's that coffee coming?"

When she entered, he faced her. "Oh, uh, I couldn't find the coffee grinds. Are you out?"

"What are you talking about?" She opened the cupboard where she kept her coffee. "The can is right here."

"Oh. Look at that. I don't know why I didn't look there."

"Me either since that's where they've always been." She tossed the can to him and he caught it.

Then he scraped his hand down the back of his neck. It reminded her of something Lex would do when he was feeling embarrassed. "I guess I got a little nostalgic being in your home again. A little sad too. I miss you, you know?"

She sighed. "Brian, this isn't a ploy to get me back, is it? Because—"

He put up his hands. "I know I messed up. I get it. You have your vampire now." He paused. "Right? That's still a thing?"

At length, she replied, "Right." He didn't need to know Lex was likely finished with her.

Brian gave a small smile. "I want you to know I'm here for you. If you ever want to, you know, try again, or anything."

"That's sweet, Brian, but we aren't right for each other. You and I are looking for different things. And I hope one day we're both able to find it."

He sighed. "I'm trying. I went on a date the other day." He paused and eyed her closely. Searching for a hint of jealousy?

She smiled brightly. "Oh yeah? Did it go well?"

He pursed his lips together. "She wasn't you."

A bit of her heart broke for him, but she didn't know what to say. "It's getting late. We should get going. If you still want coffee, maybe we can pick some up on the way."

The vagrants were supposed to meet Brian at the edge of town, outside the abandoned sugar mill, but after two hours of waiting, Kasima was getting antsy.

While the sun was still up, she'd snapped a few shots of the mill from a distance. The warm light had glinted off the broken bits of glass that had managed to cling to the windowsills, most of which had been haphazardly boarded up from the inside. Now that the moon was out, blue light shimmered off those jagged shards.

She was getting tired, ready to call it a night.

Brian checked his watch. "Where the hell are they?"

A sharp wind rustled the bushes nearby. Shadows danced in the night. They both glanced over, waiting.

When no one appeared, she said, "Maybe we should try another time."

Brian glanced back at the mill. Husks of dead trees lingered around the perimeter like old soldiers that had once proudly guarded this land but had long since surrendered to the erosion of time, their roots rotting in the rust-laden earth.

Long ago, one face of the mill had been painted a bright red. Now aged, it was chipped and flaked, more burgundy than red and battered by the elements.

Brian popped his trunk and then retrieved a flashlight, aiming it toward the mill. "Come on. We might as well get *something* out of tonight."

She hesitated. "You mean to go in there? Now?"

"Yes. My sources said this used to be a junkie hang-out, but they've all moved on. Better pastures I guess. They might have left some evidence inside."

"I don't know. Wouldn't it be better to come back in the daytime?"

He gave her a teasing look. "Don't tell me you're afraid."

She tapped her chin. "Hmm. Junkies, dealers, tramps, oh, and an abandoned building in the middle of the night. What's not to be afraid of, I wonder?"

"You've nothing to worry about, Kas, I've got you covered." He opened his coat to reveal a gun holster strapped to his belt.

She blinked. "When did you get a gun?"

"I've had it for a while. Kept it at home, mostly, but I thought it was prudent to start carrying it during my hairier investigations."

Prudent, perhaps, but a gun didn't make her feel any better about going into that mill.

"Come on. We'll be really quick. I promise. And wouldn't it be great to get a few night shots from inside? Maybe the moon shining on some dirty syringes or something?" He smiled as if that would be the greatest thing in the world.

The syringe part didn't exactly light her creative fire, but the moon *was* bright and would be streaming through those large exposed windows into the raw, steely interior. Brian was right, it was a great photo op, if nothing else, for her personal collection.

Besides, she didn't think anyone else was around. Two hours and they hadn't heard a peep but for crickets, cicadas, and the occasional owl.

Still, it *was* a big empty abandoned building. "I don't know."

"Okay, how about you stay out here with the car and *I'll* go in and take some photos." He extended his hand for her camera, her most prized possession. "The paper won't be able to give you credit for the pictures, though."

She snatched her camera back, seeing so clearly the carrot he dangled. But, damn did she want that carrot. This wasn't just a great photo op, it was a potential professional leap as well. She grumbled and stomped toward the building. "Let's make this quick."

Expression a bit victorious, Brian kept pace with her as they made their way.

Everywhere she looked, nature was reclaiming this desolate patch of land. Dried grass, leaves, and gravel crunched underfoot. Creeping vines infested much of the ground, encroaching up the sides of the mill's stained brick walls. Weeds peeked through the cracks in the concrete steps.

Inside, darkness reigned. Scant streams of moonlight squeezed through the boarded windows.

There was an eerie stillness here that sent shivers down her spine, like she had ventured into an alternative world where everything smelled of decay, mold, and refuse. In some far-off location, a slow dripping echoed as if some leaky pipe still held water.

Brian scanned the room with the flashlight. Metal scaffolding took up one wall, decorated by buckets, wood planks, and old dusty brushes. At one point, there'd been a halfhearted attempt to renovate before the mill had been abandoned completely.

"Watch where you step," Brian said, swinging his light her way.

A sinkhole had eaten away a large chunk of the room,

chunks of cement attached to rebar clung to the edge as if for dear life.

Rusted nails and trash littered the ground around it.

She kept a wide berth.

A little farther in, elaborate graffiti garnished one partially crumbled wall, the artwork vibrant against gray bricks. Just to the right of it, soot painted its way up the brick from a nearby fire pit that still contained a pile of charred debris. It looked to be only days old.

"I think people still come here," she whispered.

Brian was several feet ahead. "Probably," he muttered. "Look there." He pointed to a rickety old stairway that appeared to lead to nowhere. It just stopped where a second floor used to exist. Marching toward it, Brian declared, "It's perfect. Get a picture of me standing up there holding a syringe."

"Did you already find drug paraphernalia?"

He fished something out of his pocket. With his teeth, he tore off a piece of plastic and then spat it on the ground. Then he held up a syringe. "Even if I had, there's no way I'm touching a used one."

Flashlight in hand, he carefully made his way up the stairs. Kasima held her breath, hoping to God they held under his weight. Her mind flashed to the worst case scenario: The stairs toppling, him cracking his head, the flashlight disappearing in the rubble, along with his body. With only her. Here. In the dark. Alone. For miles.

He'd be doomed.

"Brian, please be careful."

He glanced back at her and grinned. "You worried for me, Kas? Guess that means some part of you still cares about me."

She huffed. "I would never want anything bad to happen to you, even if we weren't still friends."

He waved her concern away and continued to the top. Then he held up the syringe like a new discovery. The shot was really quite perfect. Moonlight streamed through an eroded hole in the roof, providing adequate lighting. She raised her camera, adjusted the aperture and shutter speed, and snapped a couple pictures.

"Let me get one with the flash," she said, switching it on. As she took another shot, for a split second, she caught an odd reflection from the corner of her eye.

Though her brain hadn't had enough time to process the tiny twin pinpricks of light, her intuition flared. Her pulse raced, and adrenaline pumped through her. Her body was reacting as if to danger. Then her mind caught up. Those pinpricks had been her flash bouncing off a set of eyes.

"Brian?" she called, her voice quivering. He swung his head around, registering her tone. But he was too far away to do anything. And the only flashlight, which was still in his grip, wasn't strong enough to reach her here on the ground.

Like a rodent caught in the hypnotic gaze of a snake, she stared into the utter blackness, trying to make out the threat, or lack thereof. Was her mind playing tricks? She hoped so, because Brian still hadn't made a move to help her. Could he see better from his vantage?

There was one way to know what was out there.

Her pulse spiked.

Slowly, she tilted the camera up, finger hovering over the button.

Click.

The area lit up as if by lightning.

A bloodcurdling scream ripped from her lungs.

CHAPTER 22

The light from her camera's flash dissipated, leaving behind an ebony curtain that concealed a dark, dangerous threat—which her mind could still see all too clearly.

Staring straight back at her was a grizzly man with red eyes.

Yet, as she stood there, frozen, no attack came.

Had he moved? She couldn't tell. Blood was rushing past her eardrums, muffling her hearing. The first thing that registered was the echoing drip, drip, drip of that distant pipe. Her every molecule was on high alert, yet she still couldn't force her legs into action. They were a worthless mixture of Jell-O and sludge.

Was escape even prudent?

There was no reliable light source. On the way in, trash had littered their path. If she took off into the dark, she'd risk tripping and landing on the many rusted nails, or the beds of broken glass, or that open pit that was ready to swallow her whole.

Could she fight off three-hundred pounds of psycho? That measly three-week defense course might buy her some time if she caught him in his weak spot, but she couldn't even see where his jugular was, let alone his balls.

Brian was saying something from his high vantage. Her panicked mind didn't comprehend. Her eyes were glued to that menacing darkness, trying to catch any sign of movement. Could the man see her? Was his night vision more acute? If he were human, chances were he was as blind as she. If he wasn't, the flash could have temporarily blinded him.

Her ears pricked at the sound of movement.

And still she couldn't move, the sludge in her legs hardening into concrete.

Any second now...disaster.

Or maybe not. Brian was making his way down the rickety staircase. Without the proper amount of alarm in his tone, he asked what she had screamed for. He hadn't yet seen the dark stranger. Was that man lying in wait?

"There's someone here," she squeaked out, still staring at that black abyss.

A man's throat cleared then, and his gruff voice trickled out from the darkness. "Don't be scared, miss. I didn't mean to frighten you."

She didn't respond, her terrified mind combing over his words. A quick mental sonic calculation told her the man was still in the same spot he been when her flash had gone off, or quite near there.

"To be honest, *you* scared the bejeebers out of *me*." He sounded sincere, this stranger from the dark, alone in a condemned, abandoned mill. She was nowhere near ready to let her guard down.

Brian stepped onto the landing then with that blessed flashlight in hand. She wanted to snatch it from him and keep it with her till she was safely back in her bed...which couldn't happen soon enough.

"Mack, is that you?" Brian aimed the light at the man. With a dingy hand, he shielded his eyes. "You were supposed to meet us outside."

"Must have fallen asleep," the man, Mack, replied.

Relief rushed her, and she swayed on her feet. This was the person they'd been waiting for.

He was wearing a dirty faded shirt that might have been green at one point, but now matched the grayish-brown surroundings. His jeans were ripped at the knees, white strings fanning out. Mud caked the soles of his shoes. Behind him on the ground was a ruffled wool blanket. Next to it, she spotted a bottle-shaped paper bag.

Mack rubbed his eyes with both fists.

"Where's your friend?" Brian crossed to stand beside Kasima, who had yet to shrug off her adrenaline. She wanted to smack Brian for bringing her here. *Remember the accolades.*

She clenched her still-shaking hands and took in a slow, calming breath.

"Uh." Mack's squinted gaze meandered around the room, though she didn't believe he could see any better than she in this blackness. "Buddy! You here?"

There was no reply.

Mack scratched his head. "Huh. Where'd'e go?" He threw out his arms, and blew out a hefty puff of air that smelled of gin before answering his own question. "Du'know."

Brian groaned, then rallied. "Well, let's get started. You ready to answer some questions?"

"Sure thing, boss."

Finally Kasima's adrenaline ebbed, especially when Mack retreated to his little cubby under the stairs and produced a gas lantern that cast a dim light in the room.

She didn't place a lot of stock in the reliability of Brian's 'source', but he was the investigative reporter, not her. She was just here to take great pictures. Speaking of, better get to work.

While Brian questioned the bum, having to repeat his words several times, she snapped a few photos of the two. Then she took the flashlight and ventured toward the section of the wide-open space where a couple of boards had fallen away from a window. Moonlight streamed in, landing on a mossy patch of soil. There, a small flowerbed had taken root. The blooms were closed for the night, but she could make out the vibrant orange and cool purple petals. The image she snapped was dichotomous with new life against a backdrop of broken glass and decaying debris.

Turning off her flash, she snapped another photo with the moon as her light source. That one would be eerily gorgeous.

"Come on. Let's go," Brian muttered from nearby. He sounded irritated. "This was a waste of time."

Guess the homeless drunkard wasn't the well of information Brian had been expecting.

Back at the car, Brian had her take another photo of him gazing off into the distance as though he was deep in thought with the mill in the background. She already knew it would be the one used for his article.

After putting her equipment away, they drove back to her place. In the driveway, Brian turned to her. "Thank you for today. I really appreciate it."

"You're welcome," she said politely. "Aside from being scared out of my wits by an inebriated vagabond, I actually got some nice shots for my collection." Though she wouldn't be going on any more late-night excursions with

Brian any time soon.

"I'm glad to hear it." He grinned, then the expression fell away, replaced by something more awkward. "I have another favor to ask you. It's kind of important, so please don't answer right away."

"O-kay."

"The award ceremony is tomorrow."

Warily, she replied, "Yeah."

"Originally, we had planned to go together, and, well, I kind of expected us to get back together by now, so I never asked anyone else to go, and now I'm dateless."

"You know any of the single ladies at the office would go with you." Though their relationship had failed, Brian was still a good-looking guy.

He lightly laughed. "I know, but there's no one I'm interested in at the office...aside from you." He let that hang for a second, as if to see if she'd respond. She made sure to blank her features until he continued. "I don't want to ask someone out of desperation and then end up inadvertently leading them on. You know how some women can get overly invested."

Like me? "You could always go stag. No shame in that."

He curled his lip at the suggestion. "Do you know how that would look? People will think I can't get a date to my own award ceremony."

She coughed into her hand. *His* award ceremony? She shook her head. Sure he was getting a special honor award for excellence in the field, but others would be getting similar awards.

"So what are you asking here?"

He hesitated. "Well, I was hoping you would still accompany me. Strictly as friends," he rushed out, "of course.

You'd really be helping me out."

"Brian," she sighed, "I don't know if that's a good idea."

"Because your vampire wouldn't like it? Would he stop you from doing what you wanted?" His tone turned suspicious. He still thought Lex had compelled her.

Truth was, Lex wouldn't care a lick if she posed as Brian's date. Not that he'd ever know.

"Please, Kas. Since I first learned I was being honored, I always imagined you there by my side. I really want the ceremony to be perfect."

His earnest look wore her down. "Alright, I'll go with you. As friends," she qualified.

"Friends," he repeated with a Cheshire grin.

"Okay, see you tomorrow." She got out and started heading toward her front door.

He opened his window and called out. "Thank you, Kas. I really appreciate it. I've hired a car service, so we'll arrive in style. I'll pick you up an hour before the ceremony starts."

Doing the math, she stopped and faced him. "But it'll take more than an hour to get there from here."

Brian shook his head, slowly backing his car out of her driveway. "Didn't Tanya tell you? The venue had to be moved due to the unexpected number of RSVPs."

A sinking feeling in the pit of her stomach, she said, "Moved? To where?"

"To Ever Nights."

CHAPTER 23

Over the next twenty-four hours, a battle raged within. Her stomach rioted and flipped while she mentally live-streamed steady calming thoughts. *It will be okay. I'm just doing Brian a favor. A friendly favor. Lex would understand.*

Although, it was entirely possible he wouldn't even care.

Would he assume they were back together? Would it bring him relief?

The thought shouldn't bother her so much. Yet at every opportunity, her grinding stomach reminded her that it did. It bothered her a whole hell of a lot.

If I'm lucky, he won't even be working tonight. A flimsy attempt to ease her worry, she knew, but hadn't he'd warned her he'd be busy with work—too busy to reach out to her? Even with a phone call? If only to tell her they were over?

God, how she missed his voice.

Not for the first time, she wondered: *Is he ghosting me?*

If that was his style of ending things, then he was a

coward, unworthy of her consideration.

She knew, in part, she wasn't being fair. Lex had clearly marked the parameters of their relationship, and she was the one who'd colored outside the lines. Still, a little closure would have been nice.

Every day she didn't hear from Lex was a splash of water on the seed of her resentment. Over time, that seed had blossomed and bloomed. Now it was a briar patch.

Lex could assume whatever he liked. And then he could take that assumption and shove it right up his ding-dong.

Would he be jealous? Didn't matter. They weren't a couple and he didn't have the right be jealous, not when he hadn't so much as called her to say boo. She hated that a small part of her hoped for it anyway.

She smoothed down the front of her new dress that cost a month's wage. Drop and dead and gorgeous were among the adjectives one might use to describe her. If Lex had any desire left for her, the way she looked in this dress would be a gut shot.

By the time she added the finishing touches—a pouty lip-gloss, dark coal eyes, and a flirty up do with loose curls around her neck—Brian had arrived. He'd rented a limo. Top of the line. Ostentatious, just as he liked it.

She'd thought she wanted that flashy lifestyle once. Now she could see the miserable path she'd been headed down, with a man who cared more about appearances and his own enjoyment than he did about his partner's comfort and happiness. Lex had saved her from that, whether he meant to or not. She could do better than Brian. She deserved better.

Brian stepped out of the car and checked his hair in the car's reflection. She imagined Lex with her now, rolling his eyes and shooting her a look that said *what a douche*. She almost smiled at the thought, but then anger rolled in. Lex might have shown her she could do better, but what did that matter when what she truly wanted was out of her reach?

Before Brian even got to her front door, she stepped outside to greet him. She'd expected him to politely compliment her appearance. What she got instead was way over the top.

Dropping to his knees, he placed a hand over his heart. "Oh, wow. Just, wow. You look...wow."

"Get up," she admonished. "You'll wrinkle your slacks."

He stood and brushed his knees clean. "Seriously," he added, opening the limo's door for her. "We're going to look perfect for the cameras." Tension stole through her. As with every year, this event was documented in the Tribune, among other outlets. Would a picture of her and Brian make the cover?

If Lex didn't learn of her attendance tonight, he would then.

The possibility was far-fetched, but still weighed on her, and on the way to Ever Nights, her nerves began to ratchet at the mere thought of seeing Lex. Brian offered her a glass of champagne, which she graciously accepted, and then poured one for himself. "To us."

"To you," she corrected. "Congratulations, by the way. I know you worked hard for this award." If nothing else, she could respect Brian's work ethic. He was always out tracking down leads and interviewing sources.

"I did. But let's not forget my gorgeous gal who supported me along the way." He clinked his glass against hers.

"Well, alright," she allowed. "To me, then." The bubbly liquid fizzed in her throat as she downed the glass. Brian chuckled and poured her another.

She found it surprisingly easy to view Brian in a friend capacity, something she hadn't expected. Though why should she be surprised? They'd started out friends, hadn't they? Maybe tonight would actually go smoothly.

And maybe bees nested with wasps.

Just as she polished off her second drink, they arrived at the front entrance of Ever Nights. They'd pulled out all the stops for tonight's event. A wide red carpet led from the curb, past a photo-op backdrop and up the stairs into the lobby. Skylights painted the sky in bright patterns to announce the event far and wide. A valet opened the door for her, offering his hand.

She stepped out, Brian behind her. Her eyes swept a gaggle of curious onlookers, trying to get a glimpse of any-one noteworthy. The limo had been like a promise bro-ken. The crowd's interest quickly faded, but Brian greeted the world with a Hollywood smile, his chest puffed up as though these folks had gathered for him alone. Most of them didn't spare him a second glance.

Surreptitiously, she scanned for a certain familiar sil-houette. Lex worked security. Would he be there, making sure everything ran without a hitch. He was nowhere to be found. If he was here, he was likely inside directing se-curity.

Brian gallantly offered his arm, leading her across the red carpet. Still distracted, a couple flashes blinded her. She realized they were in the photo-op section. She tried to smile. Her lips felt stretched. To her relief, Brian ush-ered her to the side so he could pose solo for the cameras. Inside, Brian was still grinning from ear to ear. He almost looked sly, high off the attention.

In the banquet hall, she and Brian found their table near the stage. As she took her seat, her head swung around, cataloguing the faces of the employees that floated around, attending guests. None boasted those sexy bedroom eyes that made her heart thunder.

Which was a relief.

She waved at Tanya and her other coworkers in attendance, all scattered throughout. Dinner was a light salad and your choice of chicken, beef, or fish. Kasima had the chicken. Brian: the fish. As he ate, he chatted up the rest of the table. Kasima paid them no mind. She couldn't keep from feeling like she shouldn't be here. Ever Nights was where she and Lex had met. It felt like sacred space. Theirs. And yet it was his territory.

After the plates were cleared, the lights dimmed, and a hush fell over the crowd. A spotlight lit up the podium and a stout man took the stage to start the ceremony, beginning by thanking everyone for coming and praising the industry as a whole, then they continued on to the awards. Kasima zoned most of it out, preoccupied with glancing back at the door every time someone entered and exited the room. Each time it was just a server or a guest scurrying off in search of a restroom. The constant spike of anticipation mixed with dread was oddly followed by disappointment.

Brian leaned in. "My moment is coming up."

She blinked up at the stage, surprised to see Mr. Dixon behind the podium now. He was talking about his all employees with a spark of pride in his eyes, how he was grateful to work with each and every one of them, boasting how he had the best team he could ask for. He was leading up to Brian's introduction.

"I really appreciate you being here with me," Brian

whispered.

Kasima smiled and patted his left hand in encouragement, startled when Brian sandwiched her hand between his. "Kasima, I wouldn't be here if it wasn't for you."

She opened her mouth to disagree, but he swiftly continued.

"I know I really messed things up between us before. I hope you'll give me a chance to make it up to you."

Her eyes darted. "Brian, I—"

"I know you've wanted this for a long time. And I'm finally ready. I think this is the perfect time to not only tell you, but to show you how much I love you." He fished something out of his pocket. She hardly heard Mr. Dixon announce Brian's name and then the heat of the spotlight poured over her just as Brian went to one knee. A unified gasp fluttered through the crowd. Brian presented her with a small felt jewelry box, opening it. "I think we should get married."

Her mouth dropped open. A thousand eager eyes bore down on her, suffocating her. Her eyes darted for escape. The room was a blur. Something touched her hand. Cool metal invaded her ring finger.

Brian stood and hooted in triumph. The crowd erupted in cheers. Kasima glanced down, taking in the horrific sight of the metal collar, choking more air from her lungs.

Someone at the table congratulated her. Brian was already gone, heading to the stage and taking the spotlight with him. A chill running over her skin, Kasima sat dazed, like she'd just been gut punched.

Then the shaking began. If anyone noticed the horror in her eyes, they likely attributed it to gleeful shock.

Brian started his speech. "Now I have two things to celebrate tonight."

The crowd roared and clapped.

Enough!

Yanking the wretched thing from her finger, she shoved it back into the box, tossed it onto Brian's chair, retrieved her purse, and then bolted out of her seat toward the exit, not caring about the curious murmurs that followed her. Brian's speech never faltered.

In the hallway, she gasped for air. Her eyes burned with the threat of tears.

The nerve!

The arrogance!

Leaning against the wall, she tried to regain her equilibrium. Had she ever truly wanted that from him? That ring on her finger had felt like a death sentence.

And to think, she'd been dreading a confrontation with Lex all night, when the real danger had accompanied her in the guise of a friend. If she had any luck at all, she could get out of here without—

When that familiar sexy baritone sounded from nearby, her world crushed in around her. "I suppose congratulations are in order."

CHAPTER 24

Lex was leaning with one foot planted against the wall behind him, his bruiser arms crossed over his black security T-shirt. The coldness in his face sent splinters of pain through her blood. Only now did she realize he could have seen everything through the security cameras.

The sight of his dark contempt pushed salty tears over the edge of her eyelids. A traitorous sob broke free.

Taken off guard, he dropped his arms and pushed off the wall. His stony features lit with concern, and for a moment it was as if he had no idea what he should do or say.

Humiliation swirled with devastation. Air left her in great heaving wallops. She tried to rein it in, but the harder she tried, the harder she cried. Growing even more embarrassed by her uncontrollable display, she covered her face with both hands.

"What is this?" Lex stepped forward and gripped her by the shoulders. She moaned louder, hating that even now, she luxuriated in that simple contact. She wanted so badly to cling to him as she broke apart.

He pulled her hands away so he could see her face. His

was a tight grimace. "Is it...are these tears of happiness?" He sounded doubtful and unsure at the same time.

The noise that left her lungs seemed to answer his question. Still looking at a loss, he wrapped her in his embrace.

So shocked by the action, her sobs instantly ceased, replaced by disbelieving sniffles. The pleasure of being held by him was so great, it snapped through her like an electric current. She shuddered.

"Do you want me to leave you alone," he asked softly, though his arms tightened around her as if in protest.

She shook her head, her breath steadying. Her fingers dug into the fabric of his t-shirt. "Please get me out of here," she managed in a coarse whisper.

With that, he leapt into action. Slinging one arm around her shoulder, he guided her forward toward the exit. Moments later, he was tucking her into the passenger seat of a yellow sports car that had just pulled up.

"Excuse me," The driver complained, looking alarmed. "What are you doing?"

After a quick exchange with Lex, the driver handed over his keys without further protest. Had he just used compulsion? Then Lex took the wheel, and Ever Nights was shrinking in the rearview mirror.

She watched him cautiously, not taking her eyes from him as he cruised down the darkened street. The atmosphere between them was thick with something she couldn't decipher. Tension rolled off him. There was a crease between his eyes and his jaw was clenched tight. Was he angry? With Brian? Or with her? Here she was, forced back into his life. Yet he'd been so gentle with her, sweeping her out of there with no rational explanation on her part.

And though he was stoic, he was still so beautiful to her. The desire to reach out and touch him was all but overwhelming. Finally she looked away, lest she betray her desires. She couldn't read too much into his actions.

He was just being kind, escorting her home. *To be rid of her again?* Still, she was grateful for these last moments with him. For this last chance to say goodbye. Perhaps now she could get the closure she'd been desperate for.

"What did he do?" Lex suddenly demanded, his tone a dangerous hiss.

She faced him. His hardened gaze was on the road ahead.

"Engagements are generally happy events," He prompted. "The crowd seemed to think so. And then his speech—"

Flashing her bare ring finger, she grated through clenched teeth, "We aren't engaged."

"I saw him put the ring on you. You accepted him."

"Don't believe everything you see through a camera." When he didn't reply, she knew she'd guessed right. "How long had you been watching me?"

"Red carpet," he admitted in a gruff tone, and she released a breath. "I knew you'd be here tonight. Was watching for you. Nearly fell off my chair when I saw you in that dress." He momentarily took his gaze from the road to rake his eyes down her body.

She swallowed hard. Was that...was that desire in his eyes?

"Then I saw who you were with. I saw you clinging to his arm and smiling. I thought..."

"Thought what?" Hope hung like a weight over her head, ready to crush her, but Lex didn't continue. "You thought we were back together?"

Curt nod.

"He asked me to come with him as a favor," she explained. "I thought he wanted to show me we could still be friends. We got along fine on assignment at the mill. If I would've known what he planned tonight..."

"Mill?"

"The old abandoned sugar mill. I took some photos for the paper while he interviewed someone."

"He took you there? That place is dangerous. Seedy people do business there at all hours."

She shivered, remembering that night with a new-found fear.

Lex went quiet for a moment, his white-knuckled grip on the wheel. "You don't...you don't love him, then?"

She scoffed. "After tonight, I loathe him."

She realized they were already pulling into her driveway. Her gut twisted. Her time was up, and it hadn't nearly been long enough. She hadn't said all the things she wanted to say.

"Will he come here tonight? Looking for you?"

She shrugged. "I don't know. Maybe. I guess it depends on how serious his proposal was or if he was just trying to humiliate me. If it was the latter, then he succeeded."

Lex shut off the engine. "He's the one who should be humiliated. What kind of idiot screws up so badly with a woman like you?"

She blinked up at him, too surprised to respond. And what should she say: *You did?* Now she wasn't so sure if that was the case.

At her door, she expected him to say goodnight, and then she would watch him drive away from her again. Instead, he asked, "May I come in?"

"Yes, of course."

They stood in the entryway for a couple heartbeats. Neither seemed sure of what to do next. Should she offer him something to drink? Was that a weird thing to offer an ex-vampire-lover? Although, maybe not-ex-vampire-lover?

"Can I get you something?" There. That was neutral.

Gazing down at her, he hooked a finger under her chin. Her pulse jumped. When she made no objection, his head dipped, and he took her lips in a tender yet demanding kiss. Fire sizzled in her veins, and heat swirled around her in a heady rush. She knew he would always cause this reaction in her, as if her very atoms had been trained to burn for him.

His hands traveled to the small of her back. The hard planes of his body pressed against the soft curves of hers. Lips pressed together, he muttered, "I've missed you."

"I missed you," she sighed, deepening the kiss, losing herself to it.

"I want you," he growled.

"Yes."

His hard palms gripping her backside, he made a sound of utter pleasure. Her body responded in a gush of warmth, and suddenly all she wanted was to feel his hot skin grappling against hers.

Gripping the silky hem of her dress, she tugged it over her head. His rough palms immediately returned to her backside, now bared but for her black thong. He lovingly caressed her plump flesh with a delicious pressure, and she could feel him growing stiff against her lower belly.

"Are you already primed for me, sweet Little Dove?" His fingers slipping past the lining of her panties. His groan reverberated when he found her slick.

She gasped at his touch. "Take me, Lex."

Large hands back on her ass, he lifted her so that she could wrap her legs around his waist. Then he kissed her hard and deep, his tongue invading her mouth.

She got the sense they were traveling. Moments later, he sat down on the couch with her straddling his legs. Their kiss grew fervid, almost desperate. She moaned into his mouth. He groaned, lust taking them both to a place of free expression, their bodies doing the talking.

With shaking hands, she reached down and fumbled with his belt buckle, undoing it and ripping the leather from the loops of his jeans. He lifted his body enough to push his jeans and boxers to the floor. While she slipped out of her panties, he shrugged off his shirt.

Back in his lap, her palms worshiped his hard, tanned shoulders, his perfect pecs, his thick arms. She luxuriated in the feel of sculpted muscle under soft skin. In turn, he worshiped her, kneading her breasts and tweaking her nipples till she couldn't stand the pressure inside her.

"So beautiful," he said, gazing up at her.

Her skin felt flushed and fevered. She was practically vibrating with need, shamelessly rubbing herself against his engorged shaft.

As if he too could wait no longer, he gripped her by the hips and slammed into her.

"Uhn!" They both cried out in pleasure. Perfection. Bliss and heat and friction, all of it drugging her mind, body, soul.

She fisted his hair, forcing him to look up at her, and suddenly she was not herself. She was a possessive, wonton, furious thing. "How dare you make me wait so long for this."

"Never again," he grunted, staring up at her with heat and lust and reverie in his eyes.

Those two words were like a promise and a declaration all at once. They both succumbed to the wild movements of their bodies and sensations that pulled snarls and moans from them both. She moaned to the ceiling while she rode him. His hot lips latched onto one of her tight nipples, heightening her pleasure with each ruthless flick of his tongue. His attention shifted to her other breast, teasing her relentlessly. Then he made a hot, sinful path of kisses up to the delicate column of her neck.

Still the needy wanton creature that she had become, she dug her nails into his scalp and held him to her, a silent command and a desperate plea rolled together. As a part of him was inside her, she wanted a part of her in him as well.

The sharp piercing of her flesh was followed by a wave of ecstasy so strong, she threw her head back on a wild scream. As he sucked her flesh, drawing her blood into him, she flew above the stars knowing only one thing: she was his.

CHAPTER 25

Drowsy and sated, Kasima lay comfortably on Lex's muscled chest. They were still on the couch, horizontal and basking in the afterglow. Eyes closed, he ran his fingers through her hair, his other hand tucked behind his head.

She reached up to touch her neck where his fangs had been. She couldn't feel any evidence of a mark. She'd heard vampires rarely left one if they could manage.

At her movement, he asked, "Did I hurt you?"

"Not at all."

He smiled then. "You get a little aggressive when you're needy."

She felt a tinge of embarrassment over that. She had been quite aggressive, mindlessly so.

"I liked it."

They spent another few minutes in comfortable silence while nagging questions swirled in her head. She wished she didn't have to broach the subject of their relationship—tonight had been great. Best night since...well, her last night with Lex—but she needed clarity. Did tonight herald a shift in their relationship? Or was this his version of closure? A final goodbye?

Her chest twisted at the thought.

Never again, he'd grated. At the time, she thought she knew what that meant. It had been so clear in the heat of lust. Now she wasn't so sure. Never again would he make her wait so long? Never again would they be together?

One thing she was sure of: they couldn't continue as FWBs. Her heart was in too deep, and this uncertainty was eating her up inside. But she wasn't ready to broach the subject. If the conversation went south, this could very well be her last moments with him.

"Something on your mind?"

"No. Why?" Apparently she'd been nervously drumming her fingers on his chest.

"You seem anxious."

"No, I'm fine." If she told him what she wanted, what she needed from him, would he leave? It felt like a clock was counting down, ready to cut their time short.

He stopped stroking her spine, and pushed to sit up. She scooted back to give him room. "When a woman says she's fine in that tone, generally the opposite is true. What's wrong?"

She bit her lip.

Catching the action, he raised a brow.

"I'm just thirsty," she hedged. "Which I blame on you. All that screaming, you made me do."

His lips twitched, but he didn't give her a full smile.

She stood and escaped to the kitchen, filling a glass from the tap. "You want anything?"

She heard the clank of his belt as though he'd slipped on his jeans. Her heart dropped into her stomach. *Oh God, is he's leaving?*

Had the clock struck zero?

Setting the glass down, she hurried back into the living room and stopped in her tracks when she saw he'd crossed to her hutch, still shirtless. Some of Spike's fur must have been sticking out of the drawer because he was now holding the bear up curiously. All the photos she'd developed of him remained scattered at the bottom of that drawer, her obsession on display.

"You stuffed him in a drawer." There was no inflection in his voice. He glanced down at all the photos, but made no comment.

"I, uh, did. Yes.

"Why?"

She supposed she couldn't delay the conversation forever. She leaned against the doorjamb and folded her arms under her naked breasts. "It hurt too much to look at him every day."

"Hurt?"

His confusion inspired her own. "Well, yes, after the way things ended."

"Ended?"

She cocked her head at him. "What else was I to assume? We were hot and heavy for weeks, and then suddenly you just ghosted. Not even a phone call. And we both know why. Hell, I even understood why. I know we weren't actually dating, but if you thought I'd—"

He put both his hands up, still clutching Spike in one. "Hold up. I never wanted things to end, and yes we were dating."

They stared at each other for a long moment.

"You told me you didn't do relationships. That you weren't looking for anything serious."

He ran a hand through his sex-messed hair. "I wasn't, but..."

"Then we went to the wedding and I…said what I said, and you said you were going to be busy with work, and then you couldn't even return my calls."

"I'm sorry about that, but I *was* busy with work. Cortez and Naia are still on their honeymoon. Cole is a fledgling who needs constant watching. Dane is busy with helping Evie. I was needed to pick up the slack. And I didn't call you because I was giving *you* space."

"I…" She opened her mouth, but that had thrown her. "You were? But why would you think I needed space?"

"You said you loved me, but you didn't mean it. I could tell you were freaking out because of it."

"You think I didn't mean it?" Her voice rose. "Whatever gave you that impression?"

"Because you looked horrified afterward. You ran off to the bathroom like you were going to puke."

"Yeah, because *you* looked horrified. Why in God's name would I say something like that when I didn't mean it?"

"Because when Naia sings…" He trailed off, choosing his words carefully. "Something happens to humans when Naia sings. Emotions…get carried away."

There was an undertone to his words that she didn't understand. Did he think a pretty song made her falsely confess love?

"Trust me," he added at her disbelieving look, "there's something, um, magic in her songs. People can't always be held responsible for the things they do or say when she's singing."

That sounded so far-fetched, but Lex sounded so believable. And when she thought back, she had felt a little strange when Naia had been on stage. "So you think because I said it when she was singing that I was just getting carried away? That it wasn't truly how I felt?"

He shrugged.

Translation: *yes*.

"I didn't want to make a big thing of it, if that was the case. I sort of thought I was leaving the ball in your court. That you'd call when you were ready."

"Lex, I..."

"And to be honest, maybe I too needed some space...I don't know. Maybe I was a bit freaked out when you said you loved me, but not because you said it, because of how it made me feel."

Voice but a whisper, she said, "How did it make you feel?"

"Like nothing I can explain. This thing between us, you and me, this is not something I ever expected." He cursed. "And I nearly screwed things up with you, didn't I?"

The utter shock from his words kept her from being able to respond.

"When you showed up with him tonight, I worried you'd decided to go back to him. I was going to confront you both. Kenzi, along with several of my bouncers, convinced me not to make a scene. When Brian noticed me, he smirked and kept you turned away. It's a miracle I didn't break the line."

She couldn't have anticipated such a strong reaction, but now imagined the scene: several security guards holding him back while Kenzi desperately tried to calm him.

"That smug expression made me sure he'd convinced you to take him back. And, as you put it, it hurt too much."

"I didn't mean to—"

"But I knew I couldn't trust my jealousy, so I retreated to the security room, watching to see if you'd show him any affection. If you truly wanted the prick, I wouldn't get in your way. Then came that proposal, and I could see the crowd was cheering." He met her gaze. "I've never known such pain."

"It wasn't a proposal. He didn't even ask. He just declared we'd get married and then went to make his speech."

At that Lex cracked a smile. "What a moron. And by that I mean me. If I had any doubt about my feelings before, tonight has blasted them away. I love you, Little Dove."

Her heart swelled with so much emotion she thought it might burst in her chest. Skirting the dining table, she threw her arms around him. "I am so in love with you."

Lex held her tight, the moment pure perfection. When he pulled back, his smile was so brilliant it was like gazing at a setting sun. A little blinding, but unbelievably beautiful, and sizzling hot.

As if she were the weight of a feather, he lifted her in his arms and carried her up the stairs to her bedroom. "Now I'm going to make love to you properly, till neither of us can move."

What she'd thought of as the worst night of her life was turning out to be her best.

CHAPTER 26

They'd made love all night, and well into the morning, till both of them were sated, passing out in each other's arms. But too soon, hateful sunrays nudged their way past the blinds. The evil sunrise meant she and Lex would be forced to extract themselves from their blissful nest in paradise. As much as she wanted to dig in and hibernate with him for the next month, they still had jobs and obligations. They couldn't hide from the world forever, tempting as it was. Especially when Lex resumed his tender kisses. At a leisurely pace, his lips made their way around her body, expertly driving her insane with desire.

She was about say to hell with work when her bedside phone rang.

A phone call this early was rare, and she answered it without thinking. "Hello?"

"Kasima?" Brian's monotone voice came from the receiver.

Lex gave her a wicked smirk and then slipped below the covers. What he did next had her blood rushing and her cheeks flushing.

"Brian! Uh, hi." She covered the receiver with her hand and tried not to make an orgasmic sound. When she caught her breath, she muttered, "Listen, this isn't a good time."

"You left without a word last night. I was worried. Is there something you'd like to tell me?"

"Uh, we'll talk later, Brian." She shoved a knuckle between her teeth as Lex's tongue swirled around a very sensitive part of her anatomy. Pleasure snapped through her, agonizingly sinful.

"Shall I come pick you up for a post-engagement breakfast, then?" His voice sounded hollow. She couldn't tell if he was pissed or just waking up for the day. Could he really think they were actually engaged after she'd ditched him?

"No, Brian. Don't come over. I'll see you later at work, Okay?" She'd only just kept herself from moaning the last, Lex's ruthless attention driving her toward orgasm. When he did that thing with his tongue she loved, she rushed out. "Okay, bye!" and then hung up the phone to snap at Lex. "You villain!"

Lex chuckled and then sucked her tender flesh between his lips. Tipping over the edge, she threw her head back and screamed.

* * *

That evening, Kasima typed the final sentence of an email and hit send. Brian hadn't shown up for work. At first she figured he was out on assignment, but was informed around nine that he'd called in sick.

Her previous night's very public and hasty exit from the event during Brian's speech stymied any post-engagement workplace jubilee. Folks gave her a wide berth, though she'd caught more than one glance at her very naked ring finger.

Kasima wondered how much Brian might have guessed about what had happened last night after she'd left the event.

Is there something you'd like to tell me?

That strangeness in his voice now held new meaning. Was he hurt? He couldn't have seen her leave with Lex, but someone else might have and relayed the information.

Though she had never intended to hurt him, Brian's gross misjudgment of their relationship was entirely his own doing. Yet she still felt partly responsible. Perhaps she shouldn't have assumed they could retain a friendly relationship.

As they'd dressed this morning, Lex had commented, "Am I going to need to do something about him?"

"No," she'd replied. "I'll take care of it." They just needed to have a blunt conversation face to face, after which Brian would have zero doubts. They were never getting back together.

As the hours passed, she filed down her daily stack of paperwork and emails while replaying her night with Lex. He loved her. Whenever that popped into her head, she caught herself absently smiling. So much happiness couldn't be contained by one person. It shouldn't be physically possible. Yet it somehow lived comfortably inside her. Had burrowed deep, snuggled in, and made a home. She finally knew how her parents felt when she'd caught them gazing dreamily at one another, their hands intertwined. She'd finally found that deep, divine connection she'd been searching for.

Who would have guessed she'd find her soulmate in a vampire? Who'd have thought he'd wind up being the sweetest being she'd ever met? Around lunchtime, he'd called her...just to see how she was doing. He'd worried Brian might have upset her at work.

Swoon.

When she told him Brian hadn't come in, she could practically hear him rolling his eyes. Then she told him, "I think I'm going to go to his house after work and have it out with him."

"I'd like to be there with you if you don't mind."

"I don't know if that's such a good idea." Would Lex's presence inspire hostility in Brian? She'd never seen Brian jealous of anyone, but with Lex, he might be.

"I'll just be there for your protection. He was one red-neck shy of an old-fashioned shotgun wedding last night."

She laughed at the absurdity of it all, then sighed. "Alright. What time does your shift end?"

"I'm scheduled for a double shift till midnight, but Cortez and Naia are back from their honeymoon, so I can have someone cover my later shift and I'll meet you at your place around six."

"Sounds good, I'll see you then."

* * *

At five, she clocked out and headed to her car. Dark clouds were building from the west. The scent of coming rain permeated the air. Lightning lit up the distant sky. Perhaps tonight she would set up her camera and finally catch that perfect storm image.

On her way home, she passed the turn that led to Brian's place. She slowed. She didn't believe a chaperone was necessary for a conversation that should be had in private. Plus she really did worry Lex's presence might needlessly needle Brian.

She nibbled her lip.

Although she thought it silly to wait, she'd promised Lex, and she wouldn't go back on her word. Even though a part of her felt it was cowardly not to face Brian alone. She'd have someone in her corner, while he had no one. At the same time, she was grateful for Lex's support.

She drove on.

As she pulled into her driveway, she found herself wishing it was already six. She itched to see him, to hear his lustrous deep voice and wrap herself in his strong embrace. She wondered how a human/vampire relationship would work in the long-term, if one day he'd ask her to turn for him. Would she? At the moment, that was a question she wasn't ready to answer. It would take a lot of consideration, and it was early yet in their relationship. There'd be time enough to broach the subject down the road.

Retrieving her cell phone from her purse, she stepped out of her car and dialed Lex.

"Hello, love," he answered, making her heart soar. In the background, she heard a set of masculine teasing. There was some scuffling. Something rubbed against the receiver like someone was trying to take it from Lex.

A man cried "Ow!"

More laughter ensued.

Lex cleared his throat into the receiver. "I'm about to leave now."

"I was just thinking." She unlocked her door and stepped inside. "Maybe we could have a little fun before we go see—

"Brian!" She gasped. Brian was sitting on one of her dining room chairs that had been pulled out to face the door. A gun lay in his lap!

Her heart plummeted into her gut.

"Kas?" Lex sounded rigid, on alert. "What's going on? Where are you?"

"Home," she said, too stunned to say more.

Brian aimed the gun at her. "Kasima, hang up the phone."

She put her hands up, but didn't disconnect the call. "Brian, what are you doing? Put the gun down."

"Toss the phone over here," he ordered, indicating the phone. "This is for your own good."

Oh, God, he's gone mad. "Brian, please—"

"Give me the phone!" His expression twisting in a way that made him look menacing. Like some alien creature was looking out through his eyes.

Icy adrenaline sent shivers through her body.

"Now!"

Eyeing the barrel of his gun, trained on her chest, she tossed the cell to him.

He caught it and lifted it to his ear. "Is this the vampire?" Pause. "Threaten me all you want. You don't get to win this one." With that he dropped the phone. It bounced once on the carpet. Then he stood and smashed it under his heel.

Her voice shook as she cried, "Brian, this is crazy. What are you doing?"

"You aren't in your right mind. I'm taking you somewhere safe till his compulsion wears off."

He *still* believed Lex had used vampire hypnosis on her. She could see her phone's screen was cracked, but was the cell still working? If the call remained connected, could Lex still hear their conversation?

If so, she had to get Brian talking. "Where are you taking me?"

"To a place where no one will find us."

At gunpoint, he directed her out the door and around the corner to where he'd concealed his car behind a line of tall overgrowth. Ordering her into the driver's seat, he entered the passenger's side and then shoved the keys into her hand. "Drive."

Gun trained on her, she started the car and pulled slowly away from the curb. Tiny pinpricks of water dotted the windshield. The drizzle was accompanied by a flash of light and rumble of thunder.

She longingly gazed into the rearview mirror. How far was Lex? He'd have been on the move as soon as he heard the fear in her voice, but Ever Nights was about thirty minutes away. Fifteen if Lex drove recklessly. And he would. He'd be in a rage, with no regard of his own safety. Vampires could take a lot of damage, but a high-impact crash would kill anyone.

She reminded herself, like all vampires, Lex had inhuman reflexes and would make it to her house without incident. Still he would arrive too late. Even though she drove well below the speed limit, her house was already out of sight. He'd have no way of knowing which way they went.

"Take this right," Brian directed her. After a few more turns, she realized he was guiding them out of town. Her heart sank with each mile that took her away from Lex.

"Brian, please listen to me—"

"No need," he interrupted. "I already know what you're going to say. You think I'm being paranoid and crazy and that the vampire isn't controlling you."

Well, basically, yeah.

"But don't you see? He's *making* you believe that way. You can't even see what he's doing to you. What he's doing to *us*. The way you were with him last night? That wasn't you. That was someone he forced you to become. He's completely changed you."

She shook her head. "You're wrong. Lex hasn't done anything—" Her mind stumbled as his words snapped back like a rubber band. "Wait, what do you mean the way I was with him last night?"

"When you were with him on your couch. You're *never* aggressive like that. It proved everything I've suspected. I *knew* something wasn't right. I *knew* it. I just needed proof."

Icy shards sliced her veins. Her grip tightened on the wheel. When she spoke next, her own voice sounded far away, her vision bowing and warping at the edges. "Brian, what did you *do*?"

"I planted a camera in your living room." He might as well be telling her *Oh, by the way, I watered your ficus.*

"You...you..." The road swam in front of her. She took several deep breaths, last night's private events playing back in her head. They were being recorded. Brian had watched her having sex with Lex.

Nausea churned in her gut and poisoned her blood.

Brian continued. "You're going to be okay. I think, given time, we can fix you. The compulsion has to wear off eventually."

"You're insane."

"One day you'll thank me for this. I guarantee it."

"No." She met his gaze, her eyes burning with hatred. "I won't."

CHAPTER 27

The abandoned mill's silhouette was a dark tomb on the horizon. *Somewhere no one will find us.*

She shivered as she pulled into the dilapidated parking lot. On the way here, Brian told her he'd been preparing for this and not to worry. He'd stocked up on provisions. They could spend months here if needed.

To him, this place was safe. To her, it was a great monster ready to swallow her whole and pick its teeth with her bones.

The car was still running, and Brian opened his door. Her limbs twitched, readying for action as a desperate plan formed. As soon as he stepped out, she'd slam the car into gear and peel away. She'd have to be fast—

Her fantasy died when he snatched the keys from the ignition. Only then did he exit, coming around to her side, the whole time, keeping her in his sights.

He opened her door and stepped back, waving her out with the gun. Fat drops of rain pelted her head and shoulders. He had her stand a few feet away so he could grab a duffle from the back seat. Then with him at her back, they marched toward the mill.

Shadows from the retreating sun slashed across the building's decayed shell, scattered rays glinting harshly off the jagged glass in windows.

She had a terrible thought that if she entered the mill, she might never leave it alive.

"Brian, this is madness. Please let me go."

"Kas, I don't want to have to gag you." He hiked the duffle higher on his shoulder.

It was dim inside the mill. Dust motes flared to life against what little light managed to squeak through the cracks and windows. That flower patch she'd photographed days ago had long since dried up, the plant's withered husk fanning out along the ground as if in its dying throes, it was desperately stretching in search of one last sip of water. Had this current storm come too late for the little guy?

As if in response, lightning snapped like a fiery whip outside. Rain hammered the building's roof, the sound amplified in the large empty space.

With the barrel, Brian gave her a light push to get her moving again. She edged around a sinkhole toward those rickety metal stairs and Mack's old hidey-hole. The bum's things had been removed, as if he'd moved on. She recognized one of Brian's suitcases leaning up against a wall. Next to the stairs, a thin mattress had been rolled out.

Brian motioned her forward onto the mattress. Her soiled shoes sank into the plush material. He dropped his duffle, unzipped it, and retrieved a set of handcuffs, tossing them to her. "Cuff yourself to the stairs."

Her hands were almost shaking too hard to do as instructed, but she managed to slap one end of the cuff on the railing and the other around her wrist. She had the presence of mind to leave it lose. However, in hopes of slipping out when Brian wasn't looking, but he was too clever for that. Once she was secured, he came forward and clicked the cuffs tighter, till they pinched.

"There, now we can relax." He stowed the gun in his belt behind his back.

Yeah, that's going to happen. "How long do you plan to keep me here?"

"Until the compulsion wears off."

"And what if it never does?"

"It will," he replied with total confidence.

"What if I'm not under any compulsion, Brian? This is kidnapping."

He just smirked and turned away to rummage through his bag. He pulled out, of all things, a bottle of wine and two glasses.

Seriously? "You think I'm going to drink with you?"

He eyed her for a moment, then returned one of the glasses. "You're missing out, it's a great year." Next he fished out a spool of nylon rope. At her look, he said, "just in case. Be good and I won't have to use this."

She jiggled her cuffs at him and then spread her palms out. *Where am I going to go?* After he filled his glass and took a sip, he retrieved a couple of sandwiches bound in familiar tight paper wrapping. "You stopped for fast food?"

He tossed one to her. She let it drop to the mattress. He rolled his eyes as he unwrapped his own sandwich. "I assumed you'd be hungry."

"Funny thing. I tend to lose my appetite when I'm kidnapped at gunpoint."

He bit into his sandwich, wiping his sleeve across his mouth, and then spoke as he chewed. "You'll see. When all this is over, you'll see I was right."

Sighing, she sank to her mat and leaned against the stairs' metal railing. She could tell there'd be no reasoning with him. Still, she had to try. "I want you to think about what you're doing, Brian. Really think about it."

He tore another piece off his sandwich with his teeth.

"Do you remember that story you did on vampires?"

"I did several. To which are you referring?"

"The one about how territorial they can be."

His chewing slowed.

"Consider the consequences of your actions. For all intents and purposes, a vampire has claimed me as his. And you took me from him. What do you think he's going to do?"

With an audible sound, Brian swallowed his bite. He glanced toward the entryway and back at her. Then he rallied. "You think I haven't thought of that? That I haven't planned this out?" Putting down his sandwich, he leaned over to pick through his bag once more. "When we came to interview Mack, I realized this was a perfect place to hide you. Out of town. Out of the way. Abandoned. And easily booby-trapped."

Booby-trapped?

"I've ensured there's only one door in."

She glanced back toward the entrance, a sick feeling in her gut.

"You remember that story I did last year about the highway bomber?"

She did. Brain was an investigative journalist. There was a reason he'd been specially honored at the awards ceremony. He researched every aspect of a story, making sure to gather all the details and his facts were accurate. Excitedly, Brian had relayed exactly how the culprit had designed his pipe bombs. She'd even joked that he could make one himself.

Outside, the wind began to howl.

"And if the bombs aren't enough, the special rounds I purchased will be." From his bag, Brian produced a sawed-off shotgun.

Bomb*s*? As in plural?

Wait. Special rounds? That sick feeling in her stomach turned sour.

"Are you mad?" A regular bullet could take out a human but would barely be a nuisance to a vampire. During the long vampire/human war, special bullets had been created that could drop a vampire in a single shot. With the fighting over, they'd been dubbed highly illegal. Just being in possession of such a bullet could earn a man five to ten, especially if caught by a VEA agent. *Vampire Enforcement Agency*. The VEA didn't mess around, and one did not mess around with them.

"Of the two of us, I think *my* clarity of thought is more reliable."

Pointing to herself, she said, "Left you for another man"—she pointed to him—"commits armed kidnapping and booby-traps his hideout with explosives. Sure, *I'm* the insane one."

"You didn't leave me for another *man*. You were duped by a vampire."

"I wasn't duped. I never would have met Lex if you hadn't insisted on going to the vampire's masquerade. He and I just clicked. That's all. He's *not* compelling me."

"Oh, no? When he compelled your boss to give you a *paid* day off."

"I asked him about that. He said he didn't."

"And you believed him?"

Lightning crashed so loud, Kasima jumped. The thunder was right on top of them, and seemed to make the building itself quiver.

Brian fished out his phone, navigated to a video, and showed her the screen. She saw Mr. Dixon sitting at his desk, Lex across from him. The angle of the camera offered only their profiles. The device must have been planted somewhere on the sidebar that displayed Mr. Dixon's prized golf trophies. "You planted a camera in Mr. Dixon's office?"

He pressed play. "If I could, I would," Mr. Dixon was saying. "But if I give Kasima an unscheduled day off, I'll have to accommodate everyone else in the office. You know what they say. Give people an inch…"

"A favor from one of the Cortez clan is nothing to sniff at," Lex replied.

"I've already experienced your annual masquerade, as well as the hottest shows and parties thrown each year. I want to experience something new, something I'm continually denied."

"And what's that?"

"I want a full night with that girl, Kenzi."

Lex went quiet for a moment. "You know we don't deal in that. Never have. Never will. If the girls are so inclined, they can be negotiated with one-on-one, but Kenzi has no need to sell herself, to you or to anyone else."

"Yes, but you could make her more…amenable to the idea."

Lex's expression darkened, and Kasima suddenly felt nervous for Mr. Dixon. Rising to his feet, Lex dug his knuckles into Mr. Dixon's desk and leaned forward. Mr. Dixon leaned back, eyes going wide.

When he spoke, there was something in Lex's voice that Kasima had never heard before. "You will never speak of this subject to Kenzi. In fact, you will not speak to her at all unless she speaks to you first, and you will show her nothing but respect."

Mr. Dixon nodded, but his gaze had gone slightly vacant.

Lex stood to his full height, looking disgusted. "You will also give Kasima the day off as requested, but with full pay."

Again, Mr. Dixon nodded.

Brian shut off his phone, giving her a pointed look. Kasima didn't know what to say. Lex *had* compelled Mr. Dixon, yet had denied it so effortlessly. Although, Mr. Dixon's behavior had been deplorable, how could she trust Lex after this? He'd compelled Mr. Dixon, and it had looked too easy. Had he really never compelled her?

"You see," Brain said, reading her expression. "You can't know for sure, can you?"

No, she couldn't.

* * *

The first explosion drew her from a restless sleep—the ground shook from the force. The second shipped terror all over her body. The blasts had come from outside.

In seconds, Brian was on his feet, shotgun in hand.

She yanked uselessly on her cuffs. "Undo me," she whispered.

When lightning flared, she flinched thinking it was another bomb. The rain was falling even harder than before, slamming like a billion little drums on the roof.

Ignoring her, Brian tilted his head, listening. She did too. Had Lex found her? Or had some poor little critter just decorated the front of the building? What if Mack had returned? How many bombs had Brian planted?

Someone cried out in pain. Then came more yelling, from several men by the sounds.

Brian cocked his weapon. "They're here."

Through the gushing wind and pounding rain, she heard someone holler, "He's badly injured! Get him out of here!"

Oh, God, had Lex been hurt in the blast? "This has gone too far, Brian. Let me go before anyone else gets hurt."

"We can't keep letting them win."

"Them? Who are you talking about?"

"Vampires. They've already infiltrated our government. Our leaders are only figureheads now. They let us believe we still have some power, but the vampires make all the decisions. They take our jobs. Our women. We have to take back control."

"You've never felt this way before. You're using rhetoric from decades ago."

"I've been interviewing veterans for an upcoming exposé. There's more to it than we ever knew. So much more. The war isn't over, on either side. There are humans who still want to fight. They're getting organized."

"We can't go back to that. The wars nearly decimated the country, Brian."

"Kasima!?" Lex yelled from some distance away. Relief flooded her at hearing his voice.

"I'm here!"

"Are you okay?" He couldn't fake the concern in his voice.

"She's fine!" Brian yelled, sounding offended. "No thanks to you."

"He has a gun with illegal ammunition!" Kasima said.

Brian bared his teeth at her. "Goddammit, Kas."

"Brian!" Another voice called. She thought it sounded like Cortez "Are there more bombs?"

Brian hesitated. "No."

Kasima didn't buy it. Apparently neither did Cortez. "Where are they?" After a silent moment, Cortez let out a string of expletives. "The whole place is wired."

Several others cursed, Lex included.

"How could he know?" Brian muttered, beginning to pace.

Kasima suspected there was more to Cortez than merely being able to read people well. "You can't win this, Brian."

"Maybe not," Brian's gaze went vacant, "but I can take them all out with us. The entire nest."

"What?"

He tapped the gun against his head, then fished something out of his back pocket. Was that a...detonator?

A razor's edge of terror serrated her gut. "Oh, God, Brian. Don't do this."

As if he knew what was about to happen, Cortez hollered, "It's going to blow! Get back!"

From outside came Lex's agonized bellow.

Brian pressed the trigger.

CHAPTER 28

A hot wave of solid air slammed into her, punching the breath from her lungs and pile-driving her into the ground. For a frightening moment, suffocation burned in her every cell, her vision dimming. Pain accompanied each desperate soot-filled gasp. More pain bloomed in her chest and there was a loud ringing in her ears, dampening all other noise. A metallic wetness coated her mouth, dripping down the back of her throat and threatening to fill her lungs.

Next to her, someone was coughing: Brian. He cursed as a great wind rushed in and swept away some of the dust and particles, revealing a massive chunk missing from one side of the mill.

She saw movement behind the smoke and ash. Bodies rushed in, climbing over dunes of burning debris. Brian fiddled with that detonator, turning it this way and that, slamming his thumb down on that button as if it might have malfunctioned. Frustrated, he threw it aside and raised his shotgun. She tried to scream, but could only gurgle painfully. Hot liquid dripped from the side of her mouth.

Another explosion had everyone ducking for cover. More debris took flight, football-sized missiles crashing all around.

The building let out an ominous groan. For a split second, everyone froze with a hive-mind-like alarm. The building was about to collapse on top of them.

Terror kick-dropped adrenaline through her bloodstream. She frantically eyed her cuffs and the metal baluster they were attached to. Bringing her leg up, she kicked at the bar with her heel. Only then did she notice the glass deeply embedded in her inner thigh. She could deal with it later. She kicked again, praying she could loosen the baluster.

Lex was still fighting the landscape to get to her when yet another explosion erupted to his left, shaking the earth and tossing bodies. She ducked her head, using her arms to shield against projectiles. Something sliced across her forearm.

Then, like a beast in its death throes, the building howled and screeched. Heavy metal beams broke free of the rafters. They slammed to the ground with stunning force, turning more fiery debris into killing weapons. She kicked that bar harder, no longer feeling the pain in her body, fueled by pure panic and adrenaline. Her lungs filled with liquid, and she gagged and coughed. Blood spurted from her mouth. Was she bleeding internally?

One last kick. The baluster snapped at one end, and she slipped the cuffs free just as all hell broke loose.

With a deafening shriek of metal on metal, the building listed to one side, like a capsizing ship ready to go under. His face twisted in a wild-eyed snarl, Brian lifted his gun, aiming for Lex, who was still several yards away and racing toward her. He wasn't even looking at Brian, eyes trained only on her. Did he not hear her warning? Did he not know the danger?

The gun went off. Lex's right shoulder reared back, the bullet ripping a gaping wound in his flesh, but he kept coming. Brian aimed again...straight at his skull!

"No!" She pushed off the ground, slamming her shoulder into Brian's gut. They both crashed to the ground. Once again, she was lacerated by pain, struggling for air. Part of the roof above torpedoed into the ground right next to her head. The force of the landing shot tiny rocks at the side of her face. She coughed and sputtered. Brian scrambled for his gun.

He would never stop.

Mustering the last of her strength, she yanked the glass from her leg and slammed the shard into Brian's jugular.

He scratched at his throat, eyes stretched wide in panic. With the mix of her blood and his, the shard had become too slippery for him to grasp, and his struggle was rendered useless. She saw in his eyes the moment he realized he was about to die.

Lex reached her then, grabbing Brian by the scruff and tossing him aside like a rag doll. Then he knelt beside her. Haloed by an orange glow, sparks dancing behind him, his expression was a mask of misery. She could only imagine how she looked. Instinctively, she knew that shard of glass she'd pulled from her thigh had sliced a major artery. That same shard had sliced a deep gash in her palm when used it to stab Brian. She was losing too much blood too fast. Already she was growing chilled in spite of the raging fires all around.

As exhausted as she was, she managed to raise a shaky hand to his face and gurgle, "Love you." Strength sapped, her arm dropped, leaving a swatch of red along his cheek.

"Don't you dare say goodbye. Don't you dare leave me!"

But he was the one leaving, moving away from her, farther and farther toward the end of an ever-darkening tunnel. "Love you," she repeated, before her vision turned dark.

A steady percussion of falling debris boomed nearby, vibrating in her bones.

Then she was floating, moving, a new kind of agony radiating through her. She was a live-wire of pure suffering, her mind screaming for death even as her lungs stubbornly fought to purge thick, sticky fluid so she could take just one more breath. Yet, after every harrowing inhalation, more fluid rushed in.

"Hold on, love. Hold on for me."

For Lex, she would try, but already she felt herself slipping away.

He called out for Cortez, his voice sounding so desperate she wanted to weep for him. Through bleary eyes, she could see his heart was breaking. He'd truly fallen in love with her. Now he was about to lose her.

With her last thought, she regretted every tender moment, every heated kiss they shared, because once she was gone, every one of them would be a festering scar on his memory, a medley of wounds he would carry with him forever.

CHAPTER 29

A hushed conversation echoed as if from beyond a veil of water, drawing Kasima to the very surface of her sub-conscious.

"...past the worst of it," a man said. "Her wounds are finally beginning to heal."

There was something wrong with her body, but she couldn't tell what it was.

"Are you sure you did enough?" This second voice was familiar and seemed to vibrate through her. She thought she felt strong arms around her.

"Do not worry. The change is imminent."

There was silence for a moment. "I know you vowed never to turn another vampire. You made the exception for Naia, saving her brother, and now for me. How can I ever repay you for this?"

"Naia is everything to me. She is my soulmate. My heart made flesh. For her, there is nothing I would not do. And without her...well, there would be no life without her." There was a slight pause with that. "Naia is to me everything that Kasima is to you. I know you have realized this."

"Mm," came a guttural response.

"Had you lost her, we would have lost you, and I plan to lose no more of my family. If you must repay me, do it by living a long and happy life."

She must have made a sound when a sharp current snapped along her nerves.

An anguished voice moaned, "She's in pain. This is my fault."

After a moment, Kasima's head swam, every part of her going blissfully numb. Was she on a morphine drip? Her body relaxed as her mind began to dim.

"There. Now she should sleep for a while. At least until the process begins."

"Thank you." The voices began to grow distant. "How is Dane doing?"

"Healing well. Almost back to his usual colorful self."

"Meaning he's back to being a pain in the ass."

The last thing she heard was two endearing chuckles before she succumbed to unconsciousness. For how long, she didn't know, but at some point, the morphine must have run out, because she registered a terrible burning sensation. She feared half her body had been fried away by the blast.

The pain only grew worse.

It was as if someone poured concentrated acid straight into her bloodstream, turning each vein into flowing shards of razor-sharp glass. The terrible sensation yanked her violently to the surface of consciousness. She heard a guttural wail and realized the sound had been ripped from her own lungs. Her muscles twisted and strained, contorting uselessly against the torture. She tried to open her eyes, to see what was happening to her, but the brightness burned her retinas, and she was forced to keep them tightly closed. Then, all at once, her body seemed to catch fire, and she screamed.

Someone was nearby, muttering in her ear. "I'm here. I've got you. It will end soon. I love you."

She wanted to focus on those beautiful tender words, and to the sweet voice that offered them, to hold him close and never let him go, but the unending torment made it impossible. It seemed to go on for hours and hours. She felt as if she was still in the mill, burning in the aftermath. Her charred husk clinging to life when death would be so much easier.

"Don't say that," a voice muttered. Had she spoken aloud? Yes, she realized. She was begging for mercy. For death.

On and on her suffering continued. Hours? Days? Weeks? She could only guess at the passing of time.

After what seemed like eons, she began to regain other sensations. She managed to decipher she was, in fact, not at the mill. She wasn't burning on a pyre of ash, though her every nerve ending might beg to differ. She was in a nondescript room. Though the lights had been dimmed, she couldn't open her eyes long enough to survey her surroundings more than that.

When the fire within blazed even hotter, and the agony grew excruciating, she realized it was Lex who murmured in her ear and stroked her hair. He was with her. Watching over her. Unable to help, he was suffering alongside her.

At last, she understood what was happening.

Her wounds had been too extensive. She'd been on the verge of death. To save her, Cortez must have agreed to turn her.

She was experiencing the traumatic change from human to vampire. It was so much worse than she had ever imagined. It was like being dropped straight into hellfire with no way out.

More acid-fire assaulted her, eating away at her organs. She wanted to curl in on herself, but feared moving. Her bones, brittle as they felt, might shatter.

All the while, Lex held her, comforted her with his voice, telling her it would be over soon.

She must have passed out at some point, because when she came to again, still burning, Lex and Cortez were in the midst of another conversation. She struggled to keep quiet and not interrupt. Listening to them speak distracted her from the pain.

"...has a natural intuition, one she may rarely have tapped into, if ever. I caught something of it the day of my wedding. As I read her mind, it was almost as if she sensed it. I felt like she nearly saw into me as I did her."

"You think she might read minds one day?" Those strong arms tightened around her. Read minds. Was that what Cortez did?

"It's hard to say. We cannot predict how her gifts could manifest, if at all. Many of you have exhibited no extraordinary gifts thus far. But I inherited my ability from my sire, and Marco inherited it from me."

After a while, Kasima figured they were finished talking, but then Lex said, "You were so selective with me. You made me wait years, made me prove myself again and again. I never asked you why?"

There came a soft chuckle. "I never needed you to prove yourself. You may not believe this, but I had decided to change you the very first day I met you, little shit that you were."

"Then why not change me that day? I know you could

have."

"First, you were far too young. Second, you didn't know what you wanted. To die a human or to live as a vampire. For someone at the edge of death, it might seem like the only option, but it's still a big decision." —pause— "It's a decision *she* never got to make." He sounded regretful over that, almost tormented. "Twice now I have turned an individual without their approval. Perhaps it is time I make amends with my own sire."

Had Cortez been turned against his will?

Lex said, "You wanted me to have the choice."

"I didn't want your illness to be the deciding factor for you, so I did everything in my power to make you healthy. Once you were, I simply awaited *your* decision."

"So the day I came and demanded to be changed...?"

"It was all I needed to hear."

Silence. Then came laughter, and Kasima could almost smile through the pain. When their humor died down, Lex asked, "So what made you decide you would change me? That first day?"

"I looked into the mind of a child and was surprised to find a wise man buried in there. There was anger, yes, but no fear of death. No self-pity for your tragic life. Only acceptance. And the love you had for your parents. You wished only to spare them the pain of watching their only child die. I saw a man who loves very deeply," Cortez told him. "That is a gift not many possess."

Once more, Kasima felt time slipping away. Her pain now came in erratic spurts rather than hideous gushes. But then a new kind of agony developed: a horrible dryness in her throat and a terrible hunger. No a *thirst*. A ravenous thirst. The kind that only a man who'd spent weeks scouring the desert for water might understand.

She managed to squint her eyes open and take in her surroundings. The room was dark but for a single lit candle, which she was grateful for. Her eyes were a thousand times more sensitive than normal. Her ears, too, seemed to pick up every noise. There was a fly in the room, flapping its little wings a million times a minute, yet she could practically count each revolution.

Then she noticed a set of prison bars, dividing part of the room. There was some kind of cage on the other side of the room. She might have been alarmed had she been alone. Her body was moving with the rise and fall of a chest. She glanced up, seeing she was draped over a sleeping Lex, his long lashes casting shadows on his skin. His arms were around her—had he ever left?—and she was clinging to him, her lifeboat in the sea of agony. Was the storm over?

A little discomfort remained, but it was dissipating with each passing second.

She reached up and swept her fingers along his jaw, roughened by stubble. He was more beautiful than ever. At her touch, his eyes flashed open. He gazed down at her, and gave her such a bright, sleepy smile; she was nearly overwhelmed with love for him,

Then his expression dropped, a crease forming between his brows. "How are you feeling? Are you well?"

She sat up, testing her limbs. When she did, Lex scooted toward the end of the bed, away from her, as if he thought she wanted space. She glanced at her hands, clenching and unclenching her fists, feeling an unearthly strength coursing through her. "I feel okay now. What happened?"

Lex appeared tormented by her question. "I couldn't get to you in time. I...Kasima...I'm so sorry. You were dying. I couldn't lose you. I just couldn't."

Much of what happened after that first explosion was still a blur, yet she vividly recalled Brian shooting Lex.

Scuffling across the mattress, she intended to peel back Lex's shirt to examine his wound, but ended up tearing the fabric at the seam. "Oops."

Lex seemed shocked by her actions at first, then he gave her that gorgeous half-grin of his. "I can see I'm going to have to invest in new shirts around you."

The skin around his shoulder was an angry purple color, but appeared to be healing well enough. She ran the pads of her fingers over his shoulder, marveling at the smoothness. He shuddered at her touch.

Her attention shifted to his face, and she was momentarily enchanted by the myriad greens in his emerald irises. There was even a thin layer of gold surrounding his pupil that she hadn't noticed before. As she studied him, that gold turned to liquid heat, and her gaze dipped to his soft, full lips.

"Everything is heightened right now," he warned. "Your vision. Your sense of smell. Even your desire. You may want to just take a moment—"

She cut him off with a searing kiss. At first his muscles stiffened with surprise, but soon returned the kiss with a desperate ardor. He pulled her onto his lap and held her so tightly to him that, if it weren't for this new-found strength, she might have been crushed.

What was left of his shirt became a pile of shredded scraps. She would have gladly done the same to his jeans, but a door opened behind her and a delicious scent. A burning hunger flared in her gut, and suddenly she was in agony once more. Her mouth watered as that succulent fragrance invaded her every thought, the desire for it taking priority.

With a snarl, she launched herself in the direction of that delectable, undeniable scent.

The metal bars halted her momentum with a loud clang, and she hissed at her prey...Kenzi?

Horrified, Kasima stumbled back. "Oh my God. I would have killed you."

Lex caught her from behind, wrapping his arms around her. "It's okay. This is why we take precautions." The cage wasn't on the other side of the room, she realized. The cage *was* the room. At least, the half that they were in.

It was then that Kasima felt her new sharp fangs, which had started throbbing at Kenzi's arrival.

Kenzi was shockingly unaffected. She held up a large, liquid-filled plastic bag, letting it dangle back and forth. "Who's a hungry baby vampire?"

When another hiss escaped her, Kasima covered her mouth with her hands. "What is wrong with me?"

"Nothing," Lex told her. "Kenzi, stop teasing her."

"Too soon?"

Extending his arm outside the bars, he demanded the bag. Kenzi handed it over and left without another word, taking that delicious, euphoric scent with her.

Shaking her head, Kasima sat back down. "I would have ripped her throat out."

Lex knelt in front of her. "It's overwhelming at first. You can learn to control it." Then he gripped her hips and hung his head. "I'm so sorry. This isn't what I wanted for you."

"Is that what I think it is?"

Lex peered up at her, then glanced at the bag, nodding.

Her hand shook as she reached out and took it from him. "H-How do I..."

"There's, uh, a straw attached to the bag." Yup, there it was, like a child's juice box. The notion made her chuckle. The chuckle turned to a giggle, the giggle to laughter, laughter to hysteria. Soon she was laughing so hard, she was gasping, her eyes watering. A painful stitch grew in her side, and still she couldn't stop.

Lex just watched her, looking as though he feared she might go mad. Maybe she was. "I'm about to drink blood out of an adult-sized juice box."

She thought Lex would find the humor in that, but only worry creased his features.

"Hey," she said. "I don't blame you for this."

Unconvinced, he remained silent.

"Here. Show me how to do this."

Eager to help, he slid up next to her and ripped the straw off the bag, then hesitated. "You're going to start laughing again, aren't you?"

She was already coving her smile. "Yup."

He shoved the straw into the top portion of the plastic, breaking the seal. And yes, she did laugh. This time, he joined her with a shake of his head and a small chuckle. "There, now take your *juice box*."

She dabbed at her eyes with her sleeve and cleared her throat. She accepted the...*gulp*...blood bag. This suddenly wasn't funny anymore. "Will I like it?"

"Yes," he said honestly.

The thought of what she was about to do made her stomach roil, and she couldn't imagine liking it one bit. She put her lips around the straw and gently pulled. Dark liquid rose. She almost lost her nerve.

Then it touched her tongue.

Her eyes went wide at the ambrosia flavor, and her lips hollowed as she sucked harder. The delicious liquid rushed into her mouth and she gulped it down. At some point, she heard herself groan. When the straw made an empty-cup sound, she fell back on the mattress, grinning foolishly. Her body grew pleasantly warm, her skin tingling. It was as if the essence of pure life now coursed through her. She felt connected to the earth as never before, like she was part of every molecule that made up the planet, the air, the universe.

Lex gazed down at her, pleased with her reaction. "Good?"

"Amazing."

Finally Lex gave her a real smile. He leaned down next to her and propped his head on his elbow. With his other hand, he drew his knuckle from her chin down the column of her neck, between her breasts. She shivered. Fuzzy poofs of pleasure exploded in her brain. "I like you," she sighed, feeling slightly drunk.

"Glad to hear it. I like you too."

She rolled to face him. "You think I'll be mad at you."

He sighed and pursed his lips. "I don't think everything has sunk in yet."

He might be right. Her energy was off the charts, and her mind was racing from one topic to another. "Did you know Brian hid a camera in my house?"

Lex blinked. "He was spying on you?"

"Not just me. He was spying on Mr. Dixon too. Probably others. I'm pretty sure he watched us have sex."

Lex's jaw clenched. "He was a bigger sleaze than I thought."

"I was super pissed at first. Less so, now that he's dead. Do you think while he was watching us, he, ahem..." Cupping her hand, she made a lewd gesture.

Amusement danced in his eyes. "If he didn't, he was

truly dead on the inside."

She laughed at that, but quickly sobered. "He showed me a recording of you and Mr. Dixon. When you asked him to give me the day off for the wedding…"

His gaze darted.

"You lied to me."

He rolled onto his back and let out a breath. "Well, shit."

"Why?"

"Did you hear what he wanted in exchange?"

"Yes. And I thought it was deplorable of him."

"That's why I didn't want to tell you. He's mostly harmless, generally a nice guy, and everyone likes him, but his infatuation with Kenzi was becoming a nuisance. I sort of lost my temper and decided to kill two birds with one stone. I didn't tell you, because I didn't want you to lose respect for your boss."

"Who cares about my dead-end-job horny boss? I think you didn't want me to lose respect for you."

He rolled back onto his side, eyeing her suspiciously. "Cortez thinks you might possess a special kind of insight. I think he might be right."

She shrugged. "I don't know about that. It's not exactly a Sherlock-type deduction, you know, considering you Wuuuved me."

"Is that what you think? We'd only started dating."

"Oh, you were *so* in love with me."

"You seem pretty confident about that."

"You won me a teddy bear from a carnival. In some parts of the world, that's basically a marriage proposal."

"Huh. So that means I've been engaged roughly…" he started counting his fingers.

She slapped his chest.

"Speaking of, Spike's been pretty worried." Lex reached for something behind the pillow, and produced her teddy bear. "I promised he could be here when you woke up."

"Spike!" She snatched him to her chest.

"Don't get handsy, now, Spike. Those belong to me."

"Oh, so you think we're engaged now?"

"Well, I did just give you a bear that I won at a carnival."

She froze, meeting his gaze. "I, uh, know we're joking around and all, but I have to ask—"

"No, that wasn't a joke, Kasima. I love you. I want to spend the rest of my life with you."

"Oh. My. God. Guess what?"

His brows creased. "What."

She tossed the bear aside. "I love you too!"

He hooked his arm around her and dragged her atop him. "That's a very good thing." Their lips crashed together as their bodies tangled. She thought he was ripped before, but now she could feel each muscle fluttering under her touch, each tendon shivering in delight for her. He was magnificent.

Mine.

She ran her nails down his chest, needing to leave her mark on him. Excitement lit his features. "Is my girl about to claim me?"

"Oh yeah." Straddling him, she undid his belt buckle and yanked it free of the loops. "I hope you're not attached to these pants."

"Couldn't give a shit about them."

She used her new strength to shred them. He made equally quick work of her clothes. And then they were blissfully skin to skin. The way his body moved against hers was pure magic, his powerful hips driving her to nirvana.

In her ear, he muttered, "I have to admit, I didn't think I'd find your little fangs so adorable."

"I think you mean sexy."

"Exactly what I meant. Adorably sexy. By the way, there have been no other bears. I promise."

"Oh God, that is so sexy." Fisting his hair, she brought his lips down to hers.

For leverage, he palmed her ass and rode her body harder, both of them panting and grinding their way to ecstasy. When he thrust impossibly deep, she buried her face in his neck and cried out, digging her nails into his back. His scent was heady, delicious, making her mouth water. She licked his flesh, placed her mouth on him, bit down.

Sweet, hot liquid rushed down her throat.

His guttural groan reverberated through her bones. Her eyes rolled back in her head. A cyclone of white-hot pleasure blasted her nerves. She threw her head back on a scream. He roared, his release joining hers. Perfect bliss, agonizing pleasure, tormenting ecstasy.

As their bodies toiled, they gazed into each other's eyes, and she felt their connection. It was in her bones, in her veins, in her blood. Because she'd...

"Holy shit. I bit you!"

He nuzzled her ear. "And I could not have enjoyed it more."

"Really?"

"Mm. My female is possessive of me. Wishes to mark me so that everyone knows who I belong to." He pulled back to peer up at her. "Now and forever."

She brought their foreheads together. "Sounds like a deal."

"A promise."

EPILOGUE

Kasima placed the last folded shirt into her suitcase before zipping it shut. Leaving Riverstone, even temporarily, was bittersweet. All her life this had been her home, her safe haven, and that wouldn't change, but a new adventure awaited. She was a little afraid, but excited at the same time.

"You ready?" Lex lumbered into the room with an overstuffed duffel bag slung over his shoulder.

She lifted her camera and snapped a photo, then shot him a wide grin. "Ready."

"I'm not taking you around the world so you can snap a million shots of me looking a sweaty mess."

"But you're so *hawt* when you're a sweaty mess."

"Mm-hm." He dropped his bag, hooked her waist and planted a sizzling kiss on her lips. The way his hands were traveling down her body, she was about to become a sweaty mess too.

"What is taking so long? Everyone's waiting to say good—oops." That delectable scent followed Kenzi into the room, making Kasima's mouth water. It had taken weeks in the cage before she could control her new, baser needs. To Kenzi's credit, she'd never taken it personally when Kasima mindlessly snapped at her over and over.

Cortez had visited daily, checking on Kasima's progress. The first time, post-change, she'd nearly been knocked off her feet, the commanding power of her sire filling her bones. She might feel connected to Lex, but she was *tied* to Cortez. She'd heard rumors, but now there was no denying the mystical power that bonded them, indescribable and indisputable. Whenever he was in close proximity, she was acutely aware of him, her every cell ready to serve. It was both comforting...and not...at the same time. If and when he commanded her, she would obey. Wouldn't matter what it was. She'd have no choice.

Such was his authority as her creator.

Truth be told, she was still wrapping her mind around that.

His clan held him in high regard, though. Which told her he was responsible with the power he wielded over all of them. To Lex, he was like a father.

However, even without that vote of confidence, the way he doted on Naia revealed the most about him. His new bride was the center of his universe. And Naia was a sweetheart, showing genuine concern for Kasima's well-being. Often she would visit the cell alongside Kenzi, offering words of encouragement as Kasima struggled with the crushing desire to break through the bars and greet one of them fang first. Sometimes Naia would sing for her, putting her at ease...because the girl was a freaking siren!

No wonder Lex hadn't believed her when she'd told him she loved him that night. Because Naia had been making everyone *feel the love* with her music. Naia herself had admitted it, apologetically. It was a secret no one knew outside the clan, which was why Lex had been so closed lip about it, as well as Cortez's mind-reading skill—another thing Kasima was still wrapping her head around.

Vampires might be known to the world, but there was so much more hidden behind the veil, and Kasima glimpsed but a fraction.

Kenzi said, "You two have all the time in the world to suck each other's faces off. Everyone's waiting."

Kenzi had insisted on throwing a going away party. Now that Kasima was more in control, Lex was taking her on a long trip to exotic far-off destinations. She could finally realize her dream of traveling the world, camera in hand.

"Are you sure you want to leave your home?" she asked Lex. "Your family?" Already she could tell how tight-knit this group was.

Kenzi answered. "Please. He can't wait to get out of here and have you all to himself. If you stay, he knows I'll corrupt you—I know all the pin numbers. Plus he probably wants to see how many hotel beds you can break together."

"Kenzi," Lex said, exasperated. "Tell everyone we'll be down in a moment."

Kenzi gave a salute and then left.

"We'll only be gone a few months," Lex said.

"Won't you be missed here? I hate to think I'm taking you away from your work."

"You're not. Now that Cole is past the worst of his change, he'll help pick up the slack." He eyed her then, learning to read her so quickly. "Are you having second thoughts?"

"It's just...I've only tested my control here, in a safe environment where any one of the clan can tackle me if I try anything fangy. I mean, in the back of my mind I'm still wondering how Kenzi would taste...and there's a thought I'd never expected to ever run through my head."

"It will get easier. And I'll always be there when you need me."

"I know you will." She kissed him again, then pulled away. "I've never traveled farther than the ocean shore. I guess maybe I'm a little nervous. I realize our town is blessed. We're in a little bubble of security, but I'm not naive. The world is still suffering from the wars. In a lot of places, there's a wild west mentality."

"*Wild west* insinuates there's a semblance of law in place," he said, not helping. "There are some areas of the world that have reverted to the dark ages, where evil reigns supreme, but I will never put you at risk. I want you to be able to follow your dreams, but if I catch even a whiff of danger, I'll drag you to the next continent so fast your head will spin. Just be sure to keep hold of that camera of yours."

He'd warned her of all this when he'd come to her with this opportunity. She'd heard the words *travel* and *world* and had been consumed with excitement. Now her nerves seemed to be getting the better of her.

"We can come home any time you like."

Home. The word filled her with such joy, she had to fight back tears. It wasn't just his family that they were leaving, it was hers as well. She felt it with every fiber of her being. She'd found where she belonged. Where she fit.

"Okay," she said, giving him a smile.

In the lobby, everyone had lined up to see them off. Naia hugged both her and Lex tight. "Be safe."

Kenzi was next. "Don't do anything I wouldn't do, and by that I mean do anything and everything."

The men exchanged handshakes, fist bumps, and back slaps.

Kasima still wasn't sure how to act around Cortez. Worse, he knew it, and he knew she knew he knew it. Whenever her mind delved into these little maddening circles, Cortez only smiled kindly at her.

"Have a wonderful trip," He told her. "I look forward to a slideshow of your work when you get back."

"One long boring slideshow coming up."

He gripped Lex by the shoulders. "If you need anything..."

Lex nodded, then gripped Kasima by the hand and led her outside. For the first leg of their journey, Cortez had lent them his chopper. The rest of their trip would be by vehicle or boat. Lex had mentioned a possible airship, but tickets were extraordinarily difficult to acquire on short notice.

Under the spinning blades, they waved at everyone piled on Ever Nights' front steps.

Kenzi called out, "Corrupt you later!"

Kasima peered up at Lex, taking in his, beautiful confident features, his strong jaw, and those mind-boggling lips that knew every inch of her body.

She was suddenly eager for the incredible adventure ahead.

The End

Continue reading for an exciting excerpt
from the first book in Kiersten Fay's
devilishly seductive Shadow Quest series
THE DEMON'S POSSESSION

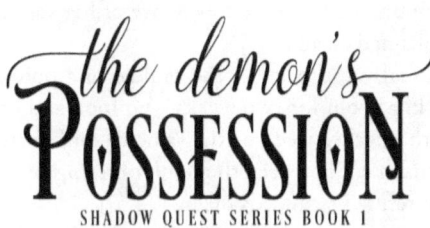

SHADOW QUEST SERIES BOOK 1

CHAPTER 1

Analia crouched in the shadows of the docking bay—
shaking with fear, anticipation—hidden behind a large
pile of cargo. Heavy adrenaline coursed through her veins.
Damp blond curls tangled around her face, falling toward
her ragged excuse for clothing and dirty bare feet. She
struggled to steady her breathing, afraid someone would
hear her. Her body threatened to collapse under the weight
of the ship's artificial gravity, as fatigue began to set in.

The sounds of the ship, like a living thing, enveloped
her. Embracing her, both as an old friend and hated foe.

Soon she would be free.

She hoped.

It was the only thing that drove her on.

She'd known a merchant ship would be docking today.
Two or three ships were scheduled every few days, in order
to maintain a variety of stock. In space, no two merchants
offered the same supplies, which meant many ships were
often commissioned simultaneously.

She watched with frustration as the blond guard stood
sentinel mere feet from her. She mentally retraced her

steps, hoping she hadn't left evidence of her spontaneous and unplanned escape.

As usual, she'd been in the middle of a punishment. Locked in a room for two weeks—no food and little water—with another week of the same to look forward to. The punishment had been the result of trying, and failing, again, to refuse Darius' advances.

Captain Darius of the *Extarga*, a.k.a the Hell Ship, had become full of rage at her continued resistance and ordered her locked away until she could accept her lot...accept him. Something she would never do.

She could never give her heart, body, or soul to someone like Darius. He was heartless and brutal.

As she had crouched on the floor of her cell, a man entered. She'd seen him before. He'd tended to her many times. Each time, she attempted a conversation, with no reciprocation.

She couldn't fault him, though. Darius strove to keep her isolated on *Extarga*, hidden away from most of the crew. Those few who had come into her presence—to bring her food or a fresh change of clothes—were ordered not to speak with her, or be *disciplined*. None had risked themselves for her conversation. Not that she didn't continue to try.

"How is your day?" she would say to whoever had been sent to her room. It was a phrase she'd heard before, through stolen moments from the ship's surveillance. "What is your name?" she would ask, hopeful for a response.

When they ignored her, she would only continue as if the conversation were two sided instead of one, telling them anything that popped into her head: her thoughts of whatever room she was in at the time or how she missed the view of space. She hadn't been allowed to see it in decades.

She drew some satisfaction from the one-sided conversation, if only a little. It always meant something to her when they lingered slightly, as though they were listening.

But in that moment she hadn't been interested in conversation, eyeing the scraps of food the man had brought for her. Scraps not even fit for an animal, but she'd take it. She was growing thin from hunger.

Though the man hadn't said a word, he had watched her as she ravaged the scraps. The first bite of food she'd eaten in a week and it had not been enough to fill her belly. She'd barely tasted it, which, by the way it had looked, hadn't been a bad thing.

Wiping her mouth, she had looked up at the man, surprised he was still there. There'd been something in his expression she had never seen before. Was it sorrow? Shame? Did he pity her? Probably. Who wouldn't?

She'd wondered what she must look like, unwashed in her tattered dress. Her feet were bare, her nails were dirty and bitten, and her hair hadn't been properly brushed for some time.

When the man turned to leave the room, he hadn't left as normal: by closing the door tight and double checking the lock. Instead, he opened the door wide and withdrew in a rush. Without even a backward glance, he had allowed the heavy door to fall closed from its own weight.

Analia didn't know what had compelled her to act in that moment, just that she had. Rushing forward, she inserted her fingers in the doorframe, just before it shut her in. She stifled a scream when the heavy door came crashing down on her.

Grinding her teeth, she resisted the urge to cradle her hand and waited.

One heartbeat. Two. Three. Her breath was labored. The first rush of adrenaline entered her system, followed by the spark of an idea. Her heart began to race at the possibilities.

What do I do now?

Then she'd remembered that several merchant ships were scheduled to dock. Perhaps...if she were lucky. If she could only make it to the docking bay. If a ship was even there, it was possible she could escape *Extarga*.

That's a lot of ifs.

She thought of the consequences if she went through with this and failed. A stream of horrific images entered her mind. She would suffer for days, weeks, maybe longer if she was caught. Never had she done anything so bold as to try to escape.

But if she didn't at least try, she knew she would regret it for the rest of her life, no matter the consequences. There may never be an opportunity like this again.

Hope flooded her, made her feel light. The idea of freedom, a better life, possibly being within her reach was a heady thought.

What if I do get free and it's worse out there?

The idea spread through her like a poison. If she did escape, and found herself on a merchant ship...what if the people on board were worse than Darius?

She pushed the thought from her mind. It couldn't be possible. Could it? Dark images swirled in her mind, picking at her resolve.

Or, what if they found out about her gift? Perhaps her unusual pointed ears were a clear sign of what she was, even if she didn't know.

Maybe under different circumstances she would have embraced her ability, but for so long she'd suffered because of it and only wished it gone. Unfortunately, as far as she knew, that was impossible. It was a part of her, through and through, blood to bone. And it was the reason Darius kept her as isolated as he did. To him, she was but an object. A piece of machinery at his disposal.

It could be that her gift was a normal trait of her people. If so, it was the only connection she had to them. She had no idea what she was or where she came from. No memory of her people. She'd been but a child when Darius had claimed her.

Analia knew what awaited her here on the Hell Ship—a lifetime of suffering until Darius siphoned every last drop of her will in his attempt to break her. Eventually he would succeed.

When she was sure the hallway was empty, she braved a peek. Then she prayed for the luck of the gods and eased the door shut till she heard the soft click of the lock move into place. Any decision she might have made to turn back disintegrated in that moment.

She glided through the corridors, toward the docking bay. Her bare feet made little noise as she went. She knew this ship better than anyone. She knew it better than Darius himself.

When Darius hooked her up to the ship, Analia had the ability to tap into the ship's heavy surveillance system. It was as though the images from the cameras were displayed directly into her mind, and she could see everything all at once. As far as she could tell, it was the only real benefit of her gift.

Though it wasn't much of a tradeoff, considering the pain of being hooked up to the ship was nearly blinding. The sensation of her energy being drawn out of her body and into the ship's power storage system was agony. To take her mind off it, she watched the crew through the cameras, envying their freedom.

It was her only joy, but right now it was her greatest enemy.

Making her way to a small control panel, she went to work infiltrating the system. For once, her ability would benefit her.

As she hooked herself up to the ship, she felt the moment she became part of it, like one colossal machine working in unison.

Analia shook her head and frowned in disgust. She really was a piece of equipment.

Everything in the ship's database was her playground. Every piece of information, every secret, and every code belonged to her. If Darius ever found out about the extent of her ability, he would surely use her to spy on his crew. There were not many under Darius' command who spoke highly of him in private conversation.

With the ship at her command, she proceeded, first, to clear an easy path to the docking bay by unlocking any door that might be sealed, and checked to see if any crew members would be in her way. After ensuring a straight path, she erased two solid weeks of recorded surveillance. Then she shut it down completely and locked the system, changing the codes before continuing toward the docking bay.

The system was only checked once every few months, and anything recorded was only viewed when there was a discrepancy. No one would think to check it until long after she'd gone. If they wanted in, they were going to have to hack the system in order to gain access. And because she *was* the system, she knew they would have a hell of a time of it.

Only once, as she carefully traversed the maze of passageways, did she come across trouble—a couple crew members, advancing toward her. She heard them before she saw them. They walked confident and loud, boots thudding on the hard shiny floor, ready to turn the corner that would put her in their line of sight.

Dread engulfed her, almost overtaking her senses. But after her moment of panic, she was able to calm her emotions, and dove for a door to her right.

Inside, the room was small and dark like a closet, but empty and unused. Her body had begun to tremble with worry; her hands were the worst, shaking uncontrollably. Opening, closing, and rubbing them together, she tried to relieve the tremors.

The voices became loud, just outside the door. She froze. Her breathing stopped. Only when the voices and footsteps continued past did her body relax.

She was tired, so tired.

Those couple of weeks without food had greatly weakened her. And she had slept badly on that cold iron floor, sometimes only falling asleep when exhaustion overruled the chill in her bones.

She pushed into the now empty corridor and continued with caution. The hallways remained quiet.

The path she had hacked allowed doors to open at her approach. With each threshold, her anxiety was reborn. Each hallway was like a repetition of the first. There was nothing distinguishing, nothing but grey walls illuminated by dim overhead lights.

With her nerves grated, she had finally made it to the docking bay.

A merchant ship was indeed docked, both ships connected and open to each other. She'd almost cried out with a surge of an unfamiliar mixture of emotions.

Joy. Relief. Anticipation.

That is, until she'd spotted the guard blocking her path. A large, strong looking male, a bored scowl etched in his features. Spiky blond hair framed his face and a black short sleeved shirt revealed his muscular arms and chest. Black pants and a pair of black boots covered his lower half. He leaned against the wall of the ship, wearing an aura of danger. Like he could rip you apart with his bare hands while maintaining that look of boredom.

Luckily, he hadn't seen her. She was already halfway hidden behind large piles of cargo. The stack of boxes towered high enough to hide a body three times her size.

She had to hold her nose to contain a building sneeze as she caught a whiff of spices.

She didn't know how long she remained in her semi-hidden position, but the time dragged. Any minute now, the docking bay would be flooded with workers, sent to gather the goods. She could only wait and hope for an opportunity, the perfect moment when no one was watching so she could hide herself away on the merchant ship. She prayed for a distraction.

The docking bay was a huge room. The ceiling stretched high overhead, and the walls were covered in white. Three floors tiered around the great round chamber. Massive machines used for lifting heavy cargo loomed above her, bolted to the thick retaining walls.

No one was currently manning them.

Usually a slave or two was brought with each delivery, though she didn't see any this time. Darius liked to acquire things, people included. Although most of the crew were free, many were slaves, and of those, mostly women. And though they were treated just as poorly as Analia, they were rarely kept as isolated.

Each crew member, slave or not, had two things in common. First, they were all handpicked by Darius, selected for their great strength, knowledge, or beauty. He demanded only the best at his command. Second, they feared their leader.

When he wasn't punishing Analia for some perceived infraction, he often forced her to watch as someone else suffered. In order, she suspected, to frighten her into submission.

It worked.

She was once forced to witness a group being *disciplined*. One of the men had been condemned to death. The other three were ordered to take his life or die themselves.

Analia never learned what they did to deserve such a punishment. They were given no weapons to carry out the act. Horror-struck, she watched as they pounded at the condemned man with only hands and feet to save their own lives. If she didn't watch, if she'd closed her eyes, then she would be on the receiving end of her own punishment.

She shook the memory away. This was her first real attempt at escape. She'd thought of it many times before, dreamt of what it would be like to be in possession of her own life. To do what she wanted when she wanted.

Oh, how she craved freedom.

To think, act, and speak with no fear of consequence. No one forcing her to use her ability until her body, drained of almost all its essence, gave out in exhaustion. No man to encroach on her body, when she hadn't the energy to fight him off.

She shook her head.

Focus.

She peeked from behind her hiding spot. The guard was still there, blocking her escape. He hadn't moved from his position since she last chanced a look. She'd never seen the man before, which meant he was a member of the merchant ship and was standing there for the sole purpose of keeping people, such as her, from trespassing.

Her plan had been simple, well...in theory. She planned to sneak onto the merchant ship, hide until it next docked, and then sneak off again, disappearing forever from Darius' reach. Easy, right?

She just needed a little more luck, just a little to get her on that ship, one step closer to freedom. She deserved it, dammit! How much more should she be made to suffer? How much more could she take?

"Calic!" a male voice shouted.

Analia jumped at the sound. She peeked to see the guard's attention diverted to something inside the other ship.

"What?" the blond guard snapped.

"The last load is stuck!" the other voice yelled. "We can't get it through the doorway! It won't fit!"

"It helps if you're smarter than the door," the blond guard muttered before yelling back, "We got it in there, didn't we?" He sighed before disappearing inside.

Her heart beat heavily in her chest. She waited a few seconds, expecting him to return quickly. When he didn't, she sucked in a breath and moved forward, hesitant at first, and then she dashed for the opening. She could hear nothing but the rush of blood in her ears and the quick thud of her wild heart.

Closer. Closer.

Her breath caught when she crossed the threshold onto the other ship. No sign of the blond guard.

She took in her new surroundings. The room was significantly smaller than the docking bay at her back, suggesting that the merchant ship as a whole was a fraction the size of *Extarga*.

There were two doorways, one to her front and one to her right. As voices came from the latter, she sprang for the opening to her front.

Spying ahead first, she moved through the door and into a long hallway. The air was warmer here, and a cushiony tan carpet tickled her feet. She was shocked by the sight of color on the walls, a mocha brown warmed by the touch of soft overhead light.

Ignoring the exhaustion and hunger that loomed over her, she moved quickly, seeing no promise of shelter. She was exposed, and if anyone spotted her now, all would be lost.

After passing through a few empty halls, guided by instinct alone, she spotted an open doorway. Beyond it, a sight she hadn't seen for a very long time.

Disbelieving, she was drawn forward.

The room was round with computer consoles wrapped around the edge. A center console near the back wall to her left stood alone. A massive window blanketed more than half the room and revealed a sight she'd been callously deprived of by Darius, a sight she had longed for.

Awe overpowered her as she gazed through the window.

Space!

Black. Deep. Vast. Speckled with pinpricks of light—endless possibilities masked in darkness. The power of it held her where she stood. Her tightly wound emotions nearly exploded at the beauty before her.

Only one thing was able to tear her eyes away and bring

her back to reality.

She was not alone.

A young dark haired male sat facing the encompassing window with his back to her. His attention was on his computer console, clicking away, oblivious to her.

"Cargo's unloaded!" a distant voice came from behind. Someone was coming toward her. "The captain wants the ship ready to go as soon as he returns!"

Her stomach tightened, and a bead of sweat ran down her spine. Slowly, she edged away from the door and crouched behind the main console, the only place where she could hide. Unfortunately, she was but partially hidden. The approaching male might not see her upon entering, but if the other man sitting at his station turned, he would spot her instantly. She watched him intensely, holding her breath.

Shit. Shit. Shit.

After glancing around once more, a frightening realization hit her, and her throat went dry. She swallowed hard.

The control room!

The heart of the ship! A room that will soon be filled with bodies ready to take their stations. And the console she was crouched behind, considering its location in the room, must belong to the captain!

In a panic, she searched for another escape. There were no other doors. There was nothing else to hide behind, in, or under.

The station she crouched behind was only a few feet from the back wall, which was drawing her attention. She got the feeling that something was there. Something she was not seeing.

Then she caught it from the corner of her eye—a small latch near the floor, not too far out of reach.

The male entered the room. "Did you hear me?" he said to the other man. "Call the crew back to their stations. We'll be departing as soon as the captain returns."

"Yeah, I heard you."

Analia scooted out of view as the male advanced into the room to attend an unoccupied console next to his colleague, leaving his back to her.

She reached out and gently lifted the latch. There was a soft click. Her breath caught at the sound. Glancing at both men, she was relieved they didn't seem to have noticed the noise.

She pulled gently, half expecting the tiny door to squeak from lack of use, but it silently revealed a small opening just big enough for her to fit through.

Shuffling through the space, she pulled the door closed behind her.

Click.

She almost growled at the sound, which seemed louder this time.

After a moment of bloodcurdling stillness, she released the breath she hadn't realized she'd been holding and surveyed her new surroundings. It was a small, cramped space, seemingly for maintenance purposes. Tubes of varying thickness ran along one wall, lit by a dim line of lights. The space was barely large enough for her to lie down with her knees bent, which, at the moment, was extremely tempting. Every muscle in her body was pulled taut. Her heart still pounded with adrenaline.

Making herself as comfortable as possible, she fought against an exhaustion that threatened to drag her into oblivion. Passing out right now would not be good. Once she felt safe, she'd relent, but not yet. The ships had yet to detach and everything could still go wrong.

She tried to listen to what was happening outside her tiny enclosure. Nothing, it seemed. She pictured the two men clicking away at their computers.

Light and dark spots began to star her vision, indicating that she was losing her battle against the overwhelming fatigue pressing down on her. She had succumbed to exhaustion enough times to know that she was lost. Still, she strained to stay awake, rubbing her eyes to reinvigorate them in a near useless attempt to keep them from closing again. Her brain pounded with the need to shut down. Only now did her heart begin to slow. Breathing was becoming easier. Body relaxing, her head lulled.

Stay awake.

Vision blurred.

The last thing she heard was the voice of a man, someone who had just entered the control room. She was unable to make out what was said, but the deep masculine timbre seemed to ease her in some way. She allowed it to roll over her, a vibrating energy that wrapped her in a cloak of security.

Or was that just exhaustion making her delusional?

Still, she couldn't deny the energy she felt from him, even from within her enclosure.

His rumbling voice boomed again. There was no making sense of his words in her tired mind.

She closed her eyes as her brain fell into blackness.

CHAPTER 2

Sebastian Uthair sat in the all too familiar spot, across from Darius in a chair similar to his, but slightly lower to the ground. Darius was half hidden behind the large wooden desk, as usual. Wood was difficult to acquire in space, vastly expensive in its raw form. Fully crafted, it sold for astronomical prices, and was generally only acquired as a means to display status or wealth.

Wealth Darius had, which was made obvious by the overabundance of wood furnishings and expensive tapestries decorating his office. But status in space was meaningless. Space was a hostile environment that required a sharp and cunning mind over prestige any day. That, and a shit load of weapons.

Most of the items in Darius' office were displayed to exude a sense of upper-class and distinction, objects placed meticulously to build a sense of importance. Sebastian saw it for what it was: a facade of an egotistical man. This man was no more important than a leaf on the wind. As a merchant, Sebastian had to deal with these all-too-self-important types constantly.

Darius dressed—same as he decorated his office—with the purpose of seeming more important than he was. His suit, expertly tailored, was made from the finest fabrics. Shoes buffed to a perfect shine. And his coffee-colored hair was molded neatly, framing his face.

He sipped his cup of steaming liquid while, in turn, scrutinizing Sebastian. Sebastian's clothes were simple. His style was more wear-whatever-you-grab and less preconceived, although today he put a little more thought into his dress. A pair of black pants—riddled with pockets, buckles, and secret places to hide his weapons—a pair of thick black boots, scuffed with overuse, and a dark coat lined with a light-grey faux fur over a simple white shirt. Around his neck he wore two heavy silver chains, which could double as weapons if needed. His short black hair was purposefully messed, allowing his horns to peek out. He too knew how to put on a show. His appearance projected danger and reinforced the common knowledge that one did not want to piss off a demon, especially this one.

Darius sat silently, giving off his usual air of superiority. Sebastian matched him with a quiet reserve, knowing what was about to come.

Negotiation time.

"I'll give you half the agreed price," Darius finally declared in a tone meant to end the conversation there. He put down his mug and picked up his pen, readying to draw up the new contract.

Two items missing from the load and the bastard thinks he should get half off!

It was rare for any merchant to feasibly acquire everything on a client's list. Especially one of Darius' lists. Most captains understood this, which was why many merchants catered to the same clients. It was the natural ebb and flow of space commerce.

Yet, so was bargaining.

Stifling his annoyance, Sebastian replied, "That would not even cover my costs." His voice was calm, a slight lift at the corners of his lips, his face a mask of arrogance.

"A few of the items I requested are missing from the load. I cannot pay the full amount we agreed upon. If I did that, every one of my merchants would bring me only half of my order and demand full price." Darius tsked.

"There are only two items I was unable to acquire and those items are damn near impossible for anyone to get. I would have to risk my life or the lives of my crew, and you are not paying me enough for that."

"I disagree." A knowing smile played across his lips. "A few short weeks ago, a competitor of yours, Kierok, I believe was his name, was able to bring me one of those items and charged me less than you quoted." A steely pause. "Perhaps I should do more business with *him*."

Sebastian knew Kierok, a rival merchant and a heartless creature. He also knew that Darius was waiting for some kind of outburst at the prospect of losing him as a customer. He probably expected Sebastian to crumble at his words and beg for whatever pay he was willing to offer.

But Sebastian could not care less if he and Darius did business. There was something abhorrent about the man. Sebastian sensed he needed to tread cautiously around him and always kept his guard up, as though he were a snake in the grass waiting for the perfect moment to strike.

"Kierok doesn't give two shits about his own crew and callously risked their lives to procure your goods. I don't work that way."

Darius studied him for a moment, frown in place. "Kierok could provide me with all the same services as you," he pushed.

Sebastian only smiled, never taking his eyes from the man in front of him. "If that's how you feel, I will have my men pack up the cargo and we'll be on our way."

Darius tried and failed to hide a sneer before saying, "Unfortunately, I cannot wait for Kierok. But I will not pay full price for partial delivery." He slammed his hand down on his desk to emphasize his point.

Sebastian shrugged, unconcerned. "I will offer to take three percent off the agreed price."

Darius, visibly agitated, leaned back in his chair. "Make it thirty percent."

"Eight percent."

Through clenched teeth, Darius replied, "I will accept no less than twenty percent off."

Sebastian pretended to weigh his options. "Then I am sorry. I'll have to decline your offer." He stood, indicating the end of negotiations and his patience. He had many other contacts that would pay adequately for his supplies.

He held out his hand in a businesslike gesture, resolution covering his features.

Darius eyed his outstretched arm with disgust. "Fifteen percent," he growled.

Offering him a fake look of indecision, Sebastian pulled his hand back and contemplated the new offer. If he had more time, he would have argued further, but he needed to be on his way. "I think I can deal with that." He didn't offer his hand again, and neither did Darius.

Darius bent to unlock a drawer low on his desk, lifting from it a small black box. He reached in and counted, then recounted the correct number of chips before tossing them on the desk in front of Sebastian.

Sebastian gathered the payment, bid Darius farewell,

and proceeded back to his ship, passing a handful of body-guards on his way out. He couldn't wait to get back. The next stop promised to be a big job, one of their biggest. He was about to negotiate a contract with the Serakians—an ancient and wise race known for their peaceful and gentle nature. When riled, however, they proved to be exceptionally fierce.

To anyone who chose to accept, the Serakians were offering a generous sum to transport a curiously small amount of cargo. Sebastian had received the notice just after he'd negotiated the contract with Darius. Now that the contract was fulfilled, he and his crew would head straight to the Serakian rendezvous point. Luckily, it wasn't too far from their current location, and should only take a week or so of travel.

The commission from this coming job could feed his crew for months, maybe a year. Sebastian was protective of his crew. He was their leader, their captain. Every action he took affected them as much as it did him. Many in his crew were next to family. Of the more than two hundred crew members more than half were loyal friends, but only two were blood relations—his sister Sonya and his brother Calic.

With a sense of satisfaction, Sebastian crossed onto his ship. Calic grunted a nod at him. Calic was his second in command. He was a tough leader, and an even tougher adversary. When they would spar, Calic held nothing back, as if he possessed a deep rage clawing for release. He demonstrated a ferocity Sebastian had never seen the likes of.

Sebastian had the same rage bubbling inside him. However, he was able to hone it differently by focusing on the survival of his crew and on each commission. He understood where the malice came from, though. They'd both been betrayed by women they loved. Calic's beloved mate and their own mother had turned their backs on them at the worst possible moment.

As a result, both Calic and Sebastian kept their women at a distance, using them for what was necessary and discarding them the moment after. The only difference between the two was that Sebastian never slept with anyone aboard *Marada*, though more than enough women lived on the ship. A few had even propositioned him. It was a strict policy he tried to enforce with everyone, including Calic. But, like many, Calic refused to submit.

"Is everything unloaded?"

Calic nodded. "Yeah, how did it go with Darius?"

"He got fifteen percent off."

"Huh. Not too bad." Calic pressed a series of buttons on the control pad and the docking hatch began to close. Metal screeched against metal as the heavy locks moved into place and a faint hiss issued as the door sealed shut.

They made their way to the bridge, where Sebastian claimed his position at the center console. As ordered, the crew was at their posts with the ship ready for departure.

An unfamiliar fragrance filled the space around him. He sniffed the air. It was feminine. "Cale! Have you had a female in here?"

Calic laughed carelessly. Conceit dripped from his words, "Depends on when you're referring to."

"Keep them out of the control room," Sebastian scolded. If Calic was going to consistently break the rules, there were plenty of more appropriate places to do it.

So help me, if he had her on my console!

Calic just shrugged in response.

Not soon enough, the ship roared to life. Sebastian was eager to get to the rendezvous and accept the contract before anyone else beat him to it. His ship was fast, but they'd been delayed due to the contract with Darius. In hindsight, he regretted accepting that commission, but the deal had already been struck, and Sebastian always fulfilled his contracts. He just hoped the delay hadn't cost him.

He wasn't too worried, however. The Serakians stipulations were extreme, to say the least. Even though the pay was great, he doubted many would be eager to take on the job.

His crew barked out their actions as the thrusters fired, surging *Marada* forward. With the course set, Sebastian eased into his seat. The crew seemed to relax along with him.

For a long while, he watched the stars as they twinkled like trapped firebugs, thinking over his checklist of supplies. They'd made several stops before meeting with Darius, stocking up in preparation for the lengthy trip ahead. He wasn't certain how long their journey would take, just that it would be a great distance. That could mean weeks or months or, gods forbid, years. He wanted to make sure they were fully prepared for whatever was required.

Even though they were currently better stocked than they'd ever been, he would still barter for more supplies from the Serakians. Being over prepared would set him more at ease with what he was about to put his crew through.

——

Analia woke. The unfamiliar rumbling of the ship reverberated through her core. How long had she been asleep? Obviously long enough that the scraps of food she'd last eaten were all but consumed by her body. The ache in her stomach punished her for it. She was weak. Struggling to even move her arms, she wrapped one around herself for added comfort. Icy chills racked her. Shivering, she stifled a groan, remembering where she was—a strange ship and an unknown crew. Her heart jumped as realization hit her.

I'm free.

It was done. She was no longer on the Hell Ship. Grinning stupidly, tears began to stream down her temples. She had to keep herself from laughing out loud. A weight seemed to have lifted from her chest, making her feel lighter.

Freedom! her mind repeated the word.

Her joy was cut short, feeling herself growing weaker by the minute. Her already cramped space seemed to grow smaller with each breath. Shifting her body in an attempt at a more comfortable position, she rested her head on the crook of her arm and stared at the blank grey wall. Once more, her stomach growled. She clutched her abdomen in an attempt to silence it.

She could only hope the crew decided to dock soon so she could escape *this* ship and disappear into a faceless crowd. Her pulse jerked at the prospect. Being away from *Extarga* was nearly intoxicating. But she knew, even though she'd escaped, she wasn't safe yet.

Getting on this craft had been easier than she could have imagined. Surely it would be just as easy getting off, right?

At the thought of Darius, she grinned anew, imagining the look on his face when he found that his precious Analia was missing.

Did I just giggle?

It was possible she was becoming delusional from thirst and hunger.

Just once, she would have loved to have seen the look of defeat on his face. To revel in the fact that she alone had bested him. Would he be engulfed in rage? Would he regret his treatment of her? Doubtful. Or would he set out straightaway to find her. Fear prickled her, and she lost her good mood. That's exactly what he would do.

They had to pull into a port soon. This was a merchant ship, after all.

Thinking back, she wondered if she'd adequately covered her tracks. Would the search take long enough for her to carry out her plan, or was he already on his way to claim her once more? She bit her lip with worry. There had been other ships to come and go. Hopefully he would seek them out first.

She found it was becoming harder to keep her eyes open. Voices trailed through the small grated door. To stay awake, she tried to concentrate on the conversation outside. It must be the captain's voice that she heard the loudest. His words were muffled. She scooted closer to the door to listen. Someone was saying something about...wards?

"Once the wards are in place, you may begin your long journey." This came from a commanding voice...a female voice.

"My men are gathering the supplies you promised." *The captain?* "They should be back shortly." He paused. "Is this it? Is this all we are to transport?"

"That is all that was requested of us. It is enough," the woman's voice proclaimed. "The contents of this box are without price. Irreplaceable. This is a very important task you undertake. Ethanule's reasoning for choosing *you* above all others is...beyond me. Know this...if this box does not reach its intended destination, you will face the wrath of my entire race, as well as Ethanule's."

Analia's curiosity was piqued.

"I assure you, Lady Hieskita, we are excellent at what we do. There is no doubt...."

"You understand your journey will take you through the warring territories. Have you no reservations about that?" the woman interrupted.

"There are ways around those zones. It would only make the trip a little longer to avoid them. And, if we must, we have maneuvered those territories many times before." The captain's reply sounded as though he was smiling at the challenge.

"You fully understand the wards then? What will happen if they're breached?"

"Yes." He tried to conceal the exasperation in his tone. "If anyone leaves or enters the ship before the package is delivered, the contract is annulled...and we are still required to deliver the package, without pay," he said robotically, emphasizing the last words. "Or risk war from both you and Ethanule."

Lady Hieskita humphed and said nothing more.

Analia laid back, alarmed by their conversation. *Wards? Long journey? No one on or off the ship!* She had to make her move now. But how?

Her mind felt dull, but she could tell there were many people out there. Too many for a clean escape, especially with her slow reflexes and weary body. More than that, she had no idea where they were. How far had they come? She realized now that she had no experience with new places, new cultures. She'd have no idea how to act, who to trust, how not to get herself killed.

Maybe she could wait it out. How lengthy could this trip be?

Thanks to Darius' favorite punishment, she found she

was able to go without food for longer and longer periods of time. But how much more could she endure? Furthermore, how much time had already past? She was so hungry. She didn't think she could hold out much longer.

By the sound of soft approaching voices, the decision to stay and wait it out was made for her. The captain took one last moment to reassure the Lady Hieskita.

"I pray for your safe journey," she replied. Then the room went silent until she began chanting. Ancient sounding words that dripped with power and energy filled the empty space around her. Energy slithered and writhed around her. It clung to her—tiny tendrils clamoring, seeking a way inside.

At first Analia resisted, using her own energy to push against it, but it pushed harder. The power didn't feel malicious, just strong. She relaxed a little, allowing the strange current to do as it wished. It softened, and then flittered through her like a warm embrace before dissipating.

When the woman's chanting died out, she said simply, "The wards are in place."

The captain said his goodbyes and thanked the woman. After a short while, a great sound rumbled.

The ship was on the move once again.

Analia's body felt colder and weaker than before. Her initial resistance to the odd energy had cost her. Breath coming in short spurts, she curled into a ball in an attempt to warm her shuddering body. When that didn't work, she allowed the weariness to overcome and she welcomed the cradling arms of unconsciousness.

——

Sebastian was damn curious about that box. Never had

a job been racked with such complications. His crew was used to docking at a space city every so often for supplies, equipment, and entertainment. They'd never gone more than a few weeks without stopping for some reason or another.

They were stocked to the brim for this trip, but it would be a trial for the crew, being on board for so long. After receiving their intended destination from Lady Hieskita, he figured the journey could take a little more than seven months, maybe ten. Once the job was completed, he would make sure they all had some much needed time away from *Marada*. Maybe find a cozy planet, brimming with fresh women.

The wards spooked him, knowing they were there yet unseen, like a parasite attached to his beloved ship. In the past, he had refused many jobs due to such restrictions in the contract. This one, however, promised to pay the equivalent of more than ten commissions combined, nearly double what he'd first thought it would be. He couldn't refuse.

To his utter shock, Ethanule had personally requested *Marada* for this mission. Why?

Ethanule was the leader of a faction of pirates. They'd done one job for him in the past; a small commission at that. There had been nothing challenging about it, nothing that should prove any real worth as a merchant or a cargo ship. Furthermore, Sebastian hadn't hid his distaste for pirates. His family openly disliked them, since their father had been brutally murdered by their kind.

But sometimes, a job is just a job.

His thoughts drifted back to the parcel. Why would Ethanule ask for him? And what could be so important that came in such a small package? That which could invoke the wrath of an entire race? This commission could either be a great achievement or his utter destruction.

Calic eyed him warily, possibly thinking the same thing. "Our course has been downloaded into the ship's navigation system, Captain."

"Good. Let's get going then. Cale, take command."

Calic nodded and assumed control of the bridge.

Sebastian left, taking the stairway outside that lead to his quarters, just above the control room. A domed window, covering half the room, ceiling to floor, revealed a vast spacescape. Unlike the one in the control room, this one did not double as an oversized communication screen, just provided a great view.

Marada itself was complete with luxuries, unusually so for a typical merchant ship. The previous owner—an extravagant and apparently rich individual—had adorned the ship with every comfort one could think of. There was a spa room with an oversized pool, and a built-in pub separate from the galley and salon. There was even a large room dressed with soil, live plants, and an artificial stream of recirculating water. The place reminded many on board of their home planets.

But what was most amazing was *Marada*'s water recycling and regeneration system, unusual for such a large ship. Where many ships used the more economical powder enzyme shower systems, *Marada* used real water. The system allowed for an abundant use of water—one of the scarcest commodities in deep space—over long periods of time. Water could be used and recycled many times over without contaminants entering the system. The only drawback was, every few decades, fresh water needed to be added to the system, siphoned from a planet that was overflowing with it.

Everything about the ship was made to provide a sense of comfort.

Even though it was constructed like a cruise ship, great attention had been paid to the internal workings as well. It was state of the art in defense and weaponry, as well as navigation. The ship came complete with an extensive database of galaxies, solar systems, stars, planets, different races, and extremely detailed information about places far out of reach.

Yes, the day he, Cale, and Sonya had stolen it, they found that they had acquired a good ship indeed. It had been five hundred years ago, the day of the betrayal, and the beginning of the war that ultimately destroyed their home planet. It was a war between his people and the war-mongers who called themselves Kayadon.

The Kayadon had come in fast, without warning. Only a select few had known what was coming, and many of those who knew chose to betray their people and their planet in favor of the infidels. People like their mother and Calic's mate. He thought of them now with venom in his heart. *Cowards.*

Shortly after the war had begun, he and his brother had received word that the fighting was nearing their village. After a quick meeting among the elders, all able men were called together. The brothers hadn't hesitated to join the fray, to protect their homes and families.

Sonya had spent hours begging to come along. She wanted to fight as badly as they had. Sebastian, being the eldest male in the family, had refused.

Not that she couldn't take care of herself. She had always been a strong fighter, trained by Sebastian himself. Her speed was incredible. She was faster than anyone in the village, including Cale. But he wouldn't let her fight because he couldn't stand the thought of losing her in battle. He had always been fiercely protective of her. Both he and Calic still were.

Readying their battle gear, Cale and Sebastian were unaware of the danger in their own home. The two women had approached as if to kiss them goodbye, but, instead, injected them with a poison that would render them weak and, therefore, useless in a fight. The poison had taken affect nearly instantaneously. Both men—disoriented, muscles slack and weak—howled in rage. Sonya too screamed her horror. "What have you done!" he recalled her saying over and over again.

"The Kayadon have come to lead us," their mother had ranted in a radical tone he'd never before heard her use. For the first time, he noticed the glossy glazed look in her eyes as she fanatically spouted her support for the invaders.

Seething with anger, and a newfound hatred, they had left the two women behind as they made their escape. The fighting was close, and they could not defend themselves. Survival instincts had taken over.

They thought to hide out in a cave or the woods till the poison passed through their systems and they once again regained their strength.

That's when they came upon *Marada*, belonging to a solitary Kayadon nobleman waiting to stake a claim on their home planet. The interloper had landed his ship far enough away from the war zone to not get involved, but close enough that he could join in the victory when it was over. The bastard never lived to see the end of the war.

After Sonya slit the man's throat, Sebastian and Calic readied the ship for takeoff. There was a short period of trial and error with the controls. Their kind had always been swift learners.

The Kayadon had quickly won the war. Their weapons had been far more advanced at the time, and they had the element of surprise. Soon after their victory, they had scorched the demon planet to the point of being uninhabitable. The Kayadon had taken what they could and enslaved many of Sebastian's people.

Sebastian shook away the memories of that terrible day. He hated that after hundreds of years later it still haunted him. He could see the anger festering within his brother too, and it had only grown over these long years. He feared that one day his brother could be lost to the rage forever.

He showered quickly and dressed before setting out again.

At present, Sonya was in charge of *Marada*'s pub. She seemed happy there. But, every once in awhile, he would see in her eyes the same look that he sometimes caught in his own, or in Cale's—a deep mourning for the loss of the home they would never know again.

Sebastian entered the pub—Sonya liked to call it The Demon's Punchbowl—and took a seat. Sonya spotted him and waved while attending Bertok, a trusted crew member who had been with them for years. Bertok shifted in his seat to nod a silent greeting at Sebastian, then turned back to his drink.

"Hey!" Sonya smiled, sashaying toward Sebastian. Her thin tail—a trait of female demons—swung side to side as she walked, making her look more seductive.

Sebastian ground his teeth at that. He suspected she did that intentionally.

Fortunately, the men on the ship were smart enough to stay away from her. They understood that he or Cale would kill anyone who dare hurt her. He also knew that Sonya resented their over protectiveness.

Sebastian smiled as she approached. "Hi, Sunny." To his amusement, she scowled at the nickname.

"What can I do for you, *Bastard*?"

He smiled wider. "I'll take some of that new stuff you got in."

"Ah, the raging inferno. It's pretty strong, even for us demons."

"Good. The stronger, the better."

Sonya poured him a generous glass and then prepared a shot for herself. She lifted the tiny glass expectantly. It was a ritual that they'd brought with them from their home planet. Whenever an unfamiliar drink was imbibed, it was always done in the company of a friend or loved one. The practice arose following a string of serial murders through the use of poison mixed with foreign alcohols.

Turned out an insane member of the demon community was going around killing off his friends. Imported alcohols had been used because a demon could easily detect poison through taste in familiar drinks, but with previously unconsumed substances that talent was nullified. Now, the simple ritual was a sign of trust and friendship.

Sebastian raised his glass.

While he sipped his drink, Sonya downed hers in one gulp, slamming her glass on the counter. "Good stuff," she declared.

Sebastian nodded his agreement.

"So," she continued. "We're stuck on the ship for some time, I hear." Again Sebastian nodded. "Well, it'll be good for business." Perking up, she poured herself another shot.

Even though Sonya was much more lenient with her pricing than the larger pubs in the space cities, whenever they docked, she always lost her clientele to the more lavish entertainment the cities provided.

She had made a profitable business out of her pub, wisely saving for her own future. Not that she was leaving her boys anytime soon.

Rather than use the ship's funds, she used pub profits to purchase whatever supplies she required, leaving herself independent of her brothers. That seemed to be important to her.

She also insisted on paying rent for her space. Sebastian had refused, but Sonya was persistent, giving him ten percent of her earnings each month. He saved everything she gave him, planning to give it all back to her one day—which, if he knew Sonya, would surely piss her off. Sebastian chuckled out loud at that. When Sonya gave him a questioning look, he just shook his head and went back to his drink.

"So what's the load this time?" she asked.

"Don't know. Something very small. Too small for the pay if you ask me. But the package is sealed and the contract is void if we take even a peek."

"Hey, sometimes the best things come in small packages. Just look at me." She did her best I'm-just-a-cute-little-demon impression, which always made him laugh. For a demon, Sonya was on the small side. So was Sebastian, for that matter, though he still towered over her.

"You're right," he said, ruffling her long, black-as-pitch hair.

She bellowed out a curse in Demonish, their native language, while swatting his hand away. Vainly, she rushed to fix the disheveled mess. Her violet eyes blazed with irritation, and a little amusement.

Sebastian continued to sip his drink reflectively, as Sonya went about her business, refilling glasses and seeing to anyone who entered.

He hoped the decision he had made to accept this commission was the right one. Sonya's words repeated in his mind. Whether the package was large or small, it was significant to someone. Significant to a lot of someones, it seemed. He couldn't help but wonder why they would trust *him* with it?

Finishing the last of his drink, Sebastian waved his goodbye to Sonya. Calic would be in charge for the next few hours so he had some time to kill before he took command again. In the gym, he worked out some of his pent up energy. A few hours later, he took a dip in the pool. Most days, he hated his downtime. He always felt he should be doing something. After the pool, he was relaxed and headed to his quarters for some rest before it came time to relieve Cale.

CHAPTER 3

Nearly a full week had passed and all was calm.

Sebastian had been working his crew hard. Round the clock detail. Each day brought them closer to their goal.

No one had complained. Everyone seemed as eager as he to get this job over with. Maybe they sensed what he did. There was something different about this commission. It was taken more seriously by everyone. Even the most careless of the crew were noticeably working harder.

Sebastian was at his command center, checking the status of their progress. For the last week, *Marada*'s engines had been churning at nearly constant full speed. It wasn't fast enough. He had hoped to be farther along than this.

Sighing, he settled into his chair, watching the vision of space at his front. It was stoic, calm, and never ending—deadly, if you weren't careful.

He imagined how different his life would be if he still lived on his home planet. If the war hadn't destroyed it, and if he'd never been deceived by those closest to him. He would have found a woman, he supposed, made a family. He would have built them an adequate home on his ancestors' land, and he would have strove every day to keep it up.

Life would have been...boring.

As it was, he loved his adventurous existence, leading his crew and meeting all the strange races of the universe. Learning and mastering all the different languages and cultures. It gave him a purpose.

A faint groan jarred him from his thoughts, barely audible against the steady rumble of the ship, but distinct. Sebastian looked around. No one else seemed to have heard it.

Another moan, this one even quieter...anguished. His brows drew together. He had definitely heard something. He sniffed, again noticing something different in the air. Had been for a while, but he hadn't thought much of it.

He stood, concentrating on the source, opening his ears to the smallest noise. All he heard was the hum of the ship. But the sound had been very close. He thought it had come from behind, but the only thing back there was the bulkhead and a small maintenance compartment.

He approached the wall and stood silent. A rasping sound came from the other side. He bent down to open the door to the small compartment and staggered back in shock as a pair of tiny bare feet came into view.

"Who's this?" he bellowed, his voice a mix of threat and confusion. His horns heated as his body reacted to the flood of demon rage.

The owner of the wee feet made no move.

Sebastian bent closer, cautiously placing his hand on a thin ankle. Still no movement. He began to pull until a feminine body emerged from the small space.

The first thing he noticed was how thin and frail she looked, as though she would break with a light squeeze. She was marked with dirt from head to toe. A dingy, piece of cloth clung to her like a second skin, barely covering her.

He shifted his gaze to her face. Her skin was pale, but flawless. She had pouty lips, full and a tempting shade of pink. Blond, curling locks draped over her bare shoulders.

The female shivered.

"Who are you?" he ground out, finally pulling himself from his stupor. He realized he was holding her upper body in his arms. When had he reached for her?

At his booming voice, her eyes flew open. If Sebastian wasn't already kneeling on the ground, he would have fallen to his knees. He was instantly lost. The ship fell away and there was only her. The blue of her eyes was indescribable. So light they unabashedly pulled him in. No color imaginable compared. Her gaze turned pleading. For what? He didn't know. But in that moment he would have given it to her.

What was wrong with him?

Too soon, the color dulled and her head lolled before she slipped into unconsciousness. Sebastian, alarmed more than he should have been, felt for a pulse.

Faint, but still there.

The natural sounds of the ship slammed into him, as his surroundings came back into focus. Some of the crew had already gathered around, apparently repeating questions he hadn't heard them ask. They looked at him expectantly and at her with curiosity.

Lifting her off the ground, Sebastian took note of her weightlessness.

"Back to your posts!" he ordered, and then carried her out of the room without another word.

The crew must have been as shocked as he was to find this tiny creature, because none of them moved at his command. He didn't care. His only focus was getting her to the doctor. So he could find out how she was able to get onto his ship, not so he could see the vivid color of her eyes again.

Racing down the hall, he hardly noticed people stopping to stare at the strange beauty in his arms. The elevator made him impatient, moving slower than he remembered. He should get someone to look at it. Finally, he reached the deck that housed sickbay. A few more passageways, and he was there. The doors parted for him, and he carefully laid her on one of the cots.

From a desk in the corner of the room, Dr. Oshwald looked up. He was a thin, lengthy man from one of the short-lived races.

It seemed to take the doctor a moment to comprehend the sudden disturbance before he rushed to Sebastian's side surveying the situation. His jaw dropped.

"Where...? Who is...?" He studied her as Sebastian had, prickling his ire.

In a pointed voice, Sebastian replied, "I don't know who she is. I just found her hiding in a maintenance compartment. She looks on the brink of death."

Dr. Oshwald went to work with a skillful determination, while Sebastian leaned against the wall, arms crossed, and watched.

The doctor came from a race of healers, their unique gifts worked on most, but not all. Sebastian had no knowledge of the mechanics behind the doctor's invaluable gift. He'd asked him about it once and the doctor had told him that it was like looking inside the body with his mind's eye. Oshwald could search out the problem and then fix it as needed.

That's what he was doing now, searching through the female's body, all the while intermediately checking her vitals in stony silence. Sebastian made his impatience known, and the doctor finally began his healing touch, placing a hand near her heart and the other at the crown of her head.

He stayed like that for a lengthy time. The whole while, she didn't stir, didn't make a sound. The breathing movements of her chest were light and barely noticeable.

A sheen of sweat began to glisten on the doctor's forehead. Finally, he removed his hands and slumped in his chair with obvious exhaustion. With effort, he wiped his forehead before he spoke. "She will live." The words were heavy. "If she'd been brought to me any later, there would have been nothing I could have done for her." Again he paused to catch his breath. "Forgive me. She took much of my energy."

Sebastian waited patiently for him to continue at his own pace.

"I've healed her body, but she has been without nourishment for a long time it seems."

"Are you saying she was in there starving to death?"

The doctor nodded.

"How long?"

"I couldn't say for sure. So many different races, so many different dietary needs. We won't know until she wakes and can answer for herself."

Sebastian knew that many races could survive long periods without food. A demon could go three or more months without nourishment. You would have yourself an irritable demon, but he would be alive. If this creature was anything like a demon, she could have been hiding on his ship for months.

As the doctor continued his business, fury began to rise in Sebastian. Before, irrationally, he had felt compassion for her. Now he had regained his senses and was livid at her trespass. How dare she think to steal herself onto his ship? Then a thought burned through him, settling deep in his gut.

What of the wards?

———

Analia fell in and out of blurred consciousness, the muted grey maintenance compartment tightening around her. She had waited too long and had run out of time. Her body was giving up. She knew she had only two choices ahead of her. Make her presence known within the tiny compartment, or resign herself to death. At least it was *her* choice to make and, though she was dying, she basked in that thought. No matter what she chose, her last action would be that of a free woman.

Inside the cramped box, she felt herself trying to leave her body. But she fought it. Why? Death would be so much easier. Suddenly, there was a warmth around her ankle, and then strong arms around her torso. A voice called her from the darkness. She sensed the presence of others with her, but strangely she didn't feel threatened.

I must finally be dead.

As she opened her eyes, she saw the most beautiful male she could have ever envisioned. He had the blackest hair and a contrasting golden shade of eyes that shimmered with some kind of emotion she was not familiar with.

His features were exquisite, and he was so warm pressed against her freezing skin. She wanted to stay in his arms forever. He must be a being of the afterlife, come to guide her through death's doors. Her body still hurt with a lingering grasp of life, but that would soon be gone.

When the man began to fade, she begged with everything she had left for him to stay with her. But he was soon gone, a dark abyss taking his place.

——

Fuzzily, she awoke. Awareness came to her slowly as her mind brushed away the thick haze. She was no longer curled in a ball on the cold hard ground. Keeping her eyes closed, she accessed her other senses to evaluate her situation.

Her chest hurt, and her limbs were heavy and unresponsive. She was lying on something that was soft but firm. A musky fragrance lingered nearby. Cautiously, she peeked from underneath her lashes.

The beautiful being that she had thought would guide her through the portals of death loomed over her. No longer were his eyes warm, but an immense coldness covered his features. She realized then that she must be alive. Fear swept through her with renewed strength, and her heart sped. His eyes flickered toward her as he noticed she was awake.

In a deep, too calm voice, he asked, "Where did you come from?"

It unnerved her because Darius would sound that way when the pain was about to start. She stifled a whimper, seeing this man as her newest threat. He could be just like Darius, especially if he found out about her gift. She wanted to curl up into a protective ball, but her arms and legs felt like lead.

Growing visibly impatient, the man waited for her answer.

She didn't know how she *should* answer. Would he take her back to *Extarga* if she told him? She thought he might. He did business with Darius and would want to stay on good terms with him. Yes, he would definitely return her to hell.

Maybe she shouldn't answer at all. Pretend ignorance of his language. Pasting a look of confusion on her face, she shook her head as if to say, *I don't understand.* The small movement was painful, causing her eyes to go temporarily blind. She let her head drop to the soft pillow.

"Sebastian, she's still recovering," a voice offered from her right.

Her gaze darted painfully to the other man. She recognized him as a doctor. Sebastian's harsh gaze didn't waver. It became darker as he silently demanded a response from her. She decided to remain quiet.

"When did you sneak onto my ship?" He emphasized the word "my." When she didn't answer, he leaned his body over her, bringing his face close to hers. His hands landed on either side of her head, boxing her in. Two inches was the only thing that separated them. "You will answer me."

The warmth of his breath rolled over her and stroked her skin, making her shiver. She stared, wide eyed. His golden glare bore into her, demanding obedience and surrender. Something protruding from his hair caught her attention.

Horns?

Her heart picked up a notch, and her breath hitched. His features were godlike, perfectly shaped. She felt the need to touch his face, but her arms still would not respond.

Then, for some reason, she became hypnotized by his lips. As she inhaled his delicious scent, her mouth watered for a taste. Ever so slowly, she inched forward. His lips parted slightly, encouraging her. With a start, she realized she was becoming...aroused?

Thankfully the doctor interjected, freeing her gaze and putting an end to...whatever it was she was about to do. "Can you speak, miss?"

Sebastian pushed away from her with a growl.

They must have given her something, she rationalized. Some kind of drug. Darius never hesitated to keep her sedated for long periods of time. Grinding her teeth, she thought this was turning out to be just another hell ship.

Then she realized why she couldn't move her arms or legs. She was strapped down. All thought left her, and she cried out, struggling against the restraints. Anger soon turned into panic as she fought uselessly to free herself.

The doctor placed his hands on her shoulders to hold her still. "It's okay. We only strapped you down so you wouldn't roll off the bed."

His attempt to calm her didn't work. As she continued to flail she could feel the skin around her wrists start to break and bleed. Breathing was becoming labored as the panic grew like a virus inside her.

"Calm yourself, woman." Amazingly, she stilled at Sebastian's clipped words. His voice, still commanding, held a hint of concern. Or was she imagining that? Staring straight at the ceiling, drawing in deep breaths, she contemplated how that one phrase had diminished her distress.

The drugs, she quickly surmised. The concern in his voice was only for his equipment and not for her well-being. She registered the feel of hot tears streaming down her face.

Sebastian continued. "The restraints will stay until I receive answers."

"How do you feel?" The doctor resumed his questioning, as if he hadn't stripped her will away with his tonics.

She locked her jaw and stubbornly refused to talk.

He then focused his attention on Sebastian, and they began speaking as if she wasn't there. "I've healed her as best I can, though I suggest she get some sustenance in her, so her body can take over the healing process. I'm not sure what species she is. The shape of her ears should give us a clue."

Analia knew her ears were abnormal, pointed with a slightly rounded tip. She had never seen anyone with ears like hers. It was the one thing that made her feel more alone than being locked away in isolation.

"What of her blood sample? Have you found anything there?"

Blood! Would they be able to determine her ability through her blood? Would there be something different about it? How could there not be? Everything about her was different. She swallowed hard.

Sebastian keenly noticed her reaction to his words and gave her a crooked smile. She hated herself for thinking it sexy.

"So you *can* understand us." It wasn't a question. "Then you can answer my questions. Where did you come from? When?"

Analia nibbled her bottom lip, sickened at not being able to better control her emotions.

Sebastian grated, "Tell me, damn you...What is your name?" She flinched. He took note of her reaction and calmed his tone. "Just give me a name."

A name wouldn't hurt. It wouldn't tell him anything about where she had come from. She hesitated for a moment and then opened her lips to speak, but stopped, however, at her dry cracked throat. She had to swallow several times before she could speak.

Noticing her discomfort, the doctor lifted a glass of water to her mouth. She turned her head away, refusing to drink. The last thing she needed was more of their concoctions in her system. Shrugging, he put the glass back down.

"My name is Analia." Her voice was pained.

"Analia," Sebastian repeated in his deep rumble. She stifled another shiver at the sound of her name on his tongue. "Let the doctor give you some water, Analia."

"No." She cleared her throat, trying to summon her own moisture.

"Why not? You must be thirsty."

"Because you've most likely drugged it. You've already given me something, I can tell, it's making me react...differently."

Sebastian glanced at the doctor. "Have you given her anything?"

The doctor shook his head. "Nothing out of the ordinary." He paused. "But, again, I haven't been able to determine her species. She may be having a reaction to one of our medicines." Focusing on her again, the doctor asked, "How are you feeling exactly?"

"I...just..." She couldn't tell him that she seemed to desire his captain. "I just feel strange." Her head fell back, and she allowed her eyes to close as a wave of dizziness washed through her.

"You need to drink some water. It will make you feel better," Sebastian commanded.

Again she refused with a simple shake of her head.

"We haven't drugged it, I promise you."

"I have no reason to take your word on it."

A tick started in his jaw. She got the feeling that he wasn't used to being disobeyed. He reached for the glass

296

and took a swift gulp. Analia watched the thick muscles of his throat work as he swallowed. "There, is that enough proof for you?"

"You could be immune," she rasped.

Growling, he shoved the glass at her. "Drink it or I'll make you drink it."

A hard dry lump stuck in her throat. She tried to reach out for the glass, but her bindings held her tight.

Frustrated, she began struggling again. Sebastian placed his hand on her stomach, and she froze completely, shocked at its gentle weight.

Afraid to look at him and risk becoming entranced once more, she kept her gaze on the ceiling. Her stomach quivered under his palm. "Remove your hand," she managed, though her voice was less commanding than she meant for it to be.

"If you promise to stay calm and take a drink, I will free you from your restraints."

Slowly, she nodded, not trusting him in the least. He began at her feet, his hands brushing her skin, leaving trails of warmth followed by a lingering coolness. Where he touched her, she felt a jolt of energy.

To her humiliation, her body began to react again. What did it think? That he was going to take her here? On the table? In front of the doctor? The thought sobered her. She didn't want anything to do with him. He was just another obstacle keeping her from her freedom.

After he unclasped her wrists, she sat up and allowed her legs to drop over the edge of the bed. As if to say *a deal's a deal*, he held out the glass. She took it and dared a sip. It tasted...okay. The small amount of liquid was quickly absorbed by her dry tongue, and she took another sip. Soon she was gulping back the cool drink with fervor, barely taking a moment to gasp for air. She hadn't realized how badly she was in need of it.

"Good girl," Sebastian said when she set the empty glass down.

Then he scooped her up in his arms. She'd been so taken by surprise at the sudden action that she'd actually wrapped her arms around his neck for support. When she realized what she was doing, she weakly pushed away from him.

She wasn't long in his grasp, as he had only crossed to the other side of the room and set her down on a thin cot within an alcove—which became like a small room when a solid beam of energy flashed between them.

A force field?

It was transparent with a slight haze, masking everything on the other side in an auburn hue.

From one prison to another!

"There. You're free of your restraints."

She made a rough noise in her throat. "You call this free?"

"It's as free as you're allowed on my ship. You've committed a serious crime by smuggling yourself onto my ship. It requires serious punishment. I'm willing to be lenient, though. If you tell me where you came from, I promise to take you back there unharmed."

"I'd rather die," she supplied.

He raised an eyebrow and waited a moment before speaking again. "You're in luck then. The punishment for your crime is death." He scanned for a reaction. When he didn't receive one, he continued. "If you don't tell me where you came from, then your only other option is to be released into space. Actually, you'd be releasing yourself into space. In my culture it would be seen as an honorable death." He crossed his arms in expectation.

Analia considered his words carefully. He was offering her death at her own hand. She'd contemplated suicide before—many, many times before. But, as closely guarded as she'd been, she never found ample opportunity. Now it was being offered to her on a silver platter.

Thinking over her life, she could only call up memories of suffering and sorrow. There wasn't a single moment that brought her joy. No memory sparked a hint of happiness to make her want to cling to this existence. Could she really push the button that would end her completely?

Yes.

Her shoulders slumped ever so slightly.

At least I had tried.

Her greatest and, sadly, sole achievement was her escape from *Extarga*. If she were dead, Darius could truly never hurt her again. The time she had spent in the small maintenance room had changed her completely. Even though she was technically still trapped, it was a small taste of what true freedom could be. It had been her choice, her decision, and no one else's, that brought her here now. She had felt the power of freedom and knew she could never go back. The moment she set one foot back on the Hell Ship would be the moment her spirit broke completely, reducing her to a mere shell of herself.

And here she was, locked up at the amusement of yet another arrogant captain. If she couldn't be physically free, then his offer was the only way to end her suffering.

With her decision resolved, she met Sebastian's gaze. "I accept your offer."

"Good. First tell me the moment you came to be on my ship."

"No. I accept your other offer." She almost smiled when his jaw dropped.

The DEMON'S POSSESSION is
available now!

Bonus Excerpt

Please enjoy this bonus excerpt from the
first book in Kiersten Fay's spellbinding
paranormal romance series
A WICKED HUNGER

CHAPTER 1

There was much in the world that Coraline Gordon feared: a revival of the revolution, being claimed by one of the countless vampire clans, dinner parties...but nothing compared to what she was about to put herself through now. Who would have imagined the most frightening event in her life would turn out to be seducing her husband?

Cora glanced out her car window at the luxurious high-rise hotel as she mentally rallied her courage. It shouldn't be such a difficult task to entice one's own husband—probably wouldn't be for any other wife—but Winston was a cold man, hard to read, fearsome at times. She knew if she didn't find a way to please him, she'd eventually be tossed back out on the streets where he'd found her. By his recent treatment, she wondered why he had married her in the first place. Was it because she'd been so destitute as to be indebted to him for her new station? Had he merely desired a picturesque wife, one that he'd molded perfectly to his taste? She'd been so pliable, wanting to please him. She hated to think she'd somehow fallen short. That he'd given her up as a failed experiment.

There had been a time when she'd cared for him more than anything, maybe almost loved him...in the beginning, anyway. Goddess of light and dark, had it only been seven months ago? She still did care for him. Craved his attention. But it wasn't the same. Soon after their week-long honeymoon, he had grown distant, burying himself in his company: Gordon Exports.

She disengaged the motor and tugged the key from its slot.

Her hand froze just inches from the ignition as indecision warred in her mind, tempting her to start the car back up and peel away before there was no turning back.

She sighed. She had attempted to be the dutiful wife, did everything in her power to make herself presentable to his wealthy friends and acquaintances. Yet somehow she had been found lacking. No longer was she invited to the gatherings, shindigs, and charity events that Winston often attended, even though she always donated the max that he would allow.

Had his friends discovered her paltry origins and unanimously shunned her for it? Subsequently, had that caused Winston to see her as the street urchin she once was? Or was there another reason for her being cast out of his society?

If only he'd inform her of what she'd done wrong, she would strive to fix it. It wasn't as if she hadn't changed so much of herself already. Her once ragged sandy-blonde hair now gleamed from the regular high-end salon treatments. Her skin was kissed by the medically induced tan that was guaranteed never to fade. All the hair but that on her head and brows had been permanently removed, leaving every inch of her like silk.

She was finding there wasn't anything she wouldn't do to regain the acceptance she'd only known for a short while. Which was why she now sat in the vintage Aston Martin that Winston had given her as a wedding present, clad in thousand-dollar lingerie that was hidden only by a long elegant trench coat. Cliché? Maybe. But she wasn't adept at being sexy, so she had to go with what she'd seen in movies.

After pocketing the key, she checked her makeup in the rearview mirror and straightened the sleek, dark wig she'd purchased this morning. Around her, folks bustled in and out of stores that lined the street. The outdoor seating area of a nearby café was packed for lunch.

She opened the car door and swung her legs out, making sure the tall heels of her knee-high boots found solid purchase before she pushed to a stand. Her heart thumped against her ribcage, but she ignored the meager protest as she crossed the parking lot.

The lobby of the five-star hotel was typical in its splendor. Gargantuan crystal chandeliers hung from the vaulted ceiling, gold-plated embellishments rested over banisters and other surfaces, beautiful artwork decorated the walls—no doubt originals, refurbished. The first few uprisings had devastated much of the world's art. What wasn't destroyed had been purchased, stolen, and horded up by wealthy collectors.

She couldn't help but note the stark contrast of her well-to-do surroundings to the one-room shack she'd shared with several other street urchins not so long ago.

The gap between the rich and poor was likened to an ocean of quicksand, nearly impossible to cross without a helping hand. And if one did manage to claw their way out of the muck, any new-found status depended on the good favor of a wealthy patron.

For her, that patron was her husband, Winston.

She hadn't openly sought his favor, though she had always thought him handsome. She would spy him here and there, strolling the streets of her neighborhood with a barrage of bodyguards while he prospected the land for new properties, or some such. No, he had come to her, wooed her, seduced her with promises of a better life and possibly a family. She had been so easily enamored. Then again, like most of the women from her district, a snap and crook of a finger would have swept her off her feet.

But it was her, not them, that Winston had set his sights on. To her that he had promised the world. Yet now those promises felt like trying to grip a puff of smoke in her palm.

Her heels clicked over the marble floor as she crossed to the elevator. Inside, she tugged her tie-belt snugly around her waist and then pressed the button for the ninth floor. Winston was in room nine-eighteen. She knew because she'd ordered the room for him before he'd left on this trip.

When the doors slid closed, she took a succession of rapid breaths. Anxiety siphoned the moisture from her throat. She swallowed, feeling her pulse rise. It was being boxed in that did it to her. She still wasn't used to the fast-paced world of the upper class. The majority of the lower classes kept to the outskirts and dilapidated districts that had been most affected by the recent wars—the areas that remained neglected, some buildings still half falling down.

Surprisingly enough, it was safer for them there, where they could watch each other's backs, where gangs ruled both by brute force and strength of number. Those who braved the city limits were either outcasts, junkies, loners, or criminals looking for a score. Either way they risked much.

She'd been a loner, for the most part.

Gangs might be safer when dealing with outsiders, but they did no good when the threat came from within. Which it often did for the weakest of the bunch.

The glassy doors opened, and a bit of her anxiety waned. As she stepped out of the elevator, a wave of dizziness assailed her. Though the floor was as sturdy as could be, her body instinctively knew how far it was from the true ground. The sensation was odd, but fleeting. Still, nausea rolled through her. Her nerves pushed adrenaline through her veins like a battering ram as she made her way down the empty hallway.

She told herself that most the buildings of today were made to withstand a nine-point-zero earthquake as well as bomb impacts. There was little chance she'd relive the terrifying disaster that took her parents and baby brother all those years ago.

Since that terrible day, she'd always hated tall buildings. She hadn't set foot in one till Winston came along— it just so happened most his business was conducted in tall buildings.

Just outside room nine-eighteen, she swallowed hard, closed her eyes, and took a deep breath. The walls weren't closing in. The ceiling wasn't about to crash down on her.

Winston always scoffed at her phobia. He called it ridiculous and embarrassing. She agreed her fear was irrational, but not unfounded. All the same, he'd instructed her to "get over it."

Right now, it didn't look like that was going to happen. Her heart had already started its familiar staccato beat, her breaths shortening. She felt hot, and a light sheen of sweat formed across her forehead. She leaned one hand on the doorjamb.

She mentally cursed. The very last thing she portrayed at this moment was sexy. Perhaps she should attempt this seduction thing when Winston returned home. As it was, he would take one glance at her and burst into laughter.

She was about to turn back down the hall when the soft murmur of voices from within the room gave her pause.

Oh, goddess, she hadn't considered he might have visitors. He *was* on a business trip, after all.

Another sound filtered through the door...a giggle of sorts, followed by a string of words Cora couldn't quite make out, yet her instincts sprang to life. The voice—the *female* voice—had sounded overtly sensual. Winston, for that was surely his deep tone, responded with a rough chuckle.

Her mind delved into a dark place, a place where every issue that had cropped up between her and Winston suddenly made sense.

But it couldn't be. Infidelity was one thing in high-society that was still frowned upon. Fear was making her jump to conclusions. Surely he was just in a business meeting or schmoozing clients.

Phobia forgotten, she raised her fist to pound on the door just as the door at her back whooshed open. Strong fingers clamped around her wrist. She started to turn to see who had stopped her and why, but the large hand left her wrist to cover her mouth. At the same time, a thickly muscled arm wrapped around her midsection and yanked her backwards. She managed a single muffled cry before she crossed the threshold and the heavy door closed her in. Her limbs flew into a panic before her brain could make sense of what was happening. She thrashed wildly, bucking to get free. But for all her struggling, her abductor might as well be made of stone.

While the man kept her still, another man dressed in dark clothing moved into her line of sight. The gun he held in her face inspired immediate capitulation. She stilled, eyes wide, heart pounding. Her own terrified gasps echoed in her ears.

In his other hand, he held up a badge. Her mind was too panicked to read the words on it, but the unique oblong shape was all too familiar. Vampire Enforcement Agency.

Another whimper crawled through her throat.

"Yeah, you know what this is, don't you?" The dark-haired man at her front said.

She managed a weak nod. Her abductors hand was still tight against her mouth.

"So you're going to cooperate, right?"

Another nod.

"No sounds, no sudden movements. Got it?"

One more nod.

"Put your hands up. My partner Mason here is going to remove your coat and search you for weapons."

Her hands shook as she obeyed. Undoubtedly, both her captors could hear the sudden rushing of her pulse. The man at her back, Mason, released her, circled around, and then pulled her tie-belt lose. She flushed and lowered her gaze to the floor as her coat fell open.

The men stared at her partially see-through bustier with a strip of black coverage over her breasts and matching sheer micro mini that revealed black string-bikini underwear. Leather boots that reached above her knees completed the ensemble.

"What did he do," Mason asked his partner, "order another hooker?"

Mason's hair was a slightly lighter brown than his companions, but cut just as short. Both men were taller than her by a half foot at least, and it was easy to imagine the compacted muscles that lie beneath their dark suits.

"When did he manage that?" his partner countered.

To her, Mason ordered, "Drop the coat and kick it toward Trent." He gestured to the other man with his head.

She let the coat slip over her shoulders and then shoved it away with her foot. Trent lowered his gun to retrieve it and began digging through the pockets.

"Hands on the wall." Not giving her much time to obey, Mason turned her around by the shoulders.

Her palms met the wall. A second later, a set of firm hands traveled along her sides and down each of her legs before retracing their steps and moving toward the undersides of her chest. Her jaw clenched. Clearly there were no weapons hidden on her person. How would she even manage such a thing?

Next, Mason pulled her arms behind her back, and metal cuffs bit into her wrists. Her stomach dropped three floors down. She wanted to ask why she was being arrested, but she was too terrified to form the question. If these men truly were vampires, simply looking them in the eye could be seen as a direct challenge.

He maneuvered her to sit on the edge of the bed.

Trent tossed her coat to the floor and held up her ID.

A set of brightly lit monitors in the corner of the room caught her eye. One displayed a split screen of the hallway from either end. The second showed different angles of a room similar to the one she was currently in. On the bed, two figures lounged. A man and a woman. The woman was dressed in a sexy outfit, not unlike her own. The man was...Winston! Shirtless, arms behind his head, smiling like she'd never seen him smile. A familiar giggle erupted from a set of tiny speakers as the woman on the screen ran her hand along his chest and then toward the clasp of his trousers.

Cora's jaw dropped. The sting of betrayal tightened the muscles in her throat.

Mason glanced at the screens, then back at her. He gripped her chin between his thumb and forefinger and tilted her head up, capturing her hurt gaze. Something like recognition fired behind his eyes. "Oh, shit. It's his wife."

Confusion mounted and she took in his features, wondering from where he might know her. He had a sharply angled jaw, a bit wide, but it fit his face perfectly. His nose was nearly straight with only the slightest bump that added a dangerous cast to his already glowering expression. His eyes were an odd bluish-grey color with the appearance of being backlit.

His brow furrowed.

She tore her gaze away, realizing she was staring directly into his eyes.

"Coraline Gordon," Trent announced, handing him her ID.

Mason didn't even look at it. Instead, he reached out and tugged the dark wig off her head. Golden locks tumbled over her shoulders.

A ripe, guttural curse made her jump. She glanced up for only a moment, wishing she hadn't. Mason's jaw was locked tight, his eyes bright with fury. A hint of his fangs verified his species.

She cringed and studied the floor as if it held the key to her survival.

A whistle rang out from Trent's direction. "Nothing against Marissa, but with a wife like that...?" He shook his head. "And the man's only been married for what? A few months?"

"Enough," Mason barked and turned toward the surveillance screens. "We have movement again."

The split screen of the hall showed three males in dark clothing, each carrying a black duffel bag, walking toward the camera.

"Dammit," Mason sighed. "This floor is supposed to be off limits to occupants." He looked to Trent. "Did we confirm that with the front desk?"

Trent's gaze widened on the screens. He pulled out his gun. "They're not here for a stay."

As the men glided swiftly down the hall, they opened their duffels and retrieved from within an automatic weapon. They stopped at room nine-eighteen. The one in front slammed his foot into the door, busting it open. Gunfire erupted. One half of Winston's head exploded while blood splattered onto the bed and walls behind him.

Cora felt dizzy from the sudden raging of her heart. A scream rang out. Had that come from her? A second scream filtered through the monitor's speakers.

"Shit!" Mason yelled. "Get down!" He pushed Cora off the mattress to the floor. With her hands still cuffed, she landed on her shoulder between the bed and the wall farthest from the door. Her body curled into a ball automatically.

The maelstrom of gunfire that came next seemed to last forever, though in hindsight, it was probably only a few seconds. The other woman's scream went silent, but echoed faintly in Cora's head. Was she dead? She was having a hard time processing that.

The only thing Cora was able to comprehend was the fact that she couldn't get enough air. What she did manage to suck into her lungs was tainted by the dusty scent of the carpet near her face. Her body shuddered violently and the cuffs dug into her skin, but she didn't dare move. Didn't dare draw attention to herself.

The gunfire ceased.

Who were the victors? She couldn't tell. Moreover, she didn't know what would benefit her more: if the strangers had survived, or the vampires.

One thing was undeniable. Winston was dead. She closed her eyes and tried to shake the gruesome image of his death away, but it seemed stained into her mind.

She began to hyperventilate.

A voice came back into the room, possibly Trent's, sounding sullen. "Human officer down, dead on scene. Suspect has been taken out by three unknown assailants." He paused. "It looked professional. One is still alive, just barely. Mace is questioning him now."

There was another pause.

"Yes, sir. Mm-hm. There was another complication. The suspect's wife showed up just before the assailants. We don't know if it's connected...Oh really?" He paused. "Oh, shit. Are you serious?"

"Serious about what?" Mason's voice sounded from the hall. Footsteps announced his reentry.

Trent's voice went low. "It's possible this wasn't an isolated incident." Then he went back to his normal tone. "Yes, sir. Be there within the hour."

"He's dead," Mason said matter-of-factly. "I didn't get anything out of him. What do you mean this wasn't an isolated incident?"

"That's all he said. Said he'd brief us when we bring in the wife."

The room went silent. She could practically feel their gazes slip to her. Her heart stopped dead before jack-rabbiting out of control. Oh, goddess! They were going to take her in. Humans who crossed the VEA didn't just go to jail—they disappeared. Panic iced her veins.

"Okay," Mason said. "You go inventory the crime scene. I'll take her down to the car."

At some point, Cora had managed to mold herself into a tight corner of the small space, but that didn't keep Mason's strong hands from lifting her up off the floor. With both palms on her shoulders, he steadied her and didn't let go till he seemed sure she wouldn't fall back over.

"Turn around," he ordered. When she did, he added, "Don't move." Then he uncuffed one of her hands.

The urge to wring her fingers around her free wrist was strong, but she kept as still as possible.

The familiar fabric of her coat came over her shoulders. Mason guided her arms through the sleeves and then turned her back around to face him. He snatched the belt string and tied the trench closed. "If it so happens you're here by coincidence, you picked a hell of a day."

If her voice box had been working she'd have told him that was the understatement of the year.

Once more, he cuffed her wrists behind her back and then guided her by the elbow out into the hall. Red splotches decorated the previously spotless walls. A body slumped lifelessly on the floor. A frightened noise escaped her lungs, and she stumbled. Mason held her steady and rushed her forward.

In the elevator, after the doors slid closed, he studied

her for a long while. She tipped her head down and became like a statue, except her breaths heaved erratically. The weight of his gaze was nearly physical. She was acutely aware of who in this small space was the predator and who the prey.

Vampires functioned on a different level than humans. They were twice as strong and thrice as primitive.

After another moment, his hand stretched toward the panel, and he pressed the button marked G for garage. This time, the ride down was not fast enough, but finally, the doors parted, revealing a badly lit space stuffed with vehicles. As he tugged her forward by the arm, her heels clicked loudly against the concrete. The sound bounced off the solid concrete walls.

He led her to an unmarked black car and then situated her in the back. She was surprised by his gentle treatment of her thus far, but then, there could be witnesses anywhere, cameras. Vampires liked to keep vampire business behind closed doors.

He slid into the driver's seat and started the engine, but kept the car in park. In the rearview mirror, their gazes locked before she turned her eyes down. The silence stretched on, and she took the time to assess the unfortunate turn of events. More likely than not, her old life was forfeit, her future precarious. Winston, for whatever reason, had caught the eye of the VEA. Never a good thing. And now he was dead.

She felt as though she should be experiencing more sorrow over that fact. In truth, she only felt numb. Maybe she was in shock. Maybe her survival instinct was overruling her emotions. Unwanted thoughts from the past bubbled up from the back of her mind.

After the disaster that had made her an orphan, she'd

been rendered a street-beggar at the age of ten. While scrounging for scraps in a back-alley dumpster, she'd caught the attention of a low-level vampire soldier.

She had tried to run, had managed a laughable attempt, but he'd caught her throat in a death grip. Not a breath later, his fangs had pierced her shoulder. When he was done nearly draining her, he'd introduced himself as one would a new acquaintance. "I'm Edgar. What's your name?"

Through her sobs, she'd whimpered out a shaky, "Coraline."

Then he'd tried to hypnotize her into following him, only to find her immune to vampire compulsion. A surprise to them both. His crazed blood-drunk eyes had grown excited. To this day, she couldn't say why that had enamored him so. Or why it made him want to torture her. Her only explanation was that vampires were sadistic by nature.

She mentally skipped over the worst of her captivity. That was where she'd learned how to go unnoticed by vampire kind, how to be still and quiet and the importance of averting one's gaze. That was where she'd learned they were more like animals than humans.

She thanked the goddess that he hadn't abused her in a sexual manner, though he did make threats of the kind. At the time, he seemed more interested in making her his personal snack pack.

Edgar had been a kind of foot soldier for a militia clan meant to squash the human uprising. When his leader discovered her chained in Edgar's quarters, he ordered a tribunal. Apparently no one in that particular clan could claim a human without express permission from the higher-ups. Edgar had made his case with her cowering by his side in front of his entire clan. He'd revealed her affinity to resist compulsion and claimed to want to keep her for further study.

Whether it had been extreme luck, or merely that Edgar was genuinely disliked by his superiors, the commander refused his request and ordered her immediate release. He'd called her a liability before bringing up that she was a minor. Cora was surprised to learn they did have some laws against such things. However, she might never understand why they hadn't just killed her then and there.

Edgar had protested and openly challenged the leader's decision. The result was Edgar's blood coating the walls. Her child's mind must have blocked out his execution, but the horror often slipped back to her in dreams.

After disemboweling Edgar, the leader had turned to her, and simply said, "Go."

Her thoughts were disrupted by the passenger side door opening. Trent folded himself into the seat. "Forensics has arrived. Clean up team's not far behind. Let's go."

CHAPTER 2

Mace watched the little human in the rearview mirror with too much interest. He always watched her with too much interest, which was why he often considered transferring to another case. Yet in all the months he'd been tailing Coraline and her rat-bastard husband, something had stopped him from doing just that, even when his unexpected infatuation had nearly blown his cover a few weeks back.

What the hell was she doing here?

Dressed like every guy's wet dream, for shit sake!

He slammed the car into reverse and then peeled out toward the exit. Trent didn't comment on his aggravated maneuver. His partner was too busy contacting Rolo, the newbie assigned to watch the Gordon house while Mace, Trent, and Marissa set up this little sting.

Marissa, though only human, had been a tough cookie, willing to snuggle up to that slime in hopes of garnering information on his dealings. Her chief was going to be pissed about losing one of his best over a vampire blood smuggling case.

The humans rarely cooperated with the VEA as it was. Now they'd be less likely to do so than ever, especially after this particular clusterfuck.

Trent's tone was clipped when Rolo answered, clearly not wanting to give too much away with Cora in the back. "You seemed to have lost something, Rolo," Trent hissed into the phone. "What the hell?"

With his superior hearing, Mace caught Rolo's answer through the tiny speaker. "What are you talking about?"

Trent sighed. "Where are you?"

"I'm where you told me to be, but I'm a little busy right now."

A faint round of gunshots vibrated the phone's speakers from the other end of the call.

"What's going on?" Trent asked.

"Just a little Mexican standoff. A group disguised as a painting crew broke into the Gordon house. They're packing some serious heat." A few more gunshots rang out. "I don't know where wifey-poo is. She never showed up after I took my shift."

"We, uh, have *the package* with us," Trent said obscurely.

"No shit? She's with you now?"

"Yes. We're heading to the police station."

Cora perked up at Trent's words. For another frustrating second, she met Mace's gaze in the mirror before lowering her head. He knew she was from the ghetto, but something in her behavior told him she had a little more experience with vampires than the average human. The suspicion only made her more intriguing.

"Do your best to capture at least one of them for questioning, then meet us at the precinct." Trent hung up. "Fuck all," he muttered. "Something serious has just gone down under our noses."

They remained silent for the rest of the ride. Mace pulled into the police garage and parked as close to the entrance as possible. Before he killed the engine, Trent was already out of the car, opening Cora's door and helping her out.

Cora had almost cried from joy when she saw the police station. The only reason for them to bring her here would be to hand her over to the human authorities instead of condemning her to vampire justice. She might yet survive this calamity.

Inside, Trent guided her to a room with dreary stone grey walls and a single table with several chairs. Then he undid her cuffs and exited, leaving her alone.

She examined her appearance in the wide, one-way mirror—standard issue, she thought. Her blonde hair was ruffled from the wig that remained back on the hotel room floor. Her light-brown eyes were stark, shell-shocked. And her coat was a little disheveled.

She was insurmountably grateful that the vampire called Mace had been kind enough to allow her to cover the outfit that now seemed like an ode to stupidity.

Why had she ever thought it was a good idea to follow Winston in an attempt to surprise him? She should have just stayed home and fretted over his return, per usual. But then, he wouldn't have returned, would he? Perhaps even now she would have been called to the door by Frederick, the butler, and greeted the police officer assigned to give her the terrible news. She would have cried and mourned and despaired.

Instead, she had to discover just how little Winston valued their marriage. The stinging realization was only muted by the horror of having witnessed his murder. It seemed silly now that she had thought seducing him would be the most terrifying thing she'd endure today.

The reflection in the mirror smacked of so much desperation, hopelessness, and misery, she had to look away. Almost without her willing it, she slipped into one of the plastic chairs, folded her arms on the table, and lowered her head into the dark crevice created by her body.

It could have been minutes or hours later when the sound of the door opening jerked her awake. She hadn't even realized how exhausted she was until slumber was stolen from her.

"Hello, Ms. Gordon." A balding man took the seat across the table.

Mason and Trent entered as well. Trent crossed to lean against the wall. Mason stood beside the officer, arms folded behind his back. Why were they still here? A sense of foreboding chased away the last of her drowsiness.

The balding man handed her a cup of water. With shaky fingers, she took it from him and downed a large gulp.

"Has someone come in to take your statement yet?" the man asked.

"No," she replied.

He glanced at the mirror and then back at her. "Well, I have a few questions for you, but I'd like to get your statement on record first. Why don't you tell me what happened?"

She blinked twice, suddenly nervous. She was going to have to explain why she'd been there. "I wanted to...surprise Winston." She wrapped her arms around her torso before continuing. "He's been working a lot lately, and we hadn't had much time for...romance—"

"Working on what?" the officer interrupted.

She hesitated. "Well, his import-export company. Anyway, I went to his room at the hotel and..." She assumed he knew exactly what happened at that point, but she went through it anyway, all the while avoiding glancing at Mason or Trent. "The next thing I knew, gunshots were going off, and I saw...I saw my husband's head...um..." Her voice quivered, making it impossible to speak for a moment.

"Can you tell me about your husband's company?"

She cleared her throat. "Not much. It's an old company. He inherited it from his parents. They transport goods in and out of the country."

"What kind of goods?"

"Anything you can think of."

"Anything illegal?"

She paused. "I...I wouldn't know. It wasn't something Winston ever talked to me about. Is that why he was being watched? Was he doing something wrong?"

Mason snorted. For a split second, she forgot herself and shot him a glare. One of his sleek eyebrows rose, and she fixed her gaze back on the human officer.

The officer continued. "If there's anything you know regarding what your husband and his associates were into, now is the time to tell us, Coraline. Even if you were involved in any way, we could—"

"Involved in what?" she asked.

The officer shared a look with Mason, and Mason took over. "We believe your husband was involved in the abduction of vampires and harvesting their blood for sale on the black market."

Cora's mouth fell open. She didn't even attempt to wipe away her dumfounded expression. Could Winston have been so stupid as to tempt the wrath of the vampire nation?

"Why would he do anything like that? Gordon Exports is a multimillion-dollar company. He had no need to—"

"Clearly, your husband got bored easily," Mason said coldly.

Her mouth clamped shut. Was that a dig at Winston's infidelity?

"It tends to happen when you want for nothing, when you're handed everything from the time of birth and never have to work for it. There's no doubt Winston was smuggling vampire blood, but we weren't sure if he was the mastermind or just a middle-man. Marissa, the woman you saw with Winston, had been seeing him regularly."

Cora flinched. The corners of her mouth tugged into a frown and a set of salty, burgeoning tears burned her eyes.

Mason's tone softened. "Her objective was to find out where the blood was coming from and who else was involved."

"How long had they been...?" She trailed off, staring at Mason's upside-down reflection in the metallic gleam of the table.

"Since before you," he replied simply.

Devastation crushed her chest.

"In fact, Marissa had been hinting about marriage just before he met you. You came as something of a surprise, actually..." Mason paused for a moment. "We weren't sure if you were involved somehow, so we assigned someone to follow you as well."

Cora's head jerked up. She'd been followed? For how long? The thought sent a shiver down her spine. "And what did you find?"

"For the most part, it seemed you were ignorant of everything. But several months ago, something was discovered. If a human had been tailing you, it would have gone unnoticed, but...the scent of vampire blood was in your veins."

Finally, she met Mason's gaze head-on. Surely he was joking. His deadpan stare bore into hers.

"That's impossible," she said.

"It's a fact. I smell it on you even now."

She shook her head. "I've never even tasted vampire blood, not even when..."

Both males canted their heads, and she knew she would be forced to finish her sentence.

"Not even when I was offered it in my youth."

After Edgar would brutalize her, he'd tear open his own wrist and present it to her, claiming his blood would heal her if she chose. She had always refused, hoping her wounds would kill her instead.

"You've ingested it within the last week," Mason insisted. "But you don't have to take my word on it. We're preparing a warrant to have your blood tested. That will not only confirm what I say, but it could identify which missing vampire it came from."

Cora's heart slammed to a halt. What would happen to her if they found something in her system? When could she have possibly ingested vampire blood? And if she had, how could she not have realized it? Didn't that stuff affect humans in noticeable ways?

She gasped as a memory knocked the wind from her lungs like a blow to the stomach. It was something she wouldn't have thought twice about had she not been forced to reconsider everything she'd known over the last seven months. She glanced at her right forefinger, at a spot that probably should brandish at the very least a scab, but the skin was smooth and even, flawless.

"What is it?" The vampire asked.

"Last Monday Winston and I were making dinner. He was cutting some carrots, and I reached over to grab the pile next to him. The knife slipped, and my finger got cut. I thought it would need stitched, but Winston wrapped it in gauze and convinced me not to worry about it. Then he finished dinner and poured me a glass of red wine." She paused at the memory of thinking how kind it had been of Winston to take such care of her. "The next morning, I checked the cut and it was already closing up. I figured it just hadn't been as bad as I'd originally thought."

Had Winston been feeding her vampire blood behind her back?

"Blood-laced wine is a popular method of consumption," Mason replied. "It masks the color and taste."

"Something happened before that," she continued as another suspicious memory assailed her. "There was a dinner party at the Montgomery home three months ago. Not a huge event, just a few people I had never met before. Ms. Montgomery had taken me upstairs to show off a new painting of her posing by the pool with her miniature chow. On our way back down, she lost her footing and fell into me. I took a hard tumble and landed wrong on my arm. I remember thinking I must have broken it. It swelled up pretty bad. But same as last week, Winston convinced me to wait before we sought medical attention. We all sat down to dinner and had wine. Before the night was over, most of the pain had dulled and the swelling had gone down. The next morning it was only a little tender."

Mason and the officer shared another look.

"I recall that gathering," Mason said. "The Montgomery's home is like a fortified castle. We couldn't get a man inside. Do you remember the names of everyone who had attended?"

"I was introduced to them all at once earlier that night, but I hadn't been able to memorize all their names. I might be able to identify some of their faces, but you could just ask the Montgomerys."

Once more the two men locked eyes.

"What?" She glanced between them.

Mason sighed. "The Montgomery home was infiltrated at the same time those assassins came for your husband."

"Oh my goddess. Are they...?"

"Dead." He said it as though he were discussing the weather.

"Hold on, now," the officer bit out. "I'm not ready for that information to be made public."

Mason ignored him. He seemed to be gauging her reaction, and she thought she knew why. "Am I a suspect?"

"You would be, if your home hadn't been targeted as well."

Her head jerked up, and she again met his intense gaze. "Targeted?"

"The operation was carried out with military precision. Synchronized to perfection. Every suspected conspirator, and several we didn't even think to add to the list, was executed."

"Mace," the officer hissed. "Would you shut your mouth?"

"She's not involved in any of it," Mason replied.

"And what makes you so sure? Her home was attacked, but she was conveniently away at the time."

"About the time Winston married her, tainted blood was circulating through the black market. People were dying from it. I believe he needed someone to test his product on before distributing it to his rich friends." He gestured toward her.

Her frown grew more pronounced.

Was that all she was? A guinea pig?

She had always wondered why Winston had chosen to marry her when he was constantly surrounded by beautiful, sometimes too obviously willing, women of his own class. Gullible guinea pig made too much sense.

The officer shook his head. "That's just your opinion until all the evidence is examined."

Mace shrugged. "Right now, there is no evidence. No leads. Only her."

The officer sighed. "Ms. Gordon, is there anything else you can tell us? Did your husband ever mention anything about his little side business?"

"No. Never."

He stood as if to leave. "If you think of anything, I won't be far. Someone will be by to take a sample of your blood and then you'll be free to go."

"Actually, she'll be coming with me."

Cora gaped at Mason.

The officer paused and swiveled his head in the same direction. His jaw tightened, and she thought he might protest.

Please protest.

Mace became stern, as did Trent, their expressions hardening. The three seemed to be having a silent conversation. Or a battle for dominance. If the VEA wanted her, she couldn't imagine there was anything the officer could do.

Apparently, he'd come to the same conclusion. "She'll be released into your custody once we get the sample."

"What does that mean, released into his custody?" She gripped the edge of the table as if she could bolt herself in place.

"This is a VEA investigation," the officer informed her. A bit of pity seeped out with his words. "We're only providing assistance."

She leaned forward. "You can't let them take me."

"Sorry, little lady." He hiked his thumb at Mason, pity quickly evaporating. "These guys are in charge. You know that."

She did. Since they'd revealed themselves to the world one hundred years ago, the vampires had *graciously* allowed the human institutions to proceed with almost no interruption, but there was no illusion that vampire law didn't overrule human law, which was the underlining cause of most of the uprisings.

"But he'll kill me," she muttered. Anyone caught with illegally obtained vampire blood was dealt a swift death. No trial necessary.

"I've no intention of killing you," Mason proclaimed.

Terror dropped her heart into her stomach. Then what did they plan for her? She knew first hand that surviving in the custody of a vampire could be even worse than death.

"Can't I stay here...in a human jail until all this is sorted out?"

Mason narrowed his gaze. "No, you can't." Then he addressed the officer in a demanding tone. "Fetch the person to administer the blood test. I want to be on our way."

The officer's features pinched slightly, almost like a sneer, but not quite. He left without a word.

Cora kept her eyes lowered to the table. Her tone came out no more than a whisper. "Please. I don't want to go with you."

The vampires made no response, which was answer enough.

CHAPTER 3

"Can't I at least get my suitcase from out of my trunk?" Cora pleaded, wanting more than anything to change into normal clothing.

She stood, hopelessly, in the police station garage, next to the same black car that had brought her here.

Mace opened the passenger side door for her. "Your vehicle and everything inside it is considered evidence at the moment. I'm afraid it will take some time to clear it."

She glanced longingly to her left, down the sidewalk that fronted the police station. A brief, ridiculous fantasy of making a run for it trickled through her mind.

She wouldn't even make it a step.

Mace waited, seemingly patient, for her to get into the car. Something in his expression told her he knew the way of her thoughts and was somewhat amused.

As she settled in the car, she wrung her fingers nervously while Mace walked around the front and took the driver's seat. The engine roared to life with the turn of the key. The sound was like an ominous prelude to an execution.

She wondered briefly where Trent was. He'd allowed Mace alone to escort her out of the police station while remaining behind with the human authorities.

In the small space of the car, sitting so close to Mace,

Cora automatically reverted back to the mindset that kept her alive during her time with Edgar. She forced her lungs to work slow and even. She tilted her head down, and went as still as a possum. From the corner of her eye she saw Mace shoot her a sidelong glance before putting the car into drive.

"Put your seatbelt on," he ordered.

She yanked the strap across her body and snapped it into place, then returned her hands to her lap just as he pulled onto the street. A moment of silence followed. She kept her eyes on her hands.

She felt the car speed up, slow down, stop, then speed up again, but never looked up, never glanced out the window.

After a long while of quiet driving, Mace said casually, "Are you trying to make me forget you're there?"

Her chin jerked slightly, but she made no response.

"Believe me. Nothing could accomplish that."

She swallowed, keeping her eyes downcast.

"Where did you learn to do that, anyway?"

Her heart stuttered, and silence crushed the space around them.

"Well, anyway, you don't have to do that. I'm not a threat to you."

He took the highway on-ramp, heading out of town. She prayed he would stop trying to engage her in conversation, but she wasn't so lucky.

After another stretch of silence, he said, "Don't you have questions about where we're going? Why you're with me? How long we've been watching you? You can ask me whatever you like."

She was sick with curiosity, but she shook her head.

"It's going to be a dull ride then, and we have a ways

328

to go."

He paused as if that should have been enough to entice her into asking. He obviously wanted to tell her, so why didn't he just get on with it?

He sighed. "I have loads of questions for you, but I don't want this to feel like an interrogation. You're a witness, not a suspect. You're no one's captive."

"Then let me go," she heard herself reply, instantly regretting her desperate tone.

"She speaks," he said on a chuckle. "And where would you go?"

She thought about that for a moment. There was only one place she could go, the large home she had shared with Winston. Thinking of him now sent a flurry of mixed emotions through her heart.

"You can't go home," Mason said, as if reading her mind. "Aside from the fact that assassins broke in with too much ease...specifically to murder you, I might add—"

"Why me? Weren't they just looking for Winston?"

"They knew exactly where Winston would be. No, they were looking for you. Still might be. These people, whoever they are....well, it's like they're cleaning up their entire operation, or perhaps eliminating the competition. We're not quite sure yet. Whatever the reason, they left no loose ends. None but you." He shot her a look. "It was more than Winston and the Montgomerys. All our suspects were targeted, and then some. Entire families were executed, children included. You can't go back there."

He allowed her a moment to take that in.

"But aside from all that," he continued, "Winston wrote you out of his will the moment you said 'I do.'"

Her head snapped up. He met her bemused expression with one of complete seriousness.

"That prenup you signed waved away any claim you might have had to Winston's wealth. He had already prepared his will before the honeymoon was over. In case of his death, the money, the cars, the three homes? It all gets split between his blood relatives. You get nothing."

A deep chasm of despair crashed in her chest. "You could be making that up."

"You know I'm not. Not after all you've learned today about your rat-bastard husband."

The venom with which Mason ended his sentence was shocking. Almost as shocking as the realization that she was now back where she'd started. Street urchin. Worse, actually—a street urchin who'd drawn the attention of the largest vampire organization known to man.

Tears billowed, quickly drenching her cheeks. Even if the vampires didn't kill her, going back to the streets might. She was too different now. Not only did she look like a *whale*—street slang for a female of means—but now she knew, really knew, what it was like to live without fear, in a soft, safe bed, not having to sleep with one eye open. Not worrying every minute of every day where her next meal would come from or having to beg for coins while trying not to resort to more desperate acts like the ladies who lined up on corners at night.

Mason said nothing as she quietly sobbed.

"You must think I'm despicable," she stammered.

"Why would I?"

"Because I'm crying more for losing the money than losing Winston."

Mason laughed. "I think you're a survivor. You married that bastard because you had no other prospects. You did it to get out of a terrible situation. Anyone would've done the same."

She sniffed, a little taken aback. "I did care for him in the beginning."

"Of course you did."

His tone grated. "I did. He was sweet and generous at first. He didn't make me feel inferior. I truly thought he loved me." She buried her face in her hands. "I feel so stupid."

Mason cursed. "Don't cry. That shithead isn't worth it."

She worked to get control before Mason grew irritated with her. And though it was bound to happen eventually, she wanted to delay seeing Mason when he'd lost his patience. Vampires were unpredictable in the best of moods.

"Did you know him or something?" she asked. "The way you talk about him, it's almost as if you hold a grudge."

Mason pursed his lips, and his eyes narrowed on the road.

"Forget it. I don't want to know. In fact, I want to know as little as possible about all of this."

"I'm afraid that's a fantasy, sweetheart. You already know more than enough."

Anxiety crawled along her skin, raising the hairs on the back of her neck. "What does that mean?"

"It means you're under our protection until we say otherwise. I'm taking you to a safe house."

A hard ball of dread pushed down on her stomach, making her nauseous. A safe house? A prison was more like it. He was going to drive her somewhere isolated and keep her there until...well, as long as he wanted.

He must have noticed her distress because he said, "You don't need to fear me. I've been assigned to keep you safe. No harm will come to you as long as you're in my charge."

She just kept from rolling her eyes. A vampire's idea of harm varied greatly from that of a human's. Before his death, Edgar had sworn to his commanding officer he'd done nothing to *harm* her. The commander hadn't even looked twice at the marks on her wrists and neck.

The scars were healed now. That was the miraculous thing about vampire bites. The evidence of them never lasted.

Mason transferred to the left lane to pass a slow-moving vehicle.

Cora turned her head to watch a graveyard of tree husks rush past. They were almost out of the upper class zone, St. Stamsworth, founded just after a devastating fire had toppled the original city. She'd heard this outer area used to be part of a national forest, boasting an array of wildlife and lush greenery. Whatever weaponry had been used during the first of the uprisings now kept any new growth from springing up out of the black-charred soil, even though Lake Tahoe still sat full as ever.

"Why were you offered vampire blood?" Mason drew her attention away from the scenery.

"Excuse me?"

"Back at the precinct, you said you'd never tasted vamp blood even when it was offered to you."

"I, uh..." She didn't want to talk about this with him. She often feared she'd somehow be blamed for Edgar's death. "It was a long time ago. I don't even remember the circumstances."

Mason frowned. "We vampires have what you humans might call a fable. Long ago, two vampires befriended a human female, and took her under their protection. She grew to care for them both, but over time, the human fell in love with one of the vampires. However, she discovered that both the vampires felt the same for her. Wishing not to hurt the one she considered only a friend, she claimed no love for either. Late one night, in secret, she went to her beloved, and the other vampire caught the two together. He became so enraged he ripped both their throats out."

Cora gasped. Why would he offer such a gruesome story? Was he threatening her? "Are you suggesting humans are deceitful or just confirming that vampires are ruthless?"

"I'm saying lies could get us both killed."

She watched his profile for a moment, and then slumped back in the chair. Vampires were always too perceptive. Most of them were walking lie detectors. "It's inconsequential, and I don't want to talk about it."

"It sounds very consequential."

She cringed away from him.

"Oh, now don't start that disappearing act again—"

Crunch.

A hard jolt shattered Cora's equilibrium.

The car listed to the side. The world tilted. Her hair fell over her face, hovering there oddly, as if defying gravity. The seatbelt pulled tightly against her chest, nearly cutting off her air supply. And the world outside the car folded over on itself, the ground kaleidoscoping in all directions. Her body jerked painfully, and agony speared her skull.

The car slid on its roof to a stop, but her body still felt like it was rolling. Muffled curses echoed through her brain. Warm liquid leaked into her eyes and blurred her vision. Where was Mace? Had he rolled the car on purpose? The driver seat was empty. Had he jumped out of the car, hoping the crash would kill her and end his babysitting stint?

"Cora?" Mason's voice sounded from outside. The passenger side door creaked open and then was nearly ripped from its hinges.

She closed her eyes, expecting the final blow of death.

"Cora, are you alright? Can you move?"

"Mace, I don't want to die."

"I know, sweetheart. Tell me, can you move your arms and legs?"

"I think so."

"I'm going to cut the seatbelt and pull you out. I'm sorry if I hurt you." He didn't wait for a response, and she tried not to cry out when he extracted her from the vehicle and laid her on the gravel. "Someone rammed us off the road," he explained, looking around. "They kept driving, but they could be back any minute. Are you okay to walk?"

"I think gas leaked all over me," she said instead of answering. She lifted her arm and wiped along her forehead. When she pulled her arm away, red coated her sleeve. She couldn't make sense of it. Red gasoline? "Oh, goddess."

"Shh. It's not as bad as you think," he said, but his eyes went tight with worry.

Something like a giggle escaped her. "Lies could get us both killed," she mocked, then laughed harder. She stopped when pain and dizziness cut into her brain. The harsh bite of exhaust and burning rubber tortured her lungs, and she coughed violently.

Her vision wavered.

"Damn, you're out of it." Mace helped her sit up.

He cinched one arm under her legs, the other around her back, then carried her from the crash site, laying her back down a few yards away.

Kneeling next to her, he retrieved his phone from his pocket and tapped Trent's name under his contacts. The line rang once, and then Trent answered, "You miss me already?"

"We have a problem."

Trent went silent and waited for him to continue.

"Someone just side-swiped us off the road, a black SUV, tinted windows."

"License plate?"

"I didn't get a chance to write it down while I was death-rolling," Mace snapped.

"Alright, untwist your panties. Is the girl okay?"

He glanced down at Cora. Her face was locked in a grimace, and blood gushed from her head wound. The sweet scent of it had his fangs descending; a purely unintentional, primal response.

"She's alive, for now."

Cora's eyes shot wide as she caught sight of his fangs, and he cursed her inherent fear of his kind. The way her voice had sounded when she'd told him she didn't want to die made him realize she'd assumed that was why he'd returned to the car. Not to help her, but to end her.

"I need to get her somewhere safe," he said, loud enough for her benefit. "Our attackers could be doubling back to check their work."

"I can have someone there in twenty minutes?"

"Not soon enough."

The roar of a motorcycle drew his gaze. The biker slowed and eased off the road toward them, looking concerned. Blessed good Samaritans.

"Besides, my ride just showed up. I'll be in touch." He hung up.

"You guys need help?" The biker zeroed in on Cora's

wound. "I have some EMT training." He dropped the kickstand with his foot and lumbered off the bike.

"Thanks, man." Mace locked eyes with him. "But I'll be taking the bike."

The compulsion went to work instantly. The biker's pupils expanded, eating away the brown of his irises. "Okay."

"You'll walk to the nearest town and call a cab to get you where you're going. After four days, you'll report the bike stolen, not before."

"Okay," the biker repeated. As soon as Mason released his stare, the man strolled away.

Mace turned back to Cora and lifted her off the ground.

She made a sound of complaint, pressing the heel of her palm to her head.

He settled her on the bike's seat, making certain she wasn't about to fall over. She glanced at the vehicle nervously.

He slipped in front of her. The engine still rumbled softly. He knew by its make that it was a fast piece of machinery, but he would take it a bit slow with Cora on the back.

"Put your arms around me and hold on tight."

She hesitated.

He pulled her arms around his torso. The act caused her chest to press up against his back. "If I feel your grip loosen, I'll cuff 'em together, understand?"

"I-I don't know how long I can hold on. Also, I've never ridden on a motorcycle."

"Don't worry, I'll be doing all the work. Hold on for as long as you can. Keep talking if you have to."

He heeled up the kickstand and eased the bike forward.

Cora tensed, as he figured she would. Her grip around his torso became vice-like, and her legs squeezed his hips. Any other time, he would have enjoyed the way she clung to him. Who was he kidding? He still enjoyed it.

Instead of heading north, he crossed the median and went south. As he picked up speed, Cora buried her head in his back. Then he kicked it into high-gear, and she let out a squeal.

Soon enough, St. Stamsworth was several miles behind them. The setting sun sent shadows stretching across the road. Mace exited the highway, deciding it might be safer to maneuver through the back roads from now on. Now that he'd had a moment to think, he had to assume that the driver of the black SUV had somehow known he and Cora would be traveling the highway at that time. The bastard had appeared from nowhere—most definitely hadn't been following them the whole way—which meant there was an informant.

Mace turned onto a gravelly road and eased off the gas a little. Here, a bit of green was fighting strong, creeping up from the black rocky ground along the roadside. A few sporadic trees sported buds along lucky branches.

Cora's grip loosened a bit. "How are you doing back there?" He yelled over the din of the wind.

She made no response.

He turned the wheel and coasted into a wooded area, not stopping till he was far enough from the road that no one would see what he was about to do.

He toed down the kickstand and twisted around to look at Cora. Her eyes drooped, and blood coated her head all the way down her right side. He feared the damage she'd sustained was more significant than he'd originally concluded. Head wounds were tricky like that. He hoped he hadn't waited too long to heal her with his blood, but he'd had to find a safe spot first.

He looped her arm around his neck and pulled her from the bike. Her body was limp, and she wasn't staring at anything in particular. A black cloud of dread moved to the forefront of his mind.

"Cora?"

She mumbled something he couldn't decipher.

He set her down, letting her lie back against the dried ground. A soft moan left her lips. Her features scrunched painfully. Then her eyelids cracked open; her pupils were pinpricks, unseeing. She was already deep in shock.

He lifted his wrist to his mouth and sank his fangs into the flesh. Then he moved his now bleeding wrist to her lips, allowing his blood to drizzle into her mouth. She flinched. With a languid touch, she tried to push his arm away.

After a moment, her vision seemed to clear and she met his gaze. Realization flashed over her. Fear replaced her previously zombified expression. She began to struggle, pushing harder against his arm and shoving her feet on the ground to move her body back.

Quelling the attempt to get away was akin to holding a bunny rabbit in place. The weight of his body pressed her into the soft turf. He reached up with his free hand and gripped the hair at her nape in his fist, tilting her head back to open her mouth wider. Instead, she clamped her mouth shut, clenching her teeth.

"You have to drink it," he said. "It will heal you. I can't risk taking you to a hospital."

She made a noise of complaint, her eyes angry and boring into his. That look chased away his dread. Better angry than dead. But when she turned pleading, his heart squeezed.

"This will heal you, not turn you," he explained. "Drink it. I won't let you up until I'm satisfied you've had enough." When she still didn't open her mouth, he threatened, "I can stay here all night." He tightened his grip on her nape.

She let out a whimper as her lips parted. He shoved his wrist between her teeth and felt the sting of her bite. And though she'd done it out of spite, the effect was a substantial amount of his blood gushing into her mouth. By reflex, she swallowed and then began to cough, trying to hack it back up.

"Don't you dare spit that out!" he growled.

She stilled. Then after a moment of trembling hesitation, she swallowed more of his blood, only gagging a couple more times.

"There's a girl." He removed his wrist from her mouth, stifling a grin at the red marks on his skin that matched the pattern of her teeth.

Cora glared up at Mason, but exhaustion stole the memory of why she was so angry with him. Her head lolled, and she was confused by the sharp scent of dirt.

"I'm so tired," she heard herself say.

"I know, sweetheart. Give me a little time to set us up with a room for the night. There's a motel about a mile back."

Her vision dimmed. Mason said something else, but she didn't hear it. When she opened her eyes again, the sky had morphed into a white, splotchy ceiling. A tiny lamp in the corner of the room gave off a soft glow. Mace hovered over her, fumbling with the belt of her coat. Automatically, her hands flew out to slap him away.

He paused, but didn't move from his position at the edge of the bed. "I drew you a bath. You look like you're straight from a massacre."

Using her elbows, she pushed to sit up. It took more effort than it should have.

The motel room was small, with only one bed. She'd consider that little nugget later. Her hand went to her forehead, which still throbbed.

"It's healing, but it needs to be cleaned," he informed her.

Healing? Her mind zeroed in on the word. "You forced me to drink your blood!"

"I did. And you don't have to sound so disgusted. It's considered a privilege among my kind."

"How dare you—"

"I already told you, if there had been any other way, I wouldn't have done it."

"When did you tell me that?"

"When you were cussing me out all the way here."

She tilted her head. She didn't remember doing that. She wouldn't have the nerve to do that.

He knelt before her and began undoing her coat belt again.

"Stop it!"

"The water is getting cold." Foregoing the belt, he reached for her left foot and started undoing the ties that ran the length of the boot. His actions were clipped, and he seemed irritated with her.

Oh, goddess! What had she said to him in her stupor? It suddenly registered that she had a very strong, very unpredictable vampire on her hands...and he was undressing her.

In a demure tone, she said, "I can do that myself."

"I'm sure you can," he replied, slipping her boot off and setting it aside. Then he started in on the second one. Soon it joined the other on the floor. When he reached for her belt once more, she cringed away from him. He stilled, but only long enough to send her a look that said she wouldn't win this battle.

She forced herself to calm.

He noted her capitulation and then resumed undoing the strap.

Her coat fell open, and a fiery blush entered her cheeks. *Damn this outfit!*

Without a word, he stood and held his hand out to her. She debated the probability of talking her way out of this. It wasn't good. Hesitantly, she slipped her hand in his, and he helped her to her feet. In the next instant, her coat plopped on the ground.

Standing now in her expensive lingerie, she kept as still as possible, focusing on the floor. Mace paused for only a second before he went to work on the rest of her garments. The micro mini fluttered to join her coat. Desperately, she wrapped her arms around herself, protecting the partly see through bustier that barely covered her breasts.

Mace let out a deep sound. She couldn't decide if it was a growl or a groan. Neither would bode well for her.

"Alright. I suppose you can keep the rest on, if you're so inclined." Again, he held his hand out for her, then led her into the bathroom. The tub was filled nearly to the top. Steam skimmed the surface.

"I don't need your help for this," she insisted.

"That cut is in an awkward place," he said. "You can't clean it properly by yourself. Besides, I owe this to you."

She dared a quizzical glance at him.

"I promised you would come to no harm, and that

promise was broken not fifteen minutes later." His features contorted into an angry mask, but swiftly melted back toward repentance. "Please let me care for you."

Figuring he would only persist in carrying out whatever he planned no matter her protests, she dipped one foot into the warm water, then the other, and sank down. The material of her outfit clung to her skin, but she was grateful for the small amount of modesty it offered.

A tingling sensation permeated over her skin. On the counter sat an opened container of bath salts and other products, one of which was probably responsible for the bouquet of floral-mint in the air.

Had Mace had time to stop by a store? How long had she been unconscious?

Sitting on the wide, flat edge of the tub was an array of items: soap, shampoo, tweezers, a plastic cup, and a sponge.

Was she really about to get a sponge bath from a vampire?

The concept was irreconcilable in her mind.

He dipped the cup into the water. "Tilt your head back," he commanded gently.

When she did, he drizzled the water over her forehead. There was a tiny sting, probably from where the liquid met her wound. He dampened the sponge next, running it over her face with an almost feather touch. Then he reached for the tweezers. She went tense.

"It's for the glass," he said. "My blood in your system has already sped the healing process. I need to remove any glass or your skin will heal over it."

She relaxed a bit—well, as much as one could relax while being half-naked and bleeding in front of a vamp. She was the picture of a tasty meal to one such as he.

"Forgive me if this hurts." His expression became serious, his brows furrowing as he methodically worked. With the tweezers, he pulled a glistening shard and dropped it into the now empty cup. It made a dull thud.

Cora counted twelve more dull thuds before Mace set the tweezers aside, dumped the glass in the trash, and then returned to rinsing the excess blood.

Next, he drizzled shampoo into his palm, lathered, then folded his fingers through her hair. She couldn't help but close her eyes as he massaged her scalp, all the while thinking how surreal this was.

His hands moved to her shoulders, and he applied a slow gentle pressure with his thumbs. She had to suppress a groan. The warmth of his skin matched the temperature of the water, and for a second, she imagined him touching her lower.

She stiffened at the thought, and he paused.

"You alright?"

"Mm-hm," she said, not trusting her voice. Her body remained tense, however, even as he continued rolling his thumbs between her shoulder blades.

What was wrong with her, conjuring up such a scene? Had rational thought been crippled by that accident?

And yet, she couldn't stop sensual pictures from invading her brain.

An internal thrumming started a low beat inside her, steadily growing stronger. She cursed her body's wayward response and fought to get it under control, clenching her muscles.

He must have assumed his actions were bothering her, because he stopped the massage and grabbed for the sponge again.

"Look at me," he commanded in a light tone.

She did so without really meaning to meet his gaze, but his grey irises captured hers. A lump formed in her throat. Was it her imagination, or did he appear turned on?

To escape from his stare, she dropped her eyes to his mouth. Not a much better idea, but at least she didn't feel like he had full access to her increasingly disturbing thoughts.

He curled his finger under her chin and moved her head to the side, then ran the soft sponge along the line of her jaw and down her neck. She closed her eyes and shuddered. Why did that feel so hedonistic?

"Mason?" She sounded breathy and a little rough.

He froze.

"Please stop...I..." She didn't know what kind of explanation she could give him. Her skin seemed hypersensitive to every nuance of his touch. Even the air, disturbed by the slightest of movements, seemed to brush her flesh like a caress. She shivered again. The thrumming that had started in her lower half was now a banging pulse that raced through her veins in a fiery rush. She needed to get her body under control.

"Right," he said, his voice more guttural than before. "You should be able to finish up." He handed her the sponge and stood. "There's a night shirt for you to change into in a bag out there. I need to run out for a little bit. Don't leave this room, and don't open the door for anyone. I'll leave my number by the phone if you need me for anything, but I shouldn't be long."

"Um, alright."

He left, closing the bathroom door behind him. She didn't fully relax till she heard the motel room door open and close.

A pent-up breath left her in a rush.

More books by Kiersten Fay

Creatures of Darkness (CoD)
A WICKED HUNGER
A WICKED NIGHT
A WICKED DEISRE

Ever Nights Chronicles (CoD spin-off)
KEEPING HIS SIREN
A VAMPIRE'S MASQUERADE

Shadow Quest Series
THE DEMON'S POSSESSION
THE DEMON SLAVE
THE DEMON RETRIBUTION
DEMON UNTAMED

For news about Kiersten Fay's books,
sign up to her exclusive readers club at
www.kierstenfay.com